Sam
(a pastoral)

by

Susan Larson

But ask now the beasts, and they
shall teach thee; and the fowls of the
air, and they shall tell thee;
Or speak to the earth, and it shall
teach thee, and the fishes of the sea
shall declare unto thee.
–The Book of Job.

Savvy Press

Published by:

Savvy Press
PO Box 63
Salem, NY 12865
http://www.savvypress.com

ISBN: 978-0-9826069-9-5
LCCN: 2012934156
Printed in the United States of America

Preface

I still dream about my horse Sam. In my dream we are cantering through the orchard on our Farm. I straddle Sam's broad bare back and hold onto a hank of his mane, because there is no bridle. The apple trees are blooming, the bees are humming in the sunshine; Sam and I are together again and we are perfectly happy.

Even though I am old and Sam is dead, brush has grown over the orchard, and other people live on our Farm, Sam is still My Horse and the Farm is still My Home.

This is an old-fashioned tale about old-fashioned things. When I was 12, around the midway mark of the last century, I moved from the suburbs of New York City to a hill farm in the wilds Upstate. There was no TV, no movie house and one radio station. Our neighbors were farm people, and they were good to us.

All I wanted then was a horse of my own; Sam was my first horse, and my last horse. Sam wasn't pretty or fast and he never won the Grand National or a ribbon in a horse show. He was just my horse. We took care of each other. He carried me where I needed to go. Some of the places we went together are on the map, and some are inside me to this day.

Dedication

To all horses everywhere. I don't understand why you put up with us humans, but thanks for your patience, forgiveness and love. To Gordon, my non-saintly Holy Man. We sure had fun didn't we?

The Family and the Farm

Whatsoever Adam called every living creature,
that was the name thereof. –Genesis 2:19

As soon as I said the Forbidden Word, my entire family stopped breathing. Mom's face turned white. Dad's face turned red.

"You always have to spoil everything," Dad said. "Don't you? DON'T you?"

"I only said…"

"It's always just one more thing you want, isn't it?"

"I only said MAYbe…"

"You selfish little pig, you never quit, do you? DO you?"

"I ONLY SAID, MAYYYBe now that we have a FARM, I could finally get a *pony*!"

"How many times have I told you, *no ponies*! Did I or did I not, expressly forbid you to even talk about ponies?"

"I didn't say *ponies*, I said *pony*, just *one* pony, just one *LOUSY PONY*!!!"

Dad threw up his hands.

"I can't take this any more, Joan! She's always pestering me for something; first it was her damn dog and now its'…"

"He's not MY dog, he's EVVIE's dog, SHE has a dog and I have NOTHING!"

"That's IT, Joan, I'm through with her!"

"Dave, she's just a kid, she doesn't know any...."

Dad started yelling and pounding the table and my sister Evvie started bawling and the dog started barking and Mom got up and hustled me out of the dining room into the kitchen.

Mom had burned dinner again, and the smell of scorched macaroni & cheese hung in the air; but it was much easier to breathe in the kitchen than in the dining room. Mom was whispering and I could barely hear her over the yelling and bawling and barking.

"Your father doesn't mean to yell at you, Ruthie. It's just that he has so many worries at work, and sometimes he...."

"Oh *I* get it now! Just because *he's* bought himself a farm it doesn't *necessarily follow* that *I* could have a pony."

"Dad has bought this nice farm for *all* of us, for our summer place," Mom said, "so can't you just be happy about that tonight, and not turn right around and ask for something more? Now Dad has two mortgages to pay, and more worries. Can't you just tell him that you're grateful?"

"I *am* grateful, I *said* I was grateful! I only said maybe, *maybe, sometime*, before I *die of old age*, I could get a pony! What good is a farm without a pony? Anyway I thought MomMom and PopPop gave him the money to buy the farm."

"*Loaned* us, they loaned us the money, so we have to pay them back."

"So why can't they loan me a pony and let me pay them back?"

"Please Ruthie, don't keep this up. No more about ponies right now, we'll discuss it some other time. Now let's go out and apologize to Dad and tell him you're grateful, all right?"

So we went back in and I told Dad I was sorry I nagged him.

"That's better," he said. "There will be no more discussion of ponies, ever, while I am head of this family. Ponies cost money, which, by the way, we don't have."

I ducked my head and my tears fell on that plate of stone cold petrified macaroni and blistered blackened cheese, and Bird's Eye Frozen Peas and Carrots shriveling up alongside them.

"Finish your dinner," said Dad.

Silence.

"I *said*, finish what's put in front of you."

"Please Dave, she's upset now, don't make her...."

"I work like a *slave* to put this food on the table and this roof over her head, and the least she can do is clean her plate and be grateful! Finish. Your. *Dinner!*"

"No."

"Dave, don't make it worse by..."

"She can't say no to me! You heard me! *Eat your dinner!*"

"*You* say no to *me* all the TIME!"

"I won't tolerate this kind of behavior, young lady."

"*I'd behave a hell of a lot better if I had a pony.*"

Dad reached over the table and slapped my face.

"I'll teach you to disobey me! Go to your room! If you continue to defy me there will be *no more riding lessons!*"

"Dave, those riding lessons are not your gift to take back, she only..."

But Dad rounded on Mom yelling How Dare She Take My Side Against Him and Mom said she's just a little kid she doesn't know any better and I ran to my room and Evvie and Robbie came too and we listened to our parents arguing.

"This is about much more than food, there's a *principle* involved," Dad shouted.

Mom whimpered that it *was* only food and you're only making things worse by forcing her, Dave.

"Do you think *I* got to leave food on my plate when I was her age? Do you think my parents handed me whatever I wanted? Do you? DO you?

Then we heard a crash and Mom screamed stop it, Dave stop it-sto-pitstopit and a noise like hands clapping and Dad slammed some doors and got into the car and drove off, probably over to his parents' house, where he always always finished everything on his plate and he always never got anything he wanted.

Horse Crazy

If Wishes Were Horses Then Beggars Would Ride. –Proverb

What I wanted was a pony. I wanted one for twelve years, which was all my life. I loved all animals, but I loved horses best of all because they are the most magnificent. They are the symbol of power and beauty all over the world. This is not just the world's opinion or my opinion, it is also God's opinion. It's in the Bible, you can look it up.

Mom told me that "Pony" was the first word I ever said. According to my Dad, it was the *only* word I ever said.

"All you think about is horses, you're *horse crazy*," he said.

"Every little girl goes through a pony phase, honey, and they all get over it, so will you," said my Mom.

"So why can't I have the pony while I'm *in* the pony phase then?"

"Because ponies are expensive – we can't afford it."

"But Mom, I want one so much."

"I know honey. Can't you find some other interest?"

No. Nobody ever loved ponies the way I did. My bones hurt from wanting a pony. Every night I dreamed about having a pony that would come when I called and carry me over the hills with the wind in my hair. Every morning I woke up wanting a pony even more.

The first time I touched a real live pony I was in first grade. My class went on a field trip to visit an orphanage. Not the storybook kind of orphanage, where the kids are forced to dress in rags and sleep in a freezing garret. This orphanage was like a little farm, with goats and chickens, and the orphans got to take care of them.

I knew I was supposed to feel sorry for these orphans, even though they lived on a farm, because they had no Moms and Dads. But I kind of envied them because in the storybooks orphans were the heroes. Orphans were plucky.

And. Plus. *The orphans had a pony.* I spotted him in the barnyard and ran right over to him.

"Ruthie Rossley come back, do you hear me?" my teacher said.

No, I didn't hear. I stroked the pony's nose. The pony nibbled my fingers and I wasn't afraid. I breathed in his sweet musky smell. We looked into each other's eyes. My heart swelled with love.

"I need to have a pony, a little spotted pony right now, can we get one? The *orphans* have one," I told my parents.

"No." said Dad. "Ponies cost money, which, by the way, we don't have."

"Where would we keep it?" said Mom.

"In the back yard. I'll take care of it," I said.

"Did you hear me say *no?*" said Dad. "Ponies need barns and pastures and hay and shoes. So that's that."

So I fell on the floor and kicked and screamed.

"Stop it Young Lady or I'll give you something to cry about."

I had plenty to cry about; my cruel parents wouldn't buy me a pony. I thought about running away and signing on as an orphan.

My family, the Rossleys, Dad, Mom, me, Evvie and our dog Robbie, lived in a little village called Marlborough outside New York City, where my Dad worked. Dad was an engineer at The Company, but he called himself "An Outdoorsman." He said the only time he was really happy was when he was tramping in the mountains Upstate. And I loved being outside, just like my Dad.

"If I didn't have you kids to feed, I'd quit my job at The Company and live up there," he would say. Dad tied his own trout flies and carved his own gun stocks and fishing rods in his shop in the basement. Most weekends he drove Upstate to go fishing and hunting with another Outdoorsman he knew named Ed Pilcher.

Sunday nights Dad would come back from Upstate with the wild smell of the mountains coming off him and sometimes he had game slung over his shoulder, grouse or pheasant, and once a year, if he had good luck, a deer. He looked so proud those times, like a Pa Ingalls, Pioneer Outdoorsman Father. I helped him dress the game. Mom wouldn't look at it, and of course Dad wouldn't let her cook it.

"Would you take me Upstate sometime?" I used to ask Dad.

"No." Dad would say. "Fishing and hunting are serious business, and I can't be bothered with kids."

He didn't take Mom either. But Mom never wanted to go because she played the organ and led the choir in church on Sunday. Evvie just liked to read. But I longed to live in the real country, wandering the woods and mountains, and the green pastures with cows and sheep in them. And to have a pony of my own.

In spite of my parent's refusal to give me a pony the first time I asked, I kept mentioning that I wanted a one, in case they thought I had outgrown my pony phase. Around Christmas and birthdays I also asked MomMom and PopPop and my Aunt Carol for a pony, and they always had answers ready, why I couldn't have one.

"You're too young."

"You'd fall off."

"It would kick you."

"You don't know anything about taking care of ponies."

"You'll lose interest and stop taking care of it."

I knew how to take care of a pony. But by the time I was nine I had read every horse book in the library at least twice. I knew about grooming, exercise, grain, hay and pasture, the different kinds of bridles and saddles, and why you mount from the left side. I memorized all the parts of a horse's body. Fetlock. Gaskin. Wither. Crest. Those words sounded magical to me.

My favorite horse book was "Black Beauty." I read it over and over. In this book Black Beauty describes what it is like to be a horse, which was pretty terrible, with people abusing him all the time. "Black Beauty" made me want to kneel down and apologize to all horses everywhere for human cruelty and try to make it up to them somehow. I made a solemn promise to Black Beauty that I would never, ever, mistreat my pony.

That is, if my parents ever got me one.

When I was nine and Christmas was coming, Dad asked me what color pony I liked best.

"Buckskin," I said. That was my current favorite.

"OK" he said, and went downstairs to his wood shop.

Finally, they were giving in! I was going to get a pony for Christmas! I stayed awake all night Christmas eve. I was shaking I was so excited. My own little buckskin pony…a soft velvety nose… the two of us, galloping free on the hilltops with the wind in our hair…

On Christmas morn, Lo and Behold, there was a buckskin pony standing under our tree. Only it was a carved wooden one, not a live one.

"Merry Christmas, here's your *pony*," Dad said "Now you can't say I never gave you a *pony*, ha ha."

I didn't say anything. I just stood there.

"What's the matter with you? I thought you liked ponies!" whined Dad.

Silence.

"You know how long I worked on that damn thing? The least you could say is….you damn ungrateful little pig, why I bother I'll never know."

I felt tears behind my eyes and words in my throat but they wouldn't come out. I just kept standing there like a post while Dad shouted names at me and yanked down the Merry Christmas signs in the windows and kicked unopened packages around the room. But I saw Mom crying.

You know, in spite of how disappointed I was, I loved that wooden horse. Dad had carved it himself and it was so beautiful, and it was big enough to sit on. I named him Buck, and I let my baby sister Evvie sit on him too, any time she wanted.

Evvie was two years younger than me, but totally different. She was the Good One. She never made a fuss, or Spoiled Everything. Evvie didn't say much but she was smart. She learned to read when she was four. She read all her books then she read all mine.

Evvie loved dogs. Of course I loved dogs too, and she loved horses, so Evvie and I read "Ginger Pye" then "Black Beauty" then "Lassie Come-Home" then "Misty of Chincoteague" out loud to each other after we got in bed at night.

Evvie asked for a dog for her 9th birthday. I asked for riding lessons for my 11th birthday.

Evvie got the dog. Robbie.

He was a collie, like "Lassie." Dad got him from the SPCA so he didn't cost any money, which, by the way, we didn't have. Our dog's former owners had chained him up outside and forgot he even existed, so the SPCA confiscated him. You could feel his bones under his coat, which was all matted together and crawling with fleas. We both cried over him thinking of how he had suffered, then we cut all the mats off and Dad bathed him in flea dip.

He was mostly Evvie's dog. At first Robbie wouldn't leave her side. He leaned up against her all the time, looking up with his sad, pleading brown eyes, as if he was afraid she would abandon him. She kept petting him and telling him not to worry, he was her dog forever.

When Robbie finally believed that Evvie meant what she said he calmed down, and just like that he learned the basic commands she taught him out of the "Lassie" dog training book. This book said that praise is better than punishment. Dad said the Lassie book was a bunch of baloney, and all animals cared about was food and not getting hit. Evvie stuck with the book. Robbie learned *come, heel, sit-stay, down-stay* and lots of extra tricks like *shake,* and *speak.* In a year he grew a fluffy brown coat with a white ruff around his neck, as handsome as the famous Lassie. Robbie slept on Evvie's bed every night, and I was not jealous.

Because I, Ruthie, got the riding lessons.

The Beggar Goes Riding

The wind of heaven is that which blows between a horse's ears.
—Proverb

Mom's Mother and Father had died when I was little, so I barely remembered them. But they had left me some money in their will to take private lessons when I turned eleven, whatever kind I wanted. Mom told me about this on my birthday, and she cried because she missed her parents, and I cried because I was so excited.

"You're just encouraging her, Joan," said Dad.

"But Dave, you know how much she wants to…" said Mom.

"This will only lead to her wanting *more and more*! She's got to learn she can't have everything," said Dad.

"I don't want *everything*, I only want *this* thing," I yelled.

Mom hustled me out to the kitchen which was smoky because she had burned the pot roast. She told me all about Dad's troubles at work. I didn't care a hoot about Dad's troubles at work. *I was going to learn to ride.*

Luckily I got real riding britches and boots second hand from my cousin Harriet who had already outgrown her pony phase. Mom signed me up for lessons at the nearest stable, one called Fox Hill Farm. The first time I walked into the Fox Hill barn, it was like waking up in another world, like Oz. Or Heaven.

Into my nose came the smells of horses and saddle soap and leather, of sweet hay and cedar shavings.

Into my ears came the lazy clop of iron horse-shoes on the cement stable aisle, and the comfy sounds of horses chomping their hay or whickering to each other.

Into my eyes came the sight of horses, two rows of them, on both sides of the aisle, and pricking up their ears turning their long wise faces to look right at me.

"We've been waiting for you Ruthie," they seemed to say.

And then. Then. Mrs. Ackerl, my teacher, boosted me up on a pony. I nearly died from happiness.

In practically no time I learned to sit a horse quietly, heels down, hands light. I learned the signals for walk, trot, and canter. Plus my teacher Mrs. Ackerl taught us how to feed and water a horse, and how to groom and tack up, that means putting the saddle and bridle on and making sure they fit just right and your horse is comfortable wearing them.

During the two hours a week I spent in the cozy horsy world at Fox Hill I lived life to the full. During the six days and twenty-two hours when I wasn't at Fox Hill, I dreamed about when I *would* be there, flying around the ring in the saddle or cuddling up against the warm body of a horse, hugging its neck, burying my nose in its mane, breathing in enough of that sweet earthy smell to last me the rest of the week.

My parents said I needed to settle down because I was too keyed up about riding.

After I had ridden at Fox Hill for a year, I still thought it was the best fun in the world, except for one thing. The school horses and ponies didn't love me. They were gentle and patient, but that was all. So many kids rode them each week they couldn't really love any of us. I started yearning again for a pony that would whicker when he saw me, and come when I called.

Then Holly Cooper, a girl in my riding class, pulled me into an empty stall one afternoon and said to me "You're a pretty fair rider, Rossley; do you want to go in with Mary Louise and me to lease a horse?"

"What's 'lease a horse'?"

"It's like renting. With three of us we'd each ride two days a week. The horse stays at the barn, but it's ours and nobody else's for a year.

Mrs. Ackerl will let you work off part of the fee doing stable chores. Would your parents let you?"

"I could ask," I said. My own horse, almost. My 12th birthday was coming up...

"*No.*"

I barely got the question out of my mouth and they were saying no.

"But I'll work in the barn every day after school! *Why* won't you let me!" I screeched at them.

"We don't think you need to have your own horse."

"We don't think it's right that you should spend all your time in a barn."

"We think you should concentrate on your schoolwork."

"We think you should have other interests."

"I don't *want* other interests, I only have *this* interest, so why *can't* I?"

"That's it!" said Dad. "I don't want to hear *any more about ponies, ever*. If you so much as say the word 'Pony,' there will be no more riding. Do you hear me?"

So that was that.

The Farm

The tree of life also in the midst of the garden. –Genesis 2:9

So up until the night that Dad made his Big Announcement that he had gone and bought himself a farm, I had never once let the Forbidden Word, PONY, cross my lips. Then for two seconds I forgot, and Dad made it clear exactly what he meant by NEVER EVER. Now, oh lucky me, I had my very own farm and my very own barn and no hope of a You Know What to go in it.

In the merry month of May, when all the papers were signed and the deed of Dad's fabulous marvelous p__y-less farm was in his hand, Mom and Dad and Evvie and Robbie and I had to drive Upstate for the weekend to stay at Dad's new farmhouse and explore Dad's uninhabited barn and forsaken pastures. I told Mom I didn't want to go, what was the sense, but she said I had to.

I glared out the car window at nothing in particular, little towns just like ours, the Taconic Parkway, then green fields and barns and cows in pastures. I saw a girl on her p__y, riding across an open hill-top with the wind in her hair. I shut my eyes.

"Wake up, Ruthie. We're in Bethel. Isn't it a quaint little town?"
Silence.

We went through the town and out the other side; then we turned off onto a dirt road. The sign said Mitchell Hollow.

"This is our hollow."

Who cared?

Robbie cared, for one. He sprang up and started yelping right in my ear.

"Quit it, willya? Down-stay!"

Then I smelled what Robbie had smelled.

We were passing a barnyard crowded with cows. I caught a sharp whiff of cow pee and manure. Then this other new smell rolled over me like a big green wave, a combination of sweet grass and apple blossoms and clover—and something wilder—spruce, pine, earth, rock, and running water. I knew it—I had smelled it on Dad on Sunday nights—it was The Smell of the Mountains.

I sat up and noticed where we were.

We were driving up a narrow valley, past a big mansion with pillars, a red barn with a sign on it, "Hunters Welcome, Bob Willett, Esq., Prop." A handsome chestnut horse in the pasture. Some hay fields. The black skeleton of burned-out house, with a new trailer sitting on cinderblocks next to it. Rusty cars in the front yard, with chickens, dogs and skinny cats sitting on them. More fields.

Thick dark woods, the hillsides crowding in close to the road, then stepping back again to make room for two wide flat meadows. The left-hand meadow was grass, the one on the right was just plowed dirt. Above that meadow a green pasture tilted up towards a mountain, and the mountain tilted up toward the sky.

"Argue Mountain. Right here is where our land begins," said Dad. There were deer in the dirt meadow; they lifted their heads and their white tails, wheeled around and bounded away, floating over the pasture fence and heading for the mountain.

"Look at those big fellas! Slap a saddle right on them!" said Dad.

"Dave, don't stir up…" Mom whispered.

I wasn't really listening. I was looking at the big silver-gray barn and the twelve black-and-white cows grazing out behind it. "Ed Pilcher's heifers," Dad said. "He's renting the field and pasture rights from me. A dollar a year."

When the car pulled into the drive Evvie and Robbie and I rolled out and hit the ground at a dead run, heading in the direction of the barn. We never even turned to look at the farmhouse with the sagging roof and rotting front porch and the outhouse in back. We ran right through the barn and into the pasture where the cows skittered out of our path, bucking and, I have to say it, farting. We ran where the deer had run, scrambling over a stone wall and up the rocky ledges into the trees. We found a narrow trail and followed it across a ledge until we came out into a little hollow. We stopped dead in our tracks.

The hollow was like a bowl scooped out of the mountainside. In that bowl was an orchard, all in bloom. Clouds of pink and white apple blossoms swayed gently above rough gray tree trunks. Birds fluttered among the flowers, and from all around came a low steady hum.

"It's bees," said Evvie. Millions of bees, drinking from the blossoms. We walked under the branches and the sweet scent of the flowers fell on us. The sky was blue and there were sky blue flowers in the grass. We lay down under the trees and looked up through the pink apple blossoms into the sky. Some of the petals fluttered down and landed on our faces. We didn't say anything, we just breathed.

We lay there till we fell asleep.

When we arrived back at the house it was the blue hour of twilight and we were stiff and damp from sleeping on the ground; we were also sunburned, briar-scratched, tired, and happy. We had company; Ed Pilcher and his son Wayne had come over after milking their cows just to welcome us to Bethel.

"You girls enjoying yourselves up in there?" said Ed.

"It's great! We saw deer! The orchard is all flowers and it smells so good!" Evvie and I were both talking and laughing at once. Ed Pilcher smiled at us and said ain't they a cute pair of little country girls.

"You girls going to get yourselves a pony to fuss with?" was the next thing Ed Pilcher said.

Silence. My whole family stopped breathing.

"Well, I'd outright give you Wayne's pony, but he ain't reliable. The pony I mean, not Wayne. I'd say Wayne's pretty reliable, he's my right hand."

Ed reached out and slapped Wayne's shoulder. Then he rubbed the nape of Wayne's neck and kept right on rubbing it. I ducked my head and looked at the floor. I had never seen a Dad pat his child before.

"But let me ask around a bit for a nice gentle pony," said Ed. "Would you like that?"

Silence. I kept looking down and held my breath.

"What'sa matter, cat gotcher tongue suddenly? You must be the only girls in the world who ain't crazy for horses. What do you think, Dave? Joan?"

Silence.

"Well. Ah. Hmm. We'll have to think about it," I heard my Dad's voice say.

I let some air out of me, little by little so nobody would hear. *We'll have to think about it* was the closest to p__y ownership that I had ever been.

The rest of the weekend I kept mum. I was not going to spoil everything again by saying p__y. I worked hard on my chores, like taking tons of cans and empty beer bottles and other junk out of the house and throwing them out at the town dump. Dad re-hung the doors and boarded up the broken windows. I helped Mom scrub the grease and dirt off the floors and walls. We had to heat up cans of beans and franks or Chef Boy-Ar-Dee on a Coleman camp stove because the house had no stove and no fridge. There was running water in the kitchen, but no shower or bath tub either.

Evvie and Robbie and I did one other important thing. We walked all around the whole Farm, following the fence line no matter where it went; up steep ledges, through birch woods and maple woods and over fields and through swamps and under brambles and across brooks. We touched every last fence post. Now the Farm was ours.

That Monday after school I got this book, "A Horse of Your Own, How to Select and Care for Your First Horse," out of the library and re-re-read it just in case. I hid the book under my pillow like a baby tooth, and I dreamed that my p__y was already on the farm, grazing in the orchard grass under the apple blossoms, just waiting for me to come find him.

Friends and Neighbors

When school got out, Mom and Evvie and I packed up and we and Robbie drove up to Bethel for the whole summer. Dad could only come up on the bus for weekends until his vacation started, but we were going up early to try to make that decrepit old house livable.

Our Farm was just as beautiful as before, only greener. So green! Ed had already cut and put in the hay from the west meadow, leaving palomino colored stubble behind. Field corn had sprouted in the east meadow that had been only plowed earth before. The heifers were still in the pasture, but—I traipsed everywhere looking—there was no p__y.

Mom and Evvie and I started fixing up the house. We painted the walls and hung curtains in the windows and bought a gas range. Mom hired Ed's nephew Steve Murphy to replace some rotten window frames and missing panes. He installed a better water pump so we could flush the toilet. Then Steve put in the toilet. The people before us had only had the outhouse, and we used it too until Steve came: it stank to high heaven and there were flies.

The phone man came and put in a phone and Mom called Ed Pilcher's wife Beatrice, to make her acquaintance. Beatrice talked so loud on the phone we could hear everything she said to Mom. Beatrice said that we should drive "over Colby Valley way" and take her pickup truck and go buy second-hand furniture "over to Carney's," so we did. The farmer's wife greeted us like old friends; we squeezed into the pickup's cab and listened while Beatrice talked, at the top of her lungs.

"Carney is a junk dealer," shouted Beatrice. "He buys up farmers' stuff at auctions when folks hit bottom and have to sell out. Business is booming for Carney these days," yelled Beatrice, "so many farmers are going under and leaving for the city.

"The Goodenows, they were the folks who farmed your place before your Dad bought it. They owed everybody so much money they had to sneak out of town at night and leave all their stuff behind," Beatrice said. "People came and took whatever they wanted from the house. Who woulda wanted it I don't know, it'd been through Carney's three times before the Goodenows dog-robbed it from the town dump."

Carney's yard was crowded with tin-roofed sheds chuck-full of beds, dressers, sofas, rocking chairs, clothes, family bibles, photo albums, you name it. Lots of stuff was too worn out for even Carney to sell, so he just let it sit out in the open, rotting away. Picking over other people's things made me feel like we were vultures. Or rats.

Mom bought some oak bedsteads, mattresses and springs; some rockers for the porch, and what Beatrice called a Living Room Suit, plus kitchen chairs and table, all for rock bottom prices. We bought some enamel pots and a big iron skillet too.

Dad came up Friday night and we picked him up at the bus station in Briggsboro. Saturday we watched him and Steve jack up the house foundation so the roof didn't sag so much. Sunday they ripped out the old front stoop and built a brand new one all in one afternoon.

Next weekend they put in a bathtub and built a fine picnic table out of some old boards stored in the barn, that Steve called "silo staves." "Silo blew over in a windstorm," Steve told us. "Them Goodenows never bothered to put it back up.

"The barn is solid though," said Steve. "Them beams is hand hewn and a foot square."

The barn was beautiful even though part of the floor was caked with old manure. There was a twelve-stanchion milking aisle and a huge haymow half full of haybales, and half full of dusty sunbeams and swallows swooping in and out feeding their babies. Evvie and I climbed into the mow and sat on the bales and planned where we'd build a stall and maybe a tack room. Being in a real barn made me feel like the p__y was really coming.

Evvie and I and our trusty dog got to know every inch of the Farm. A brook ran through the pasture and under a culvert in the road, then plunged over big rocks in a waterfall right near the house. I loved the sound of it. We found a magic ring of big beech trees on a hilltop behind the haymeadow, perfect for reading books. There was a spring below the cornfield that somebody had dug out and lined it with rocks to make a forest pool. It was clear as crystal and the water was sweet. Deer came to this pool, as well as song birds and game birds and raccoons and bunnies and fishercats and skunks. If we sat quiet at sunset we could watch them drinking. Hawks soared over the mountain by day; owls and coyotes made their eerie music by night. We loved the orchard in its little dell best of all; it was green now, and ringed all around its rim by tall white birches.

I loved being on the farm with all my heart; but I never stopped thinking about the p__y. I wondered if I should speak up and remind Beatrice to remind Ed about it; maybe he thought because I kept quiet that I didn't really care about having one. Or maybe he'd yell at me if I pestered him. Or maybe he was just kidding about the p__y all along.

Mom and Evvie and I paid social calls: the folks in the pillar mansion were away, but we met the Connors, who farmed the hollow below ours. We got down there by a shortcut—a pretty lane running through maple woods from our road to theirs. Mr. Connor showed us his barn; it was enormous, four times as big as ours, and stuffed to the roof with thousands of hay bales. There were stanchions for 50 dairy cows, and a pen for a pig; but there were no stalls for that other sort of animal. After we had admired the barn, Mrs. Connor and her mother-in-law gave us coffee and fresh made donuts in their kitchen. Grandma Connor was blind, like the Grandmother in Heidi, but she could read from blind books, and besides that she had the Second Sight. She told me I would get my heart's desire, she could see it as plain as day.

Evvie and I walked down the hollow and visited our nearest neighbor, the one who lived in the trailer next to the burned house. His name was Byron Westford. Byron Westford had come up to our house the first weekend when we were cleaning, just to say welcome to the Hollow and ask was there anything he could help us with.

Dad said Byron Westford was "a ne'er do-well." Mom said he was "a character."

Byron started every sentence with the words "Boy Jeez," which was, our Mom warned us, "an oath."

"Boy Jeez is swearing, it means…" Mom turned her voice down to a whisper, "'*By Jesus,*' and I don't want to hear either of you saying it." But when we were visiting at Byron's place, we said "Boy Jeez" anyhow. It was hard not to.

"Boy Jeez, I used to farm, but I lost m' shirt," Byron said. "I sold my herd to Glen James, that's his dairy barn down at the head of the hollow. Now, Boy Jeez, I'm a gentleman of leisure, living on the Dole."

Byron had a wife named She and twin girls named Daphne and Delilah. They lived in the trailer after their regular house burned down one night. But Byron was all alone this spring.

"She's poorly. She's down to the hospital again," he told us. "Haven't seen the girls in some toime. Living over at their cousin's, getting into some koind of trouble, Boy Jeez. So you gals are always welcome to visit. I loike the company." Byron had a funny accent.

Byron kept a pig and a flock of sheep.

"To eat," he said. "But Boy Jeez them sheep do look kind of sweet out in the medder."

But the real excitement down at Byron's was—a kind of animal with manes and tails. Byron ran a whole herd of that particular animal in his back pasture. Maybe he'd sell us one. The first time we arrived at his barnyard he had two of them tied to the paddock fence and he was harnessing them up.

"You gals want to see them work?" Byron asked.

"Sure," I said. "Do they pull a cart?"

"Stone boat. Them's competition pulling ponies."

We tried to pet them, but they swung their heads away. They weren't the nuzzling velvet-nosed kind of animal. Their eyes looked past you, and their muscles were all knobby and their manes had been mowed down to a bristly crew cut.

"Boy Jeez they won't offer to kick nor bite, but they ain't pets," said Byron. "they're workin' animals."

He wasn't kidding. When the harness was buckled the little beasts knew they were going to work and they got all snorty and prancy. The instant Byron made the hitch to the sledge loaded with cinder blocks, they lunged forward, jerking the load into motion. They dug their toes in the dirt and scrabbled and sweated and grunted across the yard. Byron called out to them: "Dandy! King!" and they pulled even harder.

"Why don't you have Belgians or Percherons, Boy Jeez, they're stronger," I asked him.

"Boy Jeez, I used to farm with big hosses! I didn't have no tractor. Can't afford to feed hosses now. Ponies is cheap to buy and they keep easy. Us old teamsters get up the pony pulls just for the hell of it. The team that pulls the heaviest load the farthest gets a cash proize, and if his woife don't take it Boy Jeez he goes over to Kennedy's Auction Barn and buys another damn pony."

I asked him Boy Jeez did he win prizes and he said Boy Jeez he did because he knew all the old-time training secrets.

"Boy Jeez, both a them ponies got to go at the same time or else they pull soideways. These Boys is crazy and knot headed, but they go good for me. I don't use the lectric like some do."

We didn't know what the lectric was, but Byron was asking us to go root for him at the next pull and of course we said Boy Jeez you bet we'll be there.

"Ed Pilcher told me he'd ask around about a...a.... pony." There. I had said the Forbidden Word out loud, to Byron. "But I think he forgot."

"Boy Jeez, he moight have, he's busy getting in his hay. Tell you what, if Ed don't find you a pony, you and me'll go to the Auction Barn and get you a noice koind one, not like these fellas. Boy Jeez, the sweetest sight I know is a young gal canterin' her pony acrost the hilltop up there in my pasture."

I really, really liked Byron.

Hoss Trading

When I bestride him, I soar, I am a hawk: he trots the air; the earth
sings when he touches it; the basest horn of his hoof
is more musical than the pipe of Hermes. –William Shakespeare

Dad's vacation had started and he was busy fishing in the mornings and doing more carpentry and painting around the house in the afternoons. When Evvie and I got home from Byron's that noontime Dad sat down to lunch looking like he had heard some bad news. "Ed called," he said. "He says his cousin Billy over in Shiloh has a—well, a pony for sale cheap. Ed says his name's Sam and he's gentle with girls."

"APONYAPONYAPONYAPONY!"

Dad groaned and rolled his eyes.

"Now Dave, you know she hasn't said anything about a pony since..."

"All right all RIGHT, Joan, I'm taking them over right now, Ed's meeting us there in half an hour."

Half an Hour! My teeth started chattering, my hands turned cold and shook. I started crying.

"Calm down, we're just going over to *look* at him," Dad said.. "We're not going to buy the first pony we *see*." But I was thinking along the lines that this might be my last chance ever, so I was going to try and get a pony today, even if it was blind, three-legged, and a little bit dead.

Evvie and I had to wait til Dad had finished his lunch. We, of course, could not eat a bite. I couldn't even talk. On the drive over I tried to imagine what a pony named Sam would look like. I had him pictured up pretty well; a girl-sized version of Man o' War; spirited, noble, and fleet. Evvie and I would think up a grand new name for him, like Shadowfax or Pegasus or Seabiscuit.

"Well, Billy, here's some customers come calling," said Ed.

Ed and Cousin Billy were waiting for us in the dooryard. Ed introduced us to Cousin Billy, who, he said, was a professional horse trainer.

"How do," said Billy, smiling at me. "So these are the girls that like horses."

"These girls are certifiably horse crazy," Dad apologized to Cousin Billy. "Ruthie here is so horse crazy she may just keel over from excitement, heh heh. Is there any cure for this behavior?"

"Ayuh," said Cousin Billy. That's how people said "yes" Upstate. "Ayuh" was all he said, but Dad took his meaning. I did too. Cousin Billy winked at me, and I winked back, and we all walked across the street to the barnyard.

"That's him over there," said Cousin Billy. I got my first glimpse of the pony we had come to try, hopefully buy.

The beast in question was snoring in the shade of Cousin Billy's silo, its head dangling between its forelegs. It was definitely NOT a pony. It was a full-sized—no, an *oversized*—horse. And it was, at first glance, the ugliest horse I had ever seen.

At second glance I saw it was a chestnut—not the burnished red-gold of Man O' War; more plain orange, like a ripe pumpkin. And it was coarse like an old plow horse, with big hairy white feet and legs like tree-trunks. Its mane and tail were scraggly and matted with burrs; they were even oranger than its coat.

Its thick ugly neck was shaped like a shoe box and its head was stuck on it at an ungraceful angle. A broad lop-sided blaze ran down the beast's face. A beard grew under its jaw, and its bristly pink lips quivered with every snore. Suddenly it jerked up its head and opened its eyes to look at us. Those eyes were not the melting brown kindly eyes of the Fox Hill ponies. They were icy *blue*!.

The homely creature swung its head to look at the people who had interrupted its nap. Its cold blue gaze swept over me and passed on to survey the others. No "I've been waiting for you Ruthie" in those eyes. The horse turned his head away from me and back into the shade.

Well, he was plug-ugly, but he was still a horse and I was desperate. I tugged at Evvie, and we walked over to him, speaking gently, saying his name Sam, Sam. The animal tossed his head in disdain and slouched off to another part of the barnyard. Ed Pilcher and Cousin Billy shooed him into a corner with spread out arms and haltered him for us. The horse stood still after that, but when we reached out to pet him he tossed his head and leaned away.

Ed and Cousin Billy said they would tack up for us because Sam was very shy about his head.

"This animal doesn't like to be bridled," said Cousin Billy. "I guess he's been yarned around a few times."

"What's yarned around?" said Evvie.

"Jerked around, rough handled, beat, probably," said Cousin Billy. "He doesn't care for men at all but he minds women and girls OK. His owner came up from the city to ride him and she never had any big trouble. She only came up a few times before she lost interest."

"Really?" said Dad. He sounded hopeful.

"She never showed him who was Boss." Said Ed.

Sam was clearly not interested in cooperating in any way, rolling his eyes and tossing his head high to get it away from Cousin Billy and the bridle. My heart sank. He was knot headed, just like Byron's ponies, only ten times as big.

"Well, sis," said Ed, "on you get." Sam stood spraddled out, looking sullen under his tack. I didn't even want to ride him; he'd be balky and mulish. But I didn't want Cousin Billy or Ed thinking I was chicken either, so I climbed into the saddle and picked up my reins.

Something happened. A vibration like electricity flowed through Sam's broad body. Sam pulled himself together, arched his neck, and strode out across the barnyard and into Cousin Billy's haymeadow as if he were carrying Ivanhoe to a joust. From deep in his chest came a low rumble, like the idle of a truck. Was he *humming*?

After we pranced around in this fashion for a while, I sort of got used to him, and thought maybe I should "apply the aids" and make him trot. Before I applied anything, Sam trotted off on his own, jouncing stiffly and awkwardly, then leveling out and picking up speed. The hum of his mighty motor was joined by the dull thuds of his feet smacking the turf.

"Hum, mum, mum, bang-bang-bang," said Sam, and we charged around cousin Billy's haylot. The horse warmed up and stopped jouncing, and I started doing my riding school figures— circles and figure eights. Sam went wherever I pointed him and did it as if his life depended on it. I sailed past my Dad and sister; their mouths were propped open in disbelief. Dad had never seen me ride. He seemed impressed. My confidence grew; I thought about maybe cantering. Before I ever touched him behind the girth with a heel, Sam tucked in his butt, lifted his front end like the prow of a ship breasting a wave, and cantered. "Snort! Snort! VROOOOM!"

"Wheeeeee!" I laughed. "Whoooeeee!"

Sam was not built for speed, but he was as strong as two oxes, and collected cantering turned out to be his specialty; his canter had a rolling feel, like riding a rocking chair across the meadow. How fast *could* he go?

"Vroom! mum mum!" said Sam, going into a thundering gallop across the whole meadow. When I thought about slowing down he came back to a canter, then trot, circled and halted, standing with one ear pointed toward me and the other toward the open field. I got off and looked at him again. Closer this time.

Sam looked better now because his orange coat had sweated to dark bronze. The mighty beast cleared his nose, chomped the bit, stretched out a mighty forefoot and pawed the ground. *"Let's go, Let's go, Let's GO!"* It was like I heard him say it.

"Well," said Ed Pilcher, "he ain't lazy. He sure can pick 'em up."

"And put 'em *down*," I said. "You wanna ride him Evvie? I'll lead ya."

"Uh, Later." she whispered. Evvie didn't know how to ride, and she was maybe a little afraid of Sam, but she knew there would be a later, definitely. We both knew we had to have this rampageous War Horse for our own. This horse was – in spite of his common looks– MAGNIFICENT.

Evvie and I walked Sam around to cool him down and then Billy brought us a curry comb and soft brush and I showed Evvie how to groom. Sam was easy with us now, but his blue eyes remained focused above our heads, looking back at the field.

"Why did they make me stop? I was just getting going!" he was almost saying it out loud.

Ed was watching us. He chuckled and said:

"One white foot, buy him,
Two white feet, try him,
Three white feet, deny him.
Four white feet and white on the nose
Take off his hide and feed him to the crows."

Ed was hinting that we should not buy Sam for anything but a rock-bottom price. Then he chuckled because he knew and we knew and Dad knew that we were going to buy Sam anyhow.

Then Ed took Dad aside and told him what he thought was a fair price.

Then Dad took Billy aside and shelled out a hundred and fifty bucks for Sam, trucking fee included. Delivery tomorrow.

Then Dad took Evvie and me aside and said "I hope you're both happy now," and we said yes thankyouthankyouTHANKYOU, and we hugged him and said he was the best Dad in the entire world.

"Hmph," grunted Dad.

Then Billy took us aside and offered us the loan of a saddle and bridle until we could shop for one of our own.

"Fuss with that horse a bit, and he'll come right around," he said.

"OK, Thanks a million," I said.

Then Ed took Evvie and me aside and told us that we should "make Sam a little afraid of us, because we had to show our horse Who Was Boss."

"OK," we said. But I figured we'd probably stick with the Lassie Method we used with Robbie. Besides, I had a hunch we would have our hands full making this particular horse afraid of anything.

When we were all done taking each other aside, Dad took us to the Agway. We bought a block of mineralized salt, and a sack of sweet feed, a rubber feed tub, a brush, a curry comb, a mane comb, a hoof pick, a green nylon halter (size L) and matching lead shank.

We went home, dumped the grain in the feed bin, hung up Bennie's tack on pegs, and put the grooming stuff in an old tin bucket. Then Evvie and I yanked out the old cow stanchions and cleaned every bit of caked-up cow manure out of the barn to make a big run-in stall. Finally we showered and sat on the porch studying "A Horse of Your Own" and waiting with all our might for Sam to arrive.

Sam Arrives

Behold, the bridegroom cometh, go ye out to meet him.
–Matthew 25:6

Cousin Billy's van pulled into the barn lane bright and early, at eight o'clock. Billy let down the ramp and led Sam out. Actually, Sam exploded out in one giant leap and never touched the ramp. He was quivering all over, bug-eyed, high-tailed and high-headed. He looked quite a bit uglier—and oranger—and wilder—than I remembered.

Evvie and I took the lead rope and greeted him with soft words and caresses, which he ignored, looking over our heads at the countryside. Billy had someplace to be, so in two minutes we were alone with our horse. We led him out to the pasture and in and out of his new stall a few times and along all the fence lines, reading the how-to-settle-them-in-to-their-new-home instructions in "A Horse of Your Own" as we went.

Finally we turned Sam loose to investigate on his own. He did another complete tour of the pasture at a high-prancing trot, sometimes screeching to a halt, nostrils whuffing, eyes flashing blue, looking. He investigated the twelve Holsteins he shared his new home with; he gazed at Connor's Holsteins in their hill pasture a half mile away; he watched Byron mowing his hay, a little late in the season, down-hollow.

The only thing he ignored was us.

Pretty soon Byron chugged up on his tractor, parked it in the lane and walked out to the barn to meet us.

"Seen the van come up. Thought I'd take a look at your new pony. Built to last, ain't he?"

I just nodded, and watched my horse thundering around the pasture.

"You ride him over at Billy's? How's he go?"

"Goes good, Boy Jeez. Stops good too."

"All you need." Byron watched Sam some more, chuckled a few times, rubbed the back of his neck, then climbed up on his tractor and chugged back down to his haylot.

Finally when Sam settled down to graze among the heifers, Evvie and I went inside to make eat olive loaf sandwiches, which we ate on the porch watching Sam and reading from chapter 2 of "A Horse of Your Own," and marveling over the fact that we were now horse owners, *caballeros,* knights of the realm.

"When can I ride?" said Evvie.

"It says here we're supposed to let him settle in for a day. Tomorrow. Or the day after. Then we'll put the bridle on."

How was I going to put the bridle on, was what I was thinking.

After lunch Evvie and I brushed Robbie and threw his ball for him so he wouldn't feel jealous, but all the while we were discussing possible horse names. But the fancy storybook names sounded silly somehow. There was only one possible name to call this horse, and that was the one he had already.

That afternoon we started fussing with Sam, just like Billy told us to, to make him come around. Robbie came with us. The horse and dog sniffed each other, and made friends; then Robbie lay in the shade of the barn and watched us clean Sam up. We picked all the burrs and tangles out of his tail with our fingers. We shampooed him using brook water and baby shampoo; we brushed his body till it shone like glass. We started training his mane to fall properly on the off-side of his neck instead of half on one side and half on the other.

"Ohhh, Sammy Sammy Sammy *Sam*," I crooned to him. "What a fine big Boy you *are*, and you are mine—and Evvie's too of course."

Sam seemed to like being the center of attention. He twitched his lips in delight when we curried his chest and scratched the insides of his ears. You would not think a horse would enjoy some stranger sticking their fingers into his ears, but Sam did. He shut his eyes, poked his neck out, twisted his head side-ways, saying "hm, mm, mm." By the middle of the afternoon Sam was showing us where to scratch. He loved a hard rub on his neck, in the middle of his forehead and—his personal favorite—the dock of his tail.

Mom came out to the barnyard and patted Sam on the nose. "He's so calm," she said. Then Dad took her to town to play piano duets with her new friend Mrs. McMahon, and he of course he went fishing. While Sam took his nap in the barn we sat guarding his slumbers and talking about his future care and training. At dusk when Sam ambled out to graze we went in to dinner and talked about it all over again.

"When are you going to stop talking about riding and ride?" Dad said. "I didn't get you that horse for you to look at."

"We're letting him get used to us first."

Dad puckered up his face and said "Oooh, I can't wide because I'll hurt my widdle horsie's feewings" in his whiny girly voice.

"Dave, don't make fun of…"

"I thought she was the one who couldn't *wait* to ride," Dad laughed.

"I'll ride, I'm going to ride, tomorrow for sure." I said.

I jerked awake at dawn the next morning. Today was *the day*; my first ride on my own horse. My stomach felt funny. Maybe I was sick. Maybe it would rain. But no, the sky was fair, with little pink clouds fading to white, and deer grazing in the hay meadow and the dew winking in the pasture grass. Sam was out feeding among the cows, looking as peaceful and as settled in as a horse could look.

"Let's go riding, I wanna ride!" said my sister.

"Me too," I said. "Do you think I don't want to ride?"

After a bite of breakfast we walked out to the pasture and lured Sam into the run-in with a half-scoop of sweet feed. I held up his green halter and he obliged me by poking his head right through it and into the tub, calmly munching away while I clipped the leadshank on and handed it to Evvie. I got the comb and brush and started cleaning Sam's near side—a side that seemed to have grown as large as the side of the barn. The off side was even larger.

I put the saddle on while he ate, and buckled it loose. Sam didn't even flick an ear. I got the bridle, and listened to my heart beating as I walked it back over. Suddenly my heart sank. This place was built for cows, not horses; the roof was only four feet or so above Sam's head. Would he rear up and crash his skull into the roof and die, like the loco mare in "My Friend Flicka?"

"Let's take him over to the picnic table," I said to Evvie. "So if he..." I couldn't finish the sentence; my throat had closed up.

Sam sauntered down the barn lane like an old moo cow, his head bobbing between Evvie and me, his ears waggling back and forth in time with his strides. My heart was thumping about three beats per waggle. I led Sam close to the stave bench, then stood on it and slowly looped the reins over his neck.

Sam tensed up and rolled a spooky-blue left eye around to glare at me. He whuffed out hard through his nose. I undid the halter and lifted the crownpiece of the bridle up in front of his nose...

"*Hmpf*!" he said, and flung that nose straight up. How could he? After I had been so nice to him.

"Should I smack him?" I asked Evvie.

"I dunno, is he being bad?"

Was he? Or was he just expecting to get yarned around? We stood there another minute. The nose stayed up, the eye stared at me. Finally I took the bridle down and reached out nice and slow with my empty hand. I stroked Sam's neck.

"Don't worry, Sam." My voice was shaking. "I won't yarn you around, ever. Ever. *I promise.*"

That eye glowered down at me and I looked up at it. I kept stroking his neck. It was as hard as stone. Another long minute went by.

The eye closed. Sam smacked his lips, made a sound like a sigh. Did I hear him say,

"*Tsk. Oh all right, if it means that much to you.*" Sam lowered his head. I held up the bridle again and he took the bit. I eased the crown piece over his ears, off side, nearside. Sam sighed again while I did up all the cavesson and throatlatch buckles; then the eye opened and looked at me. Not glaring.

"It's all right, Sam," I said. "It's all right." Sam lifted his nose up close to my face. He sniffed my hair and my mouth and touched my cheek with his whiskers. I sighed and shut my eyes. Sam was bridled. No rodeo. I had done it all myself.

Well, no, I hadn't.

Then—oh Glory Hallelujah! I got on! And I rode my good horse out into the hay meadow. The sweet morning air blew in my face and brought some tears. Fence posts and trees swept past. And, *trot!* We were flying, with the wind in our hair. And, *canter!* Sam rumbled and took off—and the earth shook beneath us!

I forgot everything in the world but Sam and me for a while. Then I saw Mom standing next to Evvie near the picnic table, smiling and waving. I trotted back, circling around them, explaining how I made Sam turn and stop and go. Except I didn't explain that he was really just doing what I wanted, as a sort of favor, without my having to make him.

"Look at him prance, he looks so spirited!" said Mom.

"But *calm*," I said.

"Well, don't let him go too fast."

Then Mom walked off down hollow to pay a call on She, who had just returned from the hospital. Evvie got on Sam and I led him around the whole farm while she got used to being up there. My sister wasn't afraid of riding any more.

Sam had come around, beyond our wildest dreams. He must have figured that Boy Jeez he had landed in Horsie Heaven, and Evvie and I were his two personal cherubs, brushing him and kissing and cooing and NOT yarning him around. Sam loved us. He wanted to be right next to us, sniffing our faces and leaning his knobbly head against our chests.

And Sam obliged us in every way. No more snorting and nose tossing and stony necks and glaring at bridling time, mercy me no.

"Foot, please," I would say. And Sam would daintily lift a foot to be picked out and did not put it down until I said OK.

"Step over please," and Sam would swing his butt sideways at a touch.

By the fourth day Sam had started following us around, bridle, halter, or no. So I figured I could quit leading Evvie around like a birthday party pony ride and let her take the reins. Evvie knew by then that Sam would just stay close to me and not run away over the hill.

"There's no shame in grabbing mane to hang onto just in case," I reminded her.

But there never was a case.

Evvie would climb on and hold the reins while I walked and trotted around the hay meadow, Sam tagging along behind, breathing down my neck. I knew he wouldn't step on me. Or on Robbie either, even when he scampered too close to Sam's big feet. Robbie was not jealous at all as we feared, he always came with us when we rode.

One time when I was trotting in front of Sam I heard Evvie screech, "Help! I'm falling off!"

I slowed to a walk. Sam slowed to a walk. "Grab mane and hook your heel on the saddle," I said.

"It's ok," Evvie said. "Sam put me back up."

"*What* did he do?"

"He sort of ootched back underneath me. When can I canter?"

Sam was not going to *allow* my sister to fall off. As far as he was concerned, you got on, you stayed on, or he'd know the reason why.

Soon Evvie was riding by herself in circles around me, in a little haymeadow near the Connor's lane that we called "The Academy." In two days she was riding figure eights and serpentines, first walking then trotting.

But Sam was getting bored going in circles. We were all itching to *go* somewhere. So the third day we rode out into the wide world; there were trails everywhere; one trail went south through the orchard into the next hollow up, called Lame Buck Hollow; one went west down to Connor's Hollow. A third one went north, right up Argue Mountain. Mysterious side trails branched off into the woods or alongside planted fields. Farmers on tractors smiled and waved. The sun shone, cool breezes blew, never a harsh word passed between us, and life was perfect.

How did Evvie and I trailride with only one horse? At first we took turns, one riding and one trotting alongside until the one on the ground got tired and we switched places. One day when Evvie was riding and I was running up a hill trying to keep up, I grabbed onto Sam's long tail and he pulled me along. Then Evvie did it too. Sam didn't mind at all. It felt as if we'd known each other all our lives.

At the Horse Show

*"My beloved is mine and I am his. He feedeth among
the lilies." –Song of Songs*

When Mom and Evvie and I were in town shopping at the Grand
Union, we saw a poster that said the County 4-H Club was putting on
a horse show that weekend. Evvie and I really wanted to go, especially now we were horse owners ourselves. We wanted to see other kids'
horses even though we knew our noble steed was better than anybody
else's—Sam was strong, smart, true, and willing—and handsome, too.

It had only taken two weeks for us to realize how beautiful Sam was.
How could we have been so blind before? Sometimes we'd sit eating
pb&js for lunch on the porch rockers, just admiring Sam's handsome
conformation as he grazed among the cows. At certain angles I could see
a curvaceous crest on his neck. In certain lights his mane looked silky.
His broad chest and round white legs and big feet were evidence of his
strength and power.

Saturday morning, Mom was going off shopping with Beatrice, and
Beatrice was going to pick her up. She and Mom talked on the phone every day and they called each other Joanie and Bea. Mom would whoop
and laugh at the things the farmer's wife said. Bea never kept her opinions to herself and she was kind of sarcastic, which Dad said he couldn't
stand in a woman. But Mom loved Bea.

Dad, however, was going to go fishing on the Otterkill, and his road lay in the direction of the 4-H fairgrounds, so he said yes he would drop us at the horse show and pick us up when he had caught his limit. We piled in with him after kissing Sam goodbye in the barn.

Dad, wearing his old hat with the home-tied flies on it, and his old tackle vest that smelled sweetly of the fish of yesteryear, kept silence. I could tell Dad was happy just thinking about trout; how to find, catch, and cook trout.

We kept silence too, about certain things. For instance we never told our parents how far from home we had gone on Sam and how we held onto his tail going up hills. Nor did we mention how Sam loved us and took care of us. Dad especially didn't need to know.

"All animals care about is food," he liked to say. "All that nonsense about dogs or horses loving you is a sentimental delusion."

Evvie and I knew better. We had no delusions whatsoever about our noble, beautiful, wonderful horse Sam.

The fair grounds were crowded with trucks and horse trailers; the hot-dog stands were selling pinky-red steamed wienies and thick-cut French fries with the skins still on. We drank in that intoxicating fairground smell of fried dough and cotton candy mingled with manure and hay and horse. We heard the call for Western Pleasure Class, so we sauntered over to the ring fence and leaned on it with the cocked heads and narrowed eyes of sophisticated Horse People, sizing up the local horse flesh.

There was already a golden haze of dust in the ring, and around and around flew the pretty, ponies—paints, appaloosas, chestnuts, buckskins, palominos with flashy blazes and socks. There were chocolate Morgans with rippling silver manes and tails, there were blue roans with black points.

Every one of them had slim legs, tea-cup sized feet, velvety little muzzles, soft kind brown eyes. For about ten minutes we said nothing, as we hung on the rail, as those fine shiny ponies flashed by.

Evvie said it.

"They're so—so—*little*."

They certainly were. We had clean forgotten what a girl's pleasure pony was supposed to look like. We had clean forgotten what *our* dream pony used to look like. Now here they all were, in front of us, a joy to behold, a dream to own, lining up and posing prettily for the judge.

I felt a terrible pang somewhere near my heart and wondered if a hot dog with ketchup and mustard and relish would make it go away. My sister and I retreated to the hotdog stand and plunked down our money. We kept some more silence as we munched our way through those weenies, weenies that tasted like ashes and dust.

We wandered back among the trailers, watching the kids in Western dress and concha belts; the kids in hunting kit, a few snooty looking young ladies in saddle-seat habits. They and their 4-H club leaders and parents were cleaning tack, shaving bot-fly eggs off ponies' legs with razor blades, braiding manes, stripping appaloosa tails down to a fashionable wisp. Those lucky kids, with their lovely horses. We didn't squint at them with cocked heads now or point out their conformation faults; we just stared.

After three hours Dad came and picked us up and held up his creel full of little speckled trouts for us to admire. He asked how was the horse show. OK, we guessed.

"Did you see any horses as nice as Sam?"

"Nah." We sat silent during the ride home, trying to digest those hotdogs, and a few other things.

As soon as we got home, my sister and I found a pair of scissors and went right out to the barn. Sam was dozing in the run-in stall. We trimmed off his beard. We braided his mane. We blunt-cut his tail and hacked the feathering off his fetlocks. Sam fell back asleep, snoring away beneath his cherubs' busy little hands. His lower lip wiggled and dangled in a particularly disgusting way, he was snoring loudly and one hip was cocked. He looked like a flatbed truck with one wheel in a ditch.

I noticed all the bot-fly eggs on the inside of his forelegs. I noticed the booming noise his feet made when he stamped the flies off. There was a sand crack in the outer quarter of his near hind hoof. It was getting bigger. His pink penis hung down between his hocks like a steamed hot dog.

We worked away in grim silence for a long time. Finally we had whittled as much off Sam as could be whittled; he was still too big and too common and too hairy, and the flies were biting and we were hot and sweaty and tired. I went to get the saddle and bridle, but Evvie shook her head.

"I don't feel much like riding."

"Me neither, I guess," I said.

We hung up the tack, and trudged up to our special sitting rock in the middle of the pasture. It looked west over our fields to Connor's hill pastures, so we called it Sunset Rock. We flung ourselves down and watched the tree shadows lengthen over the haylot and slide across the road into the cornfield.

The western sky turned pink and peach color fading to light blue further up. When it got cool, Sam came out of the barn and grazed his way up to the rock. He stood right over us. He yawned, showing us his yellow teeth and the ripply roof of his mouth. He cleared his nostrils, shook his head, lowered it so it almost touched each of our shoulders, and went back to sleep.

Venus shone over our house. Birds had stopped singing, except for a barred owl in the orchard, laughing like a fool, "who cooks, who cooks, who cooks for you-all?" The deer slipped out of the brush and came dancing onto the hay meadow on their delicate legs. The sky turned deeper blue. Still we sat there.

Finally Evvie stood up. Sam turned his head to her, pressing his nose against her chest. Evvie reached up and began to undo the braids in his mane. I stood up too and helped her. We patted Sam's big strong neck with shy pats.

When Sam went off again to graze, we went down to the house to eat supper. Venus was sliding down the sky toward the horizon and the night wind was rustling with a dark velvety sound on the mountain. The white road of the milky way wound across the sky. You could almost ride along it.

More Neighbors

"Does your horse carry double Uncle Joe, Uncle Joe?"
–Traditional song

No, Evvie and I had not bought the wrong horse. He was ours and we were his, for keeps. Plus we discovered that this horse had more talents and personal virtues than we suspected. Sam was coarse and ugly, we finally had to admit. But. He had a butter-soft mouth and his body was as flexible as rubber. He would go anywhere you pointed him, once he decided the footing was safe. So that's where we went.

Since we were going farther every day, we gave up ride-and-run and just rode Sam double bareback. We sloshed around on his back at first, and I was afraid we'd fall off and break our necks. But Sam kindly smoothed out his gaits and made sure we stuck on. He could charge straight up mountains, splash through brooks, and jump over logs and stone walls. We hung on for dear life, me grabbing mane and Evvie grabbing me and Sam balancing his cherubs nicely as we careened around the countryside, whooping and laughing and singing songs.

We made some interesting discoveries on our trips. For instance, on our first ride up the wild and mysterious Argue Mountain, we discovered an old school bus in a clearing, with a stove pipe sticking out of one window.

"Hey look, somebody lives in there!"

"Who would live in an old bus?"

We found out in a hurry when two old men popped out from behind the bus, wiping their hands on their pants. Their hands were dripping with blood all the way to their elbows, and blood was smeared all over their faces and beards. I wasn't too afraid of them, because Evvie and I were up on Sam and we could pivot on a dime and gallop away in two shakes if they tried to murder us. But they seemed really friendly and they introduced themselves as Frenchy Paree and John Mohunk, and they said Sam was one flashy looking hoss.

By then I knew where all the blood came from. Being up so high I had a bird's eye view of their back yard, and I could see a dead doe all gutted, hanging from a tree; Frenchy and Injun John were in the middle of butchering a deer they poached out of season; and we had caught them red handed. And I also figured out where the expression Red Handed came from.

When Frenchy saw me looking at the doe, he winked at me and I just winked back, to let him know I wouldn't rat on him. People who lived in a schoolbus probably needed to hunt all the time for their food.

A few days after that, riding a woods lane out of Lame Buck Hollow, we found an abandoned house. Trees were growing through the roof and the dooryard was full of brambles but the windows still had glass in them. We smelled a funny nasty smell when we went close to the house. The door was nailed shut and the windows were so dusty we couldn't see in, so we poked around outside and found some old brass buttons and pieces of dinner plates, a china doll's head, and some square little bottles with long skinny necks. We put this stuff in our pockets and set them up in our bedroom as a historical exhibit. Maybe we would go back to that house, and dig up more old things. We could go anywhere and do anything we wanted now.

It was high summer, and Dad left at dawn for the Otterkill. Ed and Wayne arrived to take a second cutting of hay. Bea came over too, and she and Mom made breakfast for the men. Bea told us to go into the fields and help out, because they were going to make a lunch and gossip and their conversations would not be fit for young ears.

"Well, girls," said Ed as we walked out to the meadow. "How's Old Sam" We took him out to the barn showed him our glorious shining steed, and I bridled him and rode him bareback in the pasture a little, just to show off.

"You girls have done real a nice job; that horse takes the bit good now, and he looks smart as paint," marveled Ed. "But his toes are getting short up front. He'll need some shoes. Let me phone up Rufus Bates for you. Rufus used to shoe Duke, and let me tell you Duke was rank to shoe. Rufus can show 'em who's Boss." And right then he turned and went back to the house and called Rufus for us.

"He'll come up tomorrow afternoon," said Ed, stooping and rolling a wisp of grass between his hands. "It's dried off good now, so let's get working."

Wayne let us ride behind him on the tractor and showed us how to mow. He said if you didn't keep your wheels lined up just right, you left a line of standing hay called a "holiday," and you were no durn good at mowing. Wayne let us try it, and Boy Jeez we left plenty of holidays. We got the big meadow all mowed, then we quit for lunch and cold lemonade.

In the afternoon the men were going to mow the smaller meadows, so we were excused; Dad was still fishing on the Otterkill, and Mom and Bea went to McMahon's. Evvie and I went riding Sam down the hollow in the golden afternoon sunlight.

"Maresey Doats and Doesey Doats,"
we sang at the top of our lungs, to the rhythm of Sam's hoof-beats.
"An' Liddle Lamsey Divey!
A Kiddley Divey doo,
Wouldn't YOOOOO?"

When we came down out of the woodsy stretch of road, Sam snorted and upped his head; half a mile away was a horse and rider. The rider waved and her horse took off and galloped towards us. Sam puffed himself up as the horse—it was the handsome chestnut from the pillar mansion—pulled up alongside us. On his back was a girl.

She was scrawny, with wispy taffy colored hair, buck teeth, and big hazel eyes. She wore a faded flower-print blouse and raggedy shorts; she was bareback, and also barefoot. One of her reins was rawhide and the other one was baling twine.

The girl threw a leg over her horse's neck and perched side-saddle staring at us, twiddling her hair with her fingers and drumming her bare heels against her mount's ribs. He never moved a muscle.

"Where'dja git that ole plow hoss?" she said at last.

"Bought him over Shiloh way," I said, imitating Byron. "Name's Sam. I'm Ruth Rossley. My sister Evvie."

"How do. Name's Jinnae Willett, his name's Rusty. I live down street in the Mitchell House, we just come home from out West visiting m'sister Paulette, and heard you was here, can I come up and see what you done with the old Good'now place?"

Jinnae swung her leg back astride, and Rusty immediately started cantering up hollow. We wheeled around and followed, cantering, rollicking, four iron shoes making cloppety-clop and four bare feet making clippety-clip.

I eased Sam abreast of Rusty. The two geldings matched strides, rolling their eyes and arching their necks, showing off to each other; Evvie and I were showing off too, both sitting up straight, elbows in, heels in position.

Jinnae did not notice. Jinnae's hands and feet and elbows and hair flapped all over the place, but not because she was insecure; she was just so relaxed. She had no form at all, but she could ride. Boy Jeez could she ride.

We waved at Ed and Wayne, who were about to drive home, slid off and turned the horses out in the pasture. The two geldings smelled noses, squealed a few times, kicking up their heels to show they were tough guys. Then they grazed side by side.

We went in the barn and showed Jinnae our stall and where we put tack and grooming stuff. Jinnae swarmed into the mow.

"Where'dja put all the cow shit was in there?" she said.

"We put the MaNOOR…"

Jinnae wasn't listening; she shimmied down and ran down the lane, toward the house. We tagged along behind.

"On the flowerbeds," Evvie called after her.

Jinnae examined the picnic table and rocked briefly in one of the rockers on the stoop. Following her was like following a butterfly that zigged and zagged and only lit down now and then.

"Where's your folks?"

"Dad's fishing. Mom went off with Bea Pilcher I think."

"D'ja got 'nything to eat?"

We went into the kitchen, slapped together some PB & J sandwiches, and poured three glasses of milk.

"M'Dad brews his own hard apple cider," said Jinnae, wolfing her sandwich. "Keeps it in a barrel in the barn. Gives you the runs if you drink too much, I hear tell, I never drunk it cause I'm still too young to get drunk. Next year though."

"I got one hundred cats with double paws, that's good luck," said Jinnae, helping herself to more milk. "I got a pet crow, and my sister Monique got a baby.

"Paulette my bigger sister was a champeen gymkhana rider in these parts, she married a horse trainer and moved to Wyomin. Paulette give me Rusty as a present, bought him over to the Kennedy Auction Barn," said Jinnae, plumping down on our new toilet to have a pee with the bathroom door wide open.

"Them Kennedys is gypsies, they always try to gyp ya," Jinnae yanked up her shorts, did not flush, and charged upstairs to our bedroom loft.

"I seen how they do," Jinnae bounced on Evvie's bed. "On auction days they stuff all the horses in this tiny little pen, in the black dark, with no food nor water." Jinnae bugged her eyes out and made her fingers into claws. "Then they take them out and knock 'em around before they go in the ring, so they scat around and everybody will think they got spirit. You want to go fishing down to Mitchell's Brook?"

She was down the stairs and heading out, slamming the back door, Evvie and I trailing after her.

I stopped dead in the yard.

"You playing some kind of trick on us, now?" I yelled. "You know you can't fish Mitchell's Brook, Jinnae Willett, it's too small anyway. My Dad tried it and hung up his line in the trees."

"C'mon then!" she yelled. Jinnae took off, her bare soles twinkling over the sharp stubble of the hayfield. Into the woods we ran. Jinnae slithered through Connor's bob-wire fence like a ferret; we snagged our clothes and had to stop to pick them loose.

"Wire strung so tight you c'n play tunes on it!" said Jinnae. We ran into a sunny pasture dotted with cow-pies and buttercups, and then– Jinnae climbed right into the brook.

"Whatcha doing? How you going to fish with no tackle?" Evvie said. But Jinnae paid no heed. She squatted down in the water and stuck her hands in under the bank and winked up at us.

"Ji-NAY!" I yelled. "Suppose a snapping turtle, suppose a snake..." but Jinnae was throwing up both her hands splashing us, except in the middle of that splash was a shiny trout, flipping around on the bank.

"Smoosh his head with a rock!" she ordered us. We smooshed.

For an hour we sat on that bank staring at Jinnae while she tossed two more trout onto the grass. Finally she climbed out and shrugged her shoulders, spreading her fingers into fans.

"You feel 'em," she said, making little tickling movements with her fingertips. "You do your fingers like this. Then you jam your thumbs in their gills and throw 'em out."

Evvie and I climbed into the brook and crouched down along the overhanging roots. Then, trying not to think about what else besides fish might be lurking under there, we stuck our hands in the shadowy water.

I couldn't get the trick of it. I'd feel something slippery, or imagine I did, and then I'd yell and snatch my hands away.

"Stobbit, you're spookin' the trout," said Jinnae. I turned to look; fish were streaking up and down the shallows of the stream. Trout were everywhere, but they were safe from the likes of me and Evvie.

It was really fun though. We headed for home vowing to be friends for life, making plans to fish some more, ride all the trails, see Jinnae's cats and the crow and the baby and the barrel.

We arrived in our dooryard just as Dad pulled in the drive. He had been skunked, the fish weren't biting at all, he said over his shoulder as he reached into the trunk for his waders and empty creel. When he turned around, we introduced him to Jinnae.

"Proud to meetcha," said Jinnae. Dad dropped his gear and shook the left paw that she poked out, and then he noticed that the right hand of this damp stringy-haired little girl was holding a length of grapevine on which hung– three fat brook trout.

Dad's smile vanished; his eyes bugged out and then scrunched up as if he was in pain. Boy Jeez, Dad was jealous of a kid, and a girl at that. But you know I was a little jealous of her too. She had a pretty horse and could ride like an Indian and lived this exciting romantic life. At the same time of being jealous, I loved Jinnae.

A Tale of Two Farriers

But he that cometh after me is mightier than I, whose shoes
I am not worthy to bear. –Matthew 3:11

The Pilchers came over to rake the hay and left before lunch. Rufus Bates arrived as promised, in the afternoon. I had seen horses getting shod at Fox Hill, but just to be sure I looked up horseshoeing in "A Horse of Your Own." There was a picture of a farrier with a pony's hind foot between his knees. The pony looked like he was asleep on three legs while the man nailed shoes onto his foot. Shoeing was a peaceful, even a boring, event in my experience.

But not, as it turned out, in Sam's.

Rufus climbed out of his truck, and I went to say how do while Evvie went to get Sam. Rufus was red-headed, red-faced and had big red arms; and he strutted around with his chest puffed up and his jaw stuck out. Rufus set up his anvil under a spreading maple tree in our door yard, and was tying on his leather apron when Evvie led Sam down the lane from the barn. Rufus sized Sam up, and although his chest and chin continued to stick out, his ruddy complexion faded to gray.

Sam sized Rufus up, his head going higher, eyes bugging out, nostrils flaring. Rufus turned abruptly and rummaged in his truck for a thick piece of nylon rope, which he tied around Sam's neck without so much as a how do.

Rufus hitched Sam up short to the maple tree-trunk. Sam began to whuff and snort. It sounded like an oncoming thunderstorm.

Rufus grabbed for the near forefoot and yanked it up. No "foot please" like we always did. Sam jerked his foot away and strained against the rope. Rufus hit Sam on the fetlock with his rasp and the horse laid his ears back and rolled his eyes.

Rufus caught Sam's foot and held it tight while Sam plunged and strained. Sam's nostrils showed their red lining and a funny membrane flicked across his eyes. Rufus managed, by sheer brute force, to hold the foot long enough to rasp it more or less smooth; then he turned to Evvie and me. He was good and mad.

"This hoss is a killer," said Rufus. "I'll get iron on his feet, but it won't be pretty. I'd sell this hoss—or shoot him—before I'd trust him. He's got them killer eyes."

I opened my mouth to defend our cuddly pet Sam, who never shied or bucked and never offered to kick nor bite. But what could I say? My horse was acting like a mad elephant. Finally, I squeaked out, "I think he needs the shoes."

Rufus, having said his piece, turned once again to the task of making Sam knuckle under. We stood there and watched while Rufus hit, cursed, and kicked our horse.

When it came time to do the third shoe, Rufus tried to hopple and lift Sam's hind foot with ropes; and the beast went berserk. He kicked at Rufus, he struggled and plunged against the hawsers that bound him. In ten seconds he was free, bolting for the barn, blood and foam spattering, and Rufus Bates holding onto the end of a rope being dragged flat on his stomach behind.

Rufus finally let go the rope. He stalked back, shirt in ribbons, to demand payment. We gave him the money for two front shoes, size three, and the extra trouble; we watched his truck roar off down hollow. Then we went into the bushes and puked up our lunch. After that we went out to the barn to comfort our horse; but when we tried to pet him he flinched and backed away. So we just sat there. Wondering if he was going to kill us.

Dad came home from the Otterkill and found out what had happened, he stomped and yelled and blamed Sam; then he blamed Evvie and me, for "making him buy the first horse we saw." Finally he blamed Cousin Billy, and called him up to give him a large portion of his mind, what did he think he was doing, selling two inexperienced girls such a vicious beast? Billy would just have to take this animal back!

Evvie and I walked out towards the barn. We were bawling. This was the end of horses in our lifetime. The end of Sam. We barely noticed the sound of approaching hoofbeats; but here came Rusty and Jinnae cantering up the edge of the cornfield. We both started bawling harder at the sight of them.

"S'matter?" Jinnae said, sliding off.

"Rufus Bates says Sam's a killer and Dad's gonna make Billy take him back." I said. Jinnae slid the bridle off Rusty and turned him out in the pasture.

"Who the heck toldja to use Rufus anyways?"

"Ed did. He called him up for us."

"Hmf. Those Pilchers don't know this much about horses. And that Rufus just bullies and jerks and yarns. Whyntcha ask Byron first, anyhow, or me? What'd that Rufus do?"

We told her. I sobbed out that I was scared of Sam now, and he was scared of us too.

Jinnae didn't say anything. She slipped into the run-in, where Sam and Rusty were standing head to tail, swishing flies. Jinnae cupped her hands over Sam's nose and walked toward his tail, running her hand along his side and down his near hind leg. Just like that, Sam's big hairy foot was resting lightly on Jinnae's scrawny little knee, and she was poking around his cut fetlock. All Sam did was cock an ear back at her.

"S'not so bad. Skin's flayed off. We can stand him in the brook to clean it up."

So we haltered Sam and made him stand awhile with the water running over his legs, while Jinnae looked at the other cuts and rope burns on him and announced that our horse would live.

"You got to tell your Dad to call up Ronan O'Ryan," said Jinnae. "He does Rusty good, and them shoes stay on tight. He's just a little guy and he's real old, but he gets 'er done."

"Could you maybe tell our Dad that?" Evvie said.

Jinnae nodded. She slipped through the barnyard fence, marched across the road and into the house. Ten minutes later she was back.

"I told him he didn't have a hoss problem he had a farrier problem. Told him to give Ronan a try. Your Mom spoke up real nice too and she got him to change his mind. No riding today, I guess. You just keep him in there a bit longer." Jinnae caught Rusty, bridled him and hauled herself on using the barn door as a mounting block, turned and rode off down hollow.

"See ya!" she waved.

We stood there holding our beloved horse, silently weeping, but this time it was thankfulness and adoration that made us do it.

Ronan came up next morning. It was cool and damp and the Pilchers, thank heavens, decided to wait a day before they baled.

"I'd rather not have them watching," I said.

"I'd rather not watch either, this time," Evvie said. I knew what she meant. I didn't think I wanted to see our horse maybe kill a little old man and then eat him.

But when Ronan O'Ryan's truck came up hollow Evvie was in the barn catching Sam and I was on the stoop waiting. Ronan O'Ryan's leathery face did not pale when Sam and Evvie came down the lane from the barn. Ronan O'Ryan walked right up, put his nose into Sam's nose and blew. Sam blew back. Ronan O'Ryan laid his hand firmly on Sam's forehead, and Sam sniffed him and sighed and shut his eyes.

"Ho Princie," said Ronan O'Ryan as he stuck his greasy finger in Sam's ear. Sam twisted his head sidewise, grunting happily. Ronan pulled Sam's ears down gently, talking to him in a soft voice, and Sam sighed again and pressed his head up against Ronan's skinny chest.

"You gals get a bucket," Ronan O'Ryan said, "put a scoop of sweet feed in it, then put in some rocks, about this size. Ho Princie."

"Here you gal", Ronan O'Ryan said to Evvie, "stand over here, same side as me and hold the lead shank. Ho Princie."

Ronan O'Ryan put the bucket down in front of Sam, who rooted around among the rocks trying to get the grain. He had to concentrate hard to do it. When he had eaten all the grain he had his hind shoes on, Ronan O'Ryan was long gone, and Sam's reputation as a killer was in serious jeopardy.

"See," Ronan O'Ryan had said as he loaded his anvil and his box of tools into the pickup, "Treat them good and they treat you good. Somebody sometime tried to yarn that hoss around, and the hoss won. He'll always win if it comes to a fight. But he'd die rather than hurt you two girls, now ain't that so?"

The Mitchell House

It was so. After Ronan came, we wondered how we could have been afraid of Sam, even for a minute. Sam had always taken care of his cherubs. He had never offered to kick nor bite. He was so picky about where he put his feet that he had never stumbled or stepped in holes or bogs. Sam had never spooked at anything: neither barking yard dogs, honking cars, kids on bikes, nor clanking farm machinery disturbed his composure. He was the Rock of Gibraltar, Byron said.

Next day we were going to help bale hay. The morning was good and hot, with little lambswool clouds frisking around the deep blue sky; red-tailed hawks floated above the mountain and orioles whistled in the elm trees. Ed and Wayne would be here as soon as the dew was off the fields.

When we heard their tractor coming up hollow, Evvie and I put on long pants and long-sleeved shirts so we wouldn't get chewed up by the sharp ends of hay sticking out of the bales, and reported for work. Evvie rode on the tractor with Ed, and I got to go help Wayne stack the hay in the mow.

Wayne set the bale elevator against the haymow edge, and we climbed up and waited for our first load. I loved being around Wayne; he was a big chunky guy with a homely face, but he was so nice. He smiled at me and told me I was a good little farm kid. Wayne was about ten years older than me and knew lots of stuff about cows and weather and machines and crops. Wayne was going to be a farmer like his dad.

Ed and Evvie drove up with a load of bales on the wagon: Evvie switched on the elevator and she and Ed started tumbling bales onto its clickety-clacking teeth, and Wayne and I started stacking.

"Hey, Ruthie," called Wayne from the other side of the mow. "You handle those little bitty green bales. I'll take these great big yellow ones, OK?" I was a little annoyed that he thought I was too soft for the tough work, but I said OK and wrapped my hands around the twine on a little stubby green bale.

I gave it a hearty tug. It didn't budge. I tugged again, grunting and straining, but I couldn't even lift it much less toss it. Tears welled up in my eyes and I sat down on the little bale breathing hard, trying not to sob. Wayne came over from his side of the mow.

"S'matter, kid? You OK?" I started to cry.

"I'm so weak I can't even lift a stupid little *bale*," I howled.

Wayne's fat pink face began to redden and pucker so that his little brown eyes practically disappeared. Finally he threw himself down in the hay with a shriek of laughter.

"Stoppit, Stoppit, STOBBIT!" I yelled.

"Try lifting wunna those bih-hih-hig yellow ones, then," he sobbed. I stomped over to a big yellow monster bale, wrapped my hands around the twine took a big breath and heaved—and the darn thing floated to my knee and up onto the stack. Easy as pie.

I looked up at big yellow bale I had just tossed, and down at the little bitty green bale stuck on the floor. Yellow. Green. Yellow. Green. Wayne was watching me, quivering and weeping quietly with mirth.

At last I got it.

"The green one's *wetter*, so it's heavier, and you KNEW it ALL ALONG, WAYNE PILCHER," I yelled. Wayne's yowls of glee got higher and louder; Ed was sitting on his tractor below, his hand shading his eyes and his shoulders shaking. Even Evvie, the little traitor, was smirking at me.

I screamed curses at them all, climbed down out of the haymow and bolted for the house. I tore up to my room and dove onto my bed, hot tears gushing. From there I could see Ed and Evvie baling more stupid hay, probably still chuckling…and here came Jinnae cantering upstreet on Rusty, waving to them. She turned into the yard and I came down to the stoop.

"Hey."

"Hey."

"Wanna go riding?"

"I'm stacking hay for Ed."

"Stacking it in the house?"

"Took a pee break, that's all."

"Why're you cryin' then?"

"I'm not crying. Because Wayne was making fun of me, if you must know. He told me to lift the little teeny green bales and I couldn't, and it was all a dirty trick."

"Everybody gets that trick done on them onst. Byron done it on me and I was mad as a snake at him. Speakin' of snakes, any checkered adders jump outa them haybales at ya?" Jinnae bugged out her eyes. "Some o' them's nine, ten foot long. Crawl right out and BITE ya. Then you die."

Jinnae paused, twiddled her hair and thought a minute.

"Oh! And Ma says she wants us to go huntin' mushrooms over Trace Holla way. We're havin' a party tonight and you girls are invited to dinner and sleep over too, you wanna? We got a snappin' turtle in the pond and it et our ducklings, just drug 'em *right under*."

"Gotta ask Ed. Gotta ask my Mom."

Ed and Wayne said go on ahead, they could handle the rest of the putting in, just the two of them. Mom said yes too, because I didn't mention the mushrooms. Plus she and Dad were playing bridge that night with the McMahons, and it would be a load off their minds to have Evvie and me stay at Jinnae's and not all alone on the Farm. Robbie had to stay home though, because of the one hundred cats.

We got Sam brushed, picked-out and bridled in short order, then we slipped onto his back from the picnic table.

"Show you a secret trail down hollow," said Jinnae. She and Rusty turned off the road into the woods, and pretty soon we were walking up a grassy track in back of Byron's fields. How had we missed this one?

"Show ya another short cut. We cross street, go through Byron's back pasture, cross Lame Buck Road, then go right up into Trace. Better than riding on the macadam! Wait till you see the 'shrooms back in there, zillions of 'em." said Jinnae.

"How do you know if they're not poison?"

"I can tell three good kinds. Regular Medder, Inky Cap, and Bleeders. Fry 'em up in drippin', they're good. High time you met the family anyhow."

"When did your Dad buy your house?" I asked. I couldn't figure out how come raggedy little Jinnae lived in a mansion.

"T'aint ourn, we just rent. It's the Mitchell House," Jinnae answered. "Mitchell owned this whole holler fifty years ago. His family still owns it. They live Downstate now."

Byron waved at us from his dooryard as we loped through his pasture. I suddenly remembered what he said to us about how he loved to see girls ride their horses up here. Boy Jeez, it had all come true! Here I was, cantering on the hilltops with the wind in my hair! I whooped and waved back.

We crossed Lame Buck Road and ducked into the shady trails of Trace Hollow. Mushrooms hid in secret spots that only Jinnae knew, and she taught Evvie and me how to tell the good kinds. The inkies grew on tree stumps, the bleeders along the trail, and the Regular Medders in pastures. Jinnae's sack, which she had used as a saddle pad on the way over, was full in no time at all

On the trail back to Jinnae's we passed the abandoned house.

"Hey, I bet you didn't know that house was there, Jinnae," said Evvie. "Ruthie and I discovered it ourselves, last month."

"I know all about that house, and don't you go over there," said Jinnae. "It's a *haunted house* and there's a *curse* on it!" she said. We laughed at her and said that only illiterate hillbillies believed that superstitious stuff. Jinnae just trotted on past the house, halted, and sat on Rusty fifty yards off, with her back to us.

We rode Sam right over to the house and got off, just to tease Jinnae. We poked around and found some fallen down sheds and rusty carpentry tools. We noticed that funny rotten sort of smell again. We yelled to Jinnae

"What's that bad smell anyway? If you know so much, who lived here? Why did they leave? Why didn't somebody else move in?"

Jinnae didn't answer and she didn't even look at us, so we gave up.

We were crossing the Lame Buck Road again before Jinnae would talk to us.

"I ain't ever goin' near that place," she said. "There's ghosts. People *die* goin in there, and that's a fact. Didn't you smell that *smell of death* over there?"

"In your stories everybody dies," I said. "We aren't afraid of ghosts, there's no such thing as ghosts."

When we got back to the Mitchell House the Willett's party was already going full blast. Jinnae introduced us to her Mom, Lu, and to her sister Monique, who was only fifteen and had a baby. We met Bob Willett, Esq. Prop, too; he was just a scrawny little guy in green work clothes and John Deere cap. His eyes looked in different directions and his head jerked every few seconds, but he was real friendly and wanted to know all about us.

Lu was friendly too, and she laughed a lot. Lu wore tight jeans and had on cakes of make-up that showed up the wrinkles in her face. She had a cigarette and a bottle of beer going at the same time. Sometimes it was hard to understand what she said because had an accent. She said she was a Canoe, or something, from Canada.

And what do you know, Frenchy and John were out in the kitchen cooking up a venison stew, so Evvie and I went to say how do. Lu was hugging them and jawing to them in French, which I could not understand even though I had taken French. We said nice to see you again and the two old men laughed and said likewise, how's your big fine shiny horse?

"He's good, where did you get the venison for the stew?" Evvie said to Frenchy. She had been sitting behind me on Sam that day we met them, and she never saw the poached doe, and I never told her either because I was sworn to secrecy.

"Oh, from out my freezer, cherie!" and Frenchy winked at me again, and I winked back at him and everybody laughed.

Everybody was in the kitchen now, laughing and hollering. Jinnae and Evvie and I sorted and cleaned the mushrooms.

"Don't cook none of them inkies," Jinnae whispered. "Put 'em aside. Everybody's too liquored up already, and if you eat inkies when you're liquored up—*you die.*"

Monique sat next to me. She was sucking on a cigarette while she jiggled her baby on her knee.

"Don't get out much these days, what with the kid and everything,"

Monique said. "But Lu's gonna sit him tonight, and I'm gonna go have me a time."

Monique had on a checked western-style shirt and tight jeans and pointy-toed leather cowgirl boots. Her hair was up in rollers under a pink bandana, and she had so much black eye liner on she reminded me of a raccoon.

"Going dancing, at a joint called Hillbilly Heaven. Wanna come with us? Meet some cute boys?" She nudged my arm and winked.

Lu kept making jokes about Monique going out on the town, and she wiggled her hips and said, "Woo-hoo." Monique snorted smoke, flicked her cigarette ash and said, "Shut the hell up, Lu."

Frenchy cooked the non-inky mushrooms in bacon grease in a big skillet and served 'em up; they were delicious and nobody died.

We sat down around a round oak dining table in a huge high-ceilinged dining room with a chandelier, and we ate that illegal venison stew. Bob broke out his famous hard cider and offered us some; we had a sip, then switched back to Kool Aid.

As everybody got more liquored up, Frenchy and John started telling stories about the old days of logging with draft horses, who would skid logs out to the roadhead. When they got unhitched, the horses would walk back up the mountain all on their own to get hitched up to another log and draw it down.

"Didn't need no teamster," Frenchy said, "just did it all by themselves."

"Quittin' time was four o'clock," said John. "Them hosses work all day like a sumbitch, goin up 'm down. But they hear the whistle blowin' over to the mill and they jes' go off home. We can't hear that damn whistle for shit, but them hosses hear it good. That's how I knew when to quit, when them big bastards don't come back up."

John was copper colored with a grey pigtail down his crooked hunched up back. He saw me looking at him and told me he was a real Injun and he was crooked because a tree had fallen on his back and broke it, and he couldn't work no more. Now he lived on the dole, which bought him almost enough booze to ease the pain, he said.

"Tell about that haunted house in Trace Hollow!" said Jinnae to Frenchy. "Them girls wouldn't believe me about them ghosts. Frenchy knows all about it, don'tcha Frenchy?" Everybody went quiet, and Lu started to nod her head and squint her eyes up.

"Yeah, Frenchy," she said, "go ahead. Tell 'em."

Frenchy had a round pink face and a curly white beard and pale blue twinkly eyes. He looked like Santa Claus usually, but right then his eyes went ice cold as he flicked them toward me and my sister, and even colder as they stared a long time at Lu. Lu kept saying "Vazzee" and pointing her chin at him in little jerks. Finally he shook his head and muttered something in French.

The Curse of the Pelletiers

Such as sit in darkness and in the shadow of death.
–Psalm 107:10

"Some folks," said Frenchy. "Some folks around here think they are somebody. They may have a big place and be a big noise in the town and elders of the church and think they are a cut above. But Frenchy knows. Frenchy knows all about them.

"They were just dumb ol' Canucks back then." (Canucks! Not Canoes!)

"Armand Pelletier, he run sheep in Trace. He was cousin to my gran ma. Built a nice house there. The wife die, but the daughter keep his house. Had a hired boy, too, his nephew Placide. When the ay-gew come, Placide's family all die except him. Armand drink too much, treat Placide bad, like a slave, work him much, feed him little, beat him ever' day, and nobody stop him, because Placide is an orphan.

"Armand's daughter Magali is of good heart, and she give to Placide to eat and knit to him some warm clothes. Placide could run off any day but he stay around for Magali.

"They become lovers and Armand find out. He beat Placide bad and throw him off the farm, and nobody hear more about him. Nobody care anyway, just another dumb Canuck. Magali marry the first man who look at her, to get away from Armand, and she have a child. This man is

Anglo and rich; he run the store in town.

"Well, one day, voila, Placide is come again at Armand's and ask for work. The old man is gone in drink, he don't want to see Placide, but he is alone, he have no choice. Armand take him back as his stock man. Not long after that the old man die of the flux.

"So what do you know, the nephew get the house and the farm, and he run it good. Then what passes but Magali's husband die of the flux too, and she get all his money. Right away she marry Placide, and she move back to Trace Hollow. Prett' soon her Anglo child get the flux and die. Soon Magali have babies by Placide. But they die too.

"The peoples commence to talk about how Placide kill Armand and the husband of Magali, maybe the Anglo child too, with poison. They talk about a curse the good God put on them, to make their babies die. People see ghosts in Trace, Armand, the Anglo, and little babies, walking around the house. The house have a bad smell, like the flux, and it don't wash away. Nobody want to do business with Placide, and then his sheeps start to die.

"Placide and Magali, you know, they try to sell out but nobody will buy. The curse, the ghosts, the smell, who knows? They leave there, buy a small farm in Colby with her money. They join up in a protestant church, they pray almighty hard, they give big money to the church, mebbe try to buy some good luck from God.

"At last they have baby boy who live. People stop talking about the murders. Their son marry the McTavish girl and they join their farms together, got half the valley now. Their son Édouard, he marry the Boyd girl, her father own the other big farm in Colby. Now Pelletiers own the valley, everything going good, they are plenty rich, now they think they are somebody.

"They commence to write their good French name the English way, they forget who they are. They forget what bad things their family did when they was French. So big in the town, they give to the poor, they try to make it up to God. But two women, a mother and daughter…they die up at the old house. They fall in the old well and drown. People talk big about the curse again and more bad things happen. Their big fancy barn in Colby burn down and they lose their stock. Nobody want to do business with them. Then their son, say he don't believe in no curse, so one time he go and try to farm in Trace, he take a tractor up in there and it fall on him and kill him.

"Them ghosts kill everybody. Them ghosts in there is French ghosts, and that's the worst kind. They hate their own blood, and they hate Anglos worse. They don't forget nothing. *Stay away from there!*" Frenchy looked hard at us and his eyes were hard as iron.

Nobody spoke. Everybody was looking at Evvie and me.

"What happened to the Pelletiers?" I said finally. "Are they all dead?"

Frenchy licked his lips and looked at his plate. I could hear the old clock, the mice in the walls. All of a sudden the hair on my neck moved like there was a tick crawling through it, and I felt cold all over. Did the ghosts know we took things from the Pelletier place?

I glanced at Evvie, and I knew that she was thinking the same as I was; we needed to go home. I began to feel scared and also sick, so we told Jinnae we'd sleep over some other time, we caught up Sam and got on, and rode away up hollow in the dark.

The Ghost in the Corn

When we got near where Byron's fields ended and the woods began, we saw pale flames flickering over the swampy places; we heard these awful shrieks and gargling noises. It could have been screech owls but it also could have been dead Pelletiers. My teeth started chattering but I was sweating at the same time. Sam never noticed; he just kept marching. Then the dead-black tunnel of the woods swallowed us and the dark closed in behind.

"I'm not scared if Sam's not scared," I whispered to Evvie. "I read that horses always know if there are ghosts around."

"Can Sam out-run ghosts?"

"Yes."

Sam walked calmly up hollow, ker-plick, ker-plock, with us crouching on his back holding our breath and listening. Ker-plick, ker-plock. It was like the dark was touching me. I could hear Evvie whimpering and breathing too fast.

After about two eternities we saw a lighter dark, where the woods thinned and our fields began. Sam broke into a jog past the cornfield and turned into the barn lane.

We slid off and Evvie opened the swing gate to the pasture. My hands were shaking so bad I could barely strip off Sam's bridle. I half-threw it on the gate, I'd get it tomorrow, I wanted to be inside the house now. As I turned around the clouds broke up and started blowing away south; and the moon came out. Suddenly we could see everything, it was so bright. I started to run down the lane, to get out from under the hard glare of that moon, because suddenly everything could see *us* too. But before I took two steps, my sister grabbed my arm and dragged me to the ground.

"*Did you see it?*" she gasped.

"What? Stop it! *What?*" I whispered.

"*There's a ghost out on the road.*"

There was. A black shadow in a man's shape was standing in the moonlight in the middle of the road. It didn't move; it just stood there waiting. Waiting for us.

Evvie whimpered under her breath like a dog; then she started squirming on her belly, crawling through the grass toward the tall corn; I squirmed after her, keeping low. In a few seconds the cornstalks closed over us, but we kept crawling.

It's really easy to lose yourself in a cornfield. We went in there a few times just for fun during the daytime and got all turned around in two shakes. But tonight it was not fun at all. The black shadows of cornstalks slithered over our backs as we crept farther and farther into the field, try-ing to be quiet. Finally Evvie stopped and we listened; all I heard was my heart racing and my teeth chattering. I had this panicky feeling that we weren't even on our own farm any more; we were somewhere on the old Pelletier place, where the haunted aisles of corn snickered and crackled and went on forever and ever...

Crackle! Snicker! Crack! The ghost was following us, brushing the stalks as it came toward us, and making little humming noises. I sprang up and bolted through the cornshadows blackwhite blackwhite black-white blackwhite. Stop. Evvie...Not here. Not anywhere. Where was she? Where was I? *Where was the ghost?*

Hold breath. Listen. Blood pounding in my ears. Rustles and cack-les– the wind, Evvie, an animal– or Armand's ghost coming for me? Jeans warm and wet. Peed my jeans.

Go sideways. Out of this aisle, across two other aisles. Listen.

Robbie barking. He's in the house, *the house*! At last I knew where it was; it seemed miles away. Go toward the house... I stood up and ran down another aisle—and crashed into—

Big! Hairy! Rank goat smell! "AAAAAAH!" I yelled and the thing barked in my face, it knocked me down and kicked me, turned around with a flash of white and scrambled away down the aisle. I got up and ran the other way as the moon went dark again. I ran blind. Footsteps behind me, man's footsteps, following.... a dog barking, near me now, Robbie, running past me... I was lost again.

Engine hum, I knew that sound—our car—Mom and Dad coming home. I was close to the road—run, run... in ten seconds I burst out of the corn and into the road screeching and waving my arms. The car stopped, the door opened and I got in, not in back but in the front into Mom's lap. Sobbing.

Mom hugged me. "Honey, what's the matter? What are you doing in the road? You're all wet! Why aren't you at Willett's?"

"Where's Evvie? Did you see her? *O Jeez it got her it got her!*"

"Ruthie, calm down, and don't swear. She's up in the house! Look, the lights are on, can't you see? What's going on here?"

We were pulling into the dooryard and tumbling out of the car yelling... No Evvie, I scrambled up the steps into the house, yelling Evvie, where are you Evvie are you OK? Even Mom and Dad were yelling now too, Evvie Evvie.

My sister had locked herself in the bathroom. She came out shaking, white as moonlight. Then Mom and Dad knew something really *had* happened, and they sat us down and made us tell them what we had been up to.

"We came home because they were telling ghost stories down at Willett's, and we...got scared." I said. "When we got back and put Sam away we saw—a ghost—so we hid in the corn."

"It chased us. I heard it coming after us into the corn," sobbed Evvie. "I couldn't find Ruthie, and then the ghost walked right past me *this close,* and I ran for the house and let Robbie out. He ran right in there barking like crazy."

"I bumped into something out there," I interrupted. "It kicked me and woofed at me."

"Probably a deer, not a ghost," said Dad.

"But there *was* a ghost, because I yelled and ran, and then I heard footsteps coming and this humming noise, and then Robbie chased it. Where's ROBBIE? Boy Jeez *the ghost got him!*"

"There are *no ghosts* out there," Dad said. "Just shadows and moonlight and a couple of hysterical girls with too much imagination."

"But we *saw* somebody standing in the road right out front!"

"It was probably Injun John or Frenchy, hiking back up to their bus. They're just harmless old men, they wouldn't hurt a fly."

I had no idea my parents were aware of the existence of Frenchy and John *or* their bus. Did they know everything we didn't tell them? Did they know we stole stuff from a haunted house and ate wild mushrooms? Did they know we had been about to spend the night in a mansion full of drunk people?

"Look," said Mom, "Here's Robbie at the door. He was probably just chasing the deer. This is all one big false alarm."

Robbie knew better than to run deer; but Mom didn't know that. I was barely listening to my parents. Their voices were coming from a million miles away.

Mom decided to fix us some warm milk. She said we were shivering and our hands were cold as ice, and we couldn't sleep in that state. At long last we were allowed to go to bed. As soon as Mom and Dad had settled for the night, my sister and I got up again. We tip-toed to our bookshelf; we grabbed the old square glass bottles, the broken china plate, and the metal buttons. We opened our window screen very quiet-ly, and tossed those items out into the brush, as far as we could throw.

Before dawn I woke up with a jerk and sat up in bed. Somebody was whispering in my ear. I put out my arm but there was *nobody there*! *The ghost was in the room*!

I yanked the covers over my head. I had heard something terrible, but now I couldn't really remember if the ghost told me or I dreamed it. This was what it was: The Pelletiers were alive. I knew where they were. But I had to keep it a secret, from Evvie and Mom and Dad, and from myself.

A Visit

*Withdraw thy foot from thy neighbor's house
lest he weary of thee and hate thee. –Proverbs 25:17*

We were all sort of scared for a while after the night the ghost chased us in the corn. Evvie and I were afraid to go to Trace Hollow, or even up Argue, in case it really was Frenchy and Injun John after all. Mom was afraid to let us go too far away on Sam. So we stuck close to home for a few days. When Mom watched us ride in the meadows, she got scared Evvie and I would fall off, but I told her not to worry—Sam was keeping us on, and we were never ever going to get dumped. But everybody falls off eventually, and we did too, and it happened at what seemed to be the worst possible moment. But as it turned out, even falling off Sam had its benefits.

This is the story of our first dump. Dad was bringing MomMom Upstate for a weekend visit. Mom asked us to sleep in the pup tent and let MomMom have our room; and she made us help her clean the whole house even though it was already clean.

"MomMom likes to have things just so," said Mom, "And I don't want to give her any excuse."

MomMom got out of the car in the dooryard, and Evvie and I hugged her and said welcome to our farm, isn't it beautiful?

MomMom said, "Where's the house?"

"This is it right here, come on up on the stoop and admire our scenic view of Argue Mountain," I said.

A funny look came over MomMom's face. She marched up the porch stairs but went straight inside. She peered into the bathroom and inspected the parlor, shaking her head and rolling her eyes. She went into the kitchen, stared at our second hand ice box and ancient stove, and then she asked Dad;

"Dave, are you getting enough to eat?"

Mom turned around and walked out the kitchen door, slamming it. We heard the car pull out and go roaring down the road. Probably Mom was going to pick up some items she forgot at the Grand Union. In the meantime, I decided this would be the perfect moment to catch Sam and show him off to MomMom.

"Well, he's not what I would ever call *handsome*," MomMom said when we led our steed into the dooryard, all brushed and tacked up. "Is he some kind of cart horse? What's the matter with his eyes? Isn't he much too big for such young girls?"

"Nah," I said, trying to sound like Byron, "there's more of him to love and Boy Jeez he's a real good goer." I flung my arm over Sam's neck and kissed his cheek.

Then MomMom told us to stop that, because, well because-

"You don't know where he's been." She said.

"Do you want to see me ride him?" Evvie asked. MomMom rolled her eyes and asked us if that horse was really safe.

"Sure," Evvie said, "we ride him all the time. He carries double, want to see?"

"Well, I don't know..."

We took off the saddle and climbed onto Sam from the picnic table. We walked and trotted circles around the hayfield while MomMom sat in the lawn chair Dad had brought her, darning Dad's socks and calling out to us to hold on tight and not to go too fast.

I whispered to Evvie.

"Let's gallop to the end of the meadow. From the halt."

"We never do that," Evvie said.

"How hard could it be? Let's do it, it'll scare her, Boy Jeez."

"OK let's do it!" whispered Evvie. Sam already knew what was coming and approved of it. He was humming, arching his neck, and collecting himself for takeoff.

"HUP!" I yelled. That was our signal to gallop. Sam laid his ears back, snorted, and took off at a dead run.

But he took the right lead, and I was expecting the left; so Evvie and I found ourselves coming off exactly together, and crashing in a heap onto the grass, exactly together.

"HUH!" we said, exactly together.

MomMom jumped up with a shriek and waddled for the house squawking and yelling "Dave, Dave, call an ambulance!"

Evvie and I lay like the dead in the grass, the breath knocked clean out of us. And Sam? Had he gone galloping merrily over the hill? No. He stopped dead, whirled around and gazed at us in wide eyed surprise. When my sister and I caught our breath, we started to laugh at how funny Sam looked, standing there wiggling his ears like he was saying,

"Oops, sorry cherubs."

The rest of MomMom's visit was not a howling success. She was not impressed by our horsemanship and derring-do. She was scared Sam was vicious; with her own two eyes she had seen him *deliberately* buck us off. She told Dad he'd do well to sell him to the first buyer.

"If that horrible horse kills you girls, don't come running to me," she told us.

MomMom was also scared there were snakes under the porch. She was scared our well water wasn't clean. "Has it been tested?" She called our house "a shack." "Is it up to code?"

While MomMom wasn't sewing buttons on Dad's shirts, she cleaned our clean counter tops and gave Mom tips on how to improve "your camp kitchen," and how to make "at least half decent food" so her son could eat "the way he was accustomed to."

Mom offered to let MomMom cook all the meals for the week-end, and Evvie and I yelled yay, let's have rib roast and scalloped potatoes. Those were MomMom's famous specialties.

"No, thank you, I guess I know my place," MomMom said.

"Well, I can't take the heat," Mom said, "So I guess I'll get out of the kitchen." So Mom didn't cook either. It *was* sort of close in that kitchen, so we ate cold cuts along with fresh corn and tomatoes from the Connor's roadside stand.

Dad took a sudden notion to go fishing and left at dawn both Saturday and Sunday and stayed away all day. Evvie and I went out riding with Jinnae; Mom went for long walks, and MomMom sat in the parlor and mended Dad's pants.

Sunday afternoon came, and it was time for Dad to drive MomMom home. As she got into the car she shook her finger at us and said,

"Mark my words, I am going to see to it that you girls get a proper saddle of your own. No child of my son's is going to ride around like a wild Indian." I thanked her and hugged her goodbye where she sat in the front seat, but she did not hug back. Her girdle had slat things in it. She felt like a cyclone fence.

A Long Ride

"What have I done to thee
that thou has smitten me?" –Numbers 22:30

Jinnae came up to teach Evvie and me how to fish with our hands, but I said I didn't want to go. I had been thinking about what MomMom had said about riding like a Wild Indian. Maybe it would be a good idea to ride in a saddle for a while and practice my equitation, so I wouldn't end up flapping all around like Jinnae.

I planned to go down our back lane to Connor's and up the pretty Connor Hollow Road. Jinnae said if you looked for it you could find a trail that wound all the way up the back side of Argue Mountain and connected again to the Mitchell Hollow road.

I didn't feel all that great. I had My Friend; that's what all the girls in seventh grade called their period. It was supposed to be such a big deal, because you were officially a woman when you got it, but mostly it was annoying, with Kotex and clip belts. Also having it gave me the cramps and made me feel slow and stupid. But I was dead set on going; today at least I would ride the *right* way.

I fumbled with every buckle tacking Sam up. To make things worse he was fidgeting, shifting around and he kept tossing his dumb head.

"STOBBIT!" I yelled. Then I saw his left ear was folded over and stuck under the crown piece. I jerked the stupid strap over the ear. I was all hot and sweaty and squirmy, but now here was Sam all tacked up, so I gritted my teeth, and heaved myself on.

Even before I got my feet in the stirrups Sam started jigging.

"*Walk ON, Dammit!*" Sam was *deliberately* jouncing me; I hunched over in the saddle trying to sit still, but the more I tried not to bounce the more I bounced. Sam kept right on jigging.

We had to pass the Academy on the way to the lane, and I was thinking maybe I should go in there and make him trot circles to loosen him up. Or maybe I'd just let him wear himself out jigging downhill to Connor's.

At the last minute I decided I couldn't stand it– I'd go into the Academy after all. I pulled the left rein; Sam's head turned obediently in the desired direction, but the rest of him continued on down the lane. I pulled harder. He bent his head around to my stirrup and glared up at me, but he didn't change course.

"I'll teach you to disobey me!" I yelled, and gave the rein a wicked yank.

In a flash the horse jerked his head up and the bony bump between his ears crashed into my forehead. Then he spun around in place a few times. I saw stars and then the ground right below me, but I locked my arms around Sam's neck, and hooked my heel hard on the saddle flap. When he finally stopped whirling, I was gagging and dizzy and hanging practically underneath his neck.

Sam stood quiet with his head back in its normal position while I hauled myself back into the saddle somehow, and sat there sobbing.

"Why are you *doing* this to me?" I blubbered. "You deliberately tried to buck me off! You are a *vicious beast,* and I am going to sell you to the *first buyer!*"

I could get off right now and call Billy and he would come with his truck and take this stupid ugly horse back.

Except. It was all my fault. I had ruined everything. I had forgotten all those promises I made to Sam and Black Beauty and all the horses in the world. I had ridden like an idiot, not giving clear commands, then jerking and yarning the reins. I had lost my temper and got in a fight with Sam and Sam was going to win every time, just like Ronan said. "*I'll teach you to disobey me,*" I had said, and Boy Jeez he disobeyed me good and proper. I wanted to run to Mom and cry in her arms and never ride again, she would understand, I was just a little kid and riding was so dangerous.

Except. I did want to ride again. I had to make things right between Sam and me. Now.

The sun kept on shining, the birds kept on singing, and Sam kept on standing there like a statue in the park, with the reins hanging in a loop on his neck. After a while I stopped crying. I could hear Mrs. Ackerl talking in my head. "Look in the direction you want your horse to go. Give him a clear idea of what you want him to do." I sucked in a few deep breaths, took my feet out of the stirrups and let my legs hang down. I picked up my reins at the buckle, looked in the direction I wanted do go, put my trembling legs on his ribs and said, in a shaky voice,

"Walk on, Sammy."

Sam turned his body and walked into the Academy. On a loose rein. No fussing. We walked once around the edge; whole school. Then Sam and I turned into the center of the field and halted. I dropped the reins again, patted his neck and said "Good Boy." I could barely hear my voice and I was crying again. I got off and led Sam back to the barn and groomed him and turned him out and put up the tack.

"That was a short ride, Ruthie," said Mom, when I came clumping in the kitchen door.

"Oh, I don't know," I said.

Farewell Summer

The last weeks of the summer were like my best dreams come true. Evvie and Jinnae and I rode our shining steeds everywhere. We even rode them swimming in the Willett pond in spite of the snapping turtle. Sam would do anything we wanted, he was perfect—except for one thing. Ever since that day of my long short ride when I had yarned his mouth, he would toss his head if I asked him to go left or stop. I was deathly afraid that I had hurt his mouth permanently, so I started riding him with just a halter, sometimes with nothing at all except his mane.

Ed's heifers escaped from the pasture, and Sam and I chased them up Argue and herded them home. Ed was real pleased that I had rescued his "gals" and real shocked to see me riding my horse with nothing but a halter and a lead rope, but Mom got scared so I had to use the bridle again, and Sam went back to tossing his head.

We went berry-picking on top of the big hill in Byron's back pasture and got zillions of berries and made jam and pies for us and for Byron too, because they were his berries. He was real grateful too, because She didn't bake no more.

We loved Byron's hill, not just because of the berries, but because we could see for fifty miles from its flat top when we galloped across it. Evvie named it "Amon Hen," the Seat of Seeing, a name she got from "The Fellowship of the Ring" by J.R.R. Tolkien.

One night in August, when Dad told us that there would be meteor showers, we three girls rode up Amon Hen to sleep out and watch the shooting stars. We turned the horses loose to graze with the sheep; we lay back on our bedrolls, smelling the grass and the wild thyme and Oswego Tea, and looking for planets and meteors. On top of the hill the stars were almost at eye level, and what with the meteors streaking down we felt like we were floating upwards right into heaven.

After school started back in Marlborough, we still went up to The Farm weekends. Ed and Dad hired Byron to check on Sam and the heifers every day till hunting began. Before Opening Day of deer season Wayne would trailer the cattle home, and Evvie and I would ride Sam to Colby Valley to board for the winter. We had to ride over there before hunting season because hundreds of flatlanders came Upstate deer hunting. Farmers locked their stock up during deer season, because the stupid flatlanders couldn't tell a cow or a horse from a deer and blasted away at anything that moved, including each other.

"They spoil it for the rest of us," Ed said. "Two guys shot up a woman hanging out her laundry a few years back. She lived to tell about it, but them Gol-durn hmf hmf hmf fools shoulda been locked up and throw away the key." Ed never cussed like Byron. He was a pillar of the Church and so was Bea.

And it came to pass on the second Sunday in October that Evvie and I took our last ride of the year, over to Ed's by way of Trace. The day was hazy and dead quiet, with every sugar maple in the county looking as if it was on fire. The hayfields were still deep green and the cornfields were sere and stubbly; the crickets trilled their long sad note. The smell of turning aspen leaves and wood-smoke from people's stoves hung over the hollows. We rode slow and kept silence with the woods, soaking it all up for winter.

When we had slid off Sam's back at Pilchers and turned him out into the yard, he stuck around near us as if he knew we were going away. We pulled his ears and hugged his head and he gently itched his cheek bones on our shoulders. We heard a chuckle. Ed was leaning on the swing gate, his blue eyes twinkling.

"By Gum," he said, "that hoss really does seem to like you!"

"Nah, I guess he's just used to us now," I said. Then Ed said come have a bite, so we went into Bea's warm kitchen to drown our sorrows in tumblers of new milk and fresh-baked brownies. Then we went home. No, not home. Just Downstate.

Christmas at MomMom's House

He doth nothing talk of but his horse. –Shakespeare

We went back to our regular life Downstate: school, birthday parties, Scouts, Hallowe'en, Thanksgiving. I told everybody in my class about Sam and the great times we had on the farm, and invited my best friend Liz Hodges to come up sometime.

"All you care about anymore is your horse and that dumb farm," she said.

"All you talk about anymore is boys," I said back. We stayed friends, but now that I was deep in my Horse Phase I was not going to come out of it any time soon.

I went to see my old riding pals and take a lesson over at Fox Hill, paying for it by mucking out and cleaning tack, but after that one time I stopped going. Holly Cooper had her own horse now, and she was off competing in shows; and besides, Mrs. Ackerl told me she didn't approve of my horsemanship.

"You've been riding bareback," she said.

I hung my head and said Well, yes I had.

"You have ruined your form. Your seat is deep, the hands are light, but the legs, horrible! Can't you get your heels down? How will you ever get your horse to move forward?"

I don't know, I said. Getting Sam to move forward was not a problem that had come up, except that once. And I didn't care about trotting round and round in a dusty old arena. The schoolie I was riding shuffled like he was half asleep, not like Sam rumbling and thundering across the top of Amon Hen with the wind in our hair. I didn't want to ride any other horse but Sam.

Even Christmas seemed kind of dull that year. Except for Christmas Day, when we all gathered at MomMom's for one of her delicious dinners. And of course our traditional Christmas family fun and games. After MomMom's perfect turkey and gravy and heavenly whipped potatoes, and MomMom's special greenbeans and boiled onions, and angel food cake with strawberries and whipped cream, Dad would lean back in his chair and start spreading Christmas cheer by comparing his MomMom's cooking to Mom's.

"Mother, what can I say, you're a GREAT. GREAT. COOK. Almost as good as *Joanie here.*" Mom would duck her head and tell Dad softly that she didn't need to be reminded about how she didn't measure up to MomMom. Sometimes Dad would stop at that, and sometimes he'd switch over to his other traditional Yuletide story, which was about his college girl friend. He would talk about this beautiful girl he met on a ski trip on Christmas vacation his senior year, and how MomMom had just loved her and hoped he would marry her.

"Gee, every year about this time I think…maybe I should have listened to my Mother's advice and married her after all, ha ha," Dad would say. "But then I met Joan, and she acted so desperate to get herself a man that I took pity on her and married *her* instead."

Then everybody would laugh, me included, and Mom would cry and run out of the room. But this year I finally understood how she felt. Because I now knew what the term "yarning around" meant. I had seen Rufus do it. I had it done to me by Wayne Pilcher. I had done it myself. If I had been Mom I would have thrown a plateful of MomMom's perfect food right in Dad's face.

On the other hand I got a wonderful Christmas present; MomMom made good on her threat to buy me a saddle. She presented it to me after dinner, when we were opening presents. She told us she never wanted to see us riding bareback like savages again, and PopPop threatened to take the saddle back if we didn't keep it in perfect condition.

"And," PopPop said, "I want you both to work to become the best riders in the State. Why bother doing anything unless you are Number

One?"

"That means there would only be one person in the State riding," I said.

"Don't you give any backtalk to your grandfather on Christmas," said Dad. "Or there won't be even one person riding."

"And she will get her mouth washed out with soap," added MomMom.

Mom didn't say anything. She was in the bathroom again. Maybe she had had enough yarning around to last until next Christmas.

On Christmas Night I lay in bed wondering what the Farm looked like in the snow, and whether Frenchy and Injun John were having Christmas dinner at Willett's or were they nestled all snug in their bus halfway up Argue Mountain. What were Jinnae and Byron and She and the Pilchers and all the horses doing to spread Christmas Cheer?

A Serious Fight

Evvie was growing out of her Horse Phase. She didn't want to talk about Sam and next year on the trail any more.

My sister would rather spend her time cuddling with Robbie, dreaming up poetic names for her favorite spots on the farm. I have to say her names were just right, like Amon Hen. She also named our beech grove "Lothlorien," after the Elvish realm in "The Lord of the Rings." She called the shadowy woods trail between our orchard and Lame Buck Hollow "Mirkwood." The trail behind Byron's was "The Greenway," and the back lane down to Connor's became "Lovers' Lane" from "Anne of Green Gables."

Some places refused to be named. Everybody in my family tried to come up with the perfect name for the Farm, like Mountain View Farm, Roaring Brook Farm, but they all seemed wrong somehow, like when we tried to re-name Sam. Eventually we all gave up and called the Farm the Farm.

When I tried to get Evvie to discuss Sam's head tossing problem, she just changed the subject. Evvie didn't know anything about how I yarned Sam around that day, but I wanted to tell her and didn't want to tell her. Finally I got a rise out of her.

"Sam hates the bit," Evvie said. "When you stop him he gets all mad and jouncy and throws his head up."

"When *I* stop?" I said, "Why is it always *my* fault? How about when *you* halt, he tosses his head the same. He's in a snaffle bit. It's the mildest bit."

"The bit hurts him. We should just use the halter."

"We're not allowed to, remember? Maybe we should use a martingale and make him put his head down."

"The bit hurts him; it's cruel. Besides, riding is not fair to the horse."

"WHAT? Boy Jeez are you crazy!"

I should have known. Evvie had just cried her way through a horse book called "White Mane." In it a little kid rides a wild stallion with no saddle or bridle. Then, when they have to give up their freedom, they decide they would both rather die. So they swim out to sea and never come back.

On top of that, Evvie's fifth-grade class just finished doing a unit on the Emancipation of the Slaves and Harriet Tubman, the brave black woman who ran the Underground Railroad. Evvie had come home upset because her teacher said that the cruel slave masters used to tie iron bits in the mouths of disobedient slaves, *as punishment*.

My sister started boo-hooing again, right now, thinking of all the injustice in the cruel cruel world. Then she said that even *owning* a horse was wrong.

"So, what should we do with *Sam* then?" I asked her. "Tell him we're sorry and turn him loose? Just keep him to look at, like Duke? Sell him over to Kennedys? Eat him? Hey *there's* a great idea! Sam Chops!" Evvie kept right on blubbering.

"Besides," I wheedled, "Sam *likes* being ridden. Don't you think he has fun, charging around the country?"

"It's cruel," she said again, puckering up and hugging Robbie. The dog went limp, flopping into her lap grinning at me. He always sided with *her*.

"*You said that already*," I told her. "You can't just say it *again*."

"It's slavery," yelled Evvie. "We make Sam work and hurt him, and he has no say-so."

"Come ON, of course Sam has a say-so," I yelled. "Just ask Rufus Bates whether or not Sam has a say-so. Lookit, Sam lets us get on. He keeps us on. He doesn't buck. He doesn't bite. He puts his face on us just like Robbie is doing to you now."

"I think it's cruel."

"What about Jinnae?" I yelled at her. "Don't you want to ride around with her any more?"

Boo Hoo.

"If we don't ride Sam, he will probably go *direct to the slaughter house*! Who else would want him, who else would love him? He's just an ugly old plow horse in the eyes of the world!"

"It's cruel."

"DAMMIT EVVIE!"

Mom came hustling upstairs when she heard me bellow the oath, and told me not to raise my voice and not to use those words, please.

"Evvie said I was in favor of slavery and cruelty to animals!"

"I did not," said Evvie.

"Did too," I said.

"Not."

"Too."

Mom asked us to take deep breaths and tell her what the trouble was. Then we told her everything. Or almost.

"Well, Evvie, and Ruthie," she said, "you both have tender hearts and a sense of fair play. But I here's what I think. A horse isn't a pet, like a dog, it's…"

"A slave," said Evvie. I shot her my dirtiest look.

"Horses, cows, goats, sheep are made to—well, to serve," said Mom. "They are put on this earth to work for us, and we have a responsibility to treat them kindly. Maybe it's not *completely* fair, but you give Sam such good care, so he is a luckier and happier horse than most. But he has to earn his keep."

"That's the same excuse the people who owned the slaves used," Evvie put in.

"EVVIE WILL YOU COME OFF IT!"

Mom hushed me and said, "Ruthie, the slaves were human beings with a God-given right to be free, but a horse has to be owned by somebody. Sam can't run around loose in New York State. There are *laws.*"

Evvie had to agree with this point, but it did not answer the question of were we hurting our horse for our own selfish fun. If it really *was* cruel, how could I say I loved animals and still do it? I had hurt Sam and, even though I was really sorry, it made me practically a slave owner.

"Girls," Mom sighed, "you will find out that both horses and people have to do many things in this life that they won't want to do. But we have to do them anyway and just grin and bear it."

"What things?" I said.

"You'll find out. When you're older."

"But don't you even believe Sam loves us?"

"I don't know if he can think about such things. He's a real-life horse, not a story book horse like Black Beauty. He can't talk and tell us how he really feels."

"*I* happen to believe he loves us," I said. "I believe he likes it when we ride him. And he can *too* think!"

I didn't go so far as to say that Sam talked, but I believed he did. In one part of my head I could hear Sam talking to me, not with words exactly but with his whole self. He had said *"Oh all right, if it means that much to you."* He had said, *"Ooops, sorry cherubs"* When we fell off. And when he reached out his forefoot out and pawed, I had heard him say, *"Let's go, let's Go, let's GO!"*

In another part of my head I wondered if this lovey-dovey talking-horse stuff was just wishful thinking. I had fooled myself into believing Sam was beautiful, so maybe I was fooling myself into believing Sam loved me riding him. I could remember a day when he didn't love it at all.

"Wait till your father gets home," said Mom.

Dad's Philosophy of Life

As I would not be a slave, so I would not be a master.
–Abraham Lincoln

That night, after the dinner dishes were washed and Dad got a fire going in the fireplace, we asked he did he think it was cruel and slavery to ride horses? Dad chuckled. He put down his "Field & Stream," leaned back in his easy chair, and began.

"Is it cruel and slavery or not? Well. We live in a dog-eat-dog world, where The Strong prey upon The Weak, and The Smart have dominion over The Stupid. Those are the simple facts. You can believe in a fairy tale world of hearts and flowers, or you can face those facts.

"When you face facts you see that Fear and Hunger are the only forces in the world. There's no such thing as love. Nobody, man nor beast, works because he loves it. I get up and commute to the office every day because I am afraid of getting fired and going hungry. If I could arrange things to suit myself, I wouldn't have a wife and kids, ha ha, and right now I'd be asleep under a palm tree in the South Sea Islands with a few lines out to catch fish for dinner.

"And you girls, you go to school every day not because you love it but because you're afraid you'd get a licking if you didn't. And you would, too, rest assured, ha ha.

"Every animal in the world—and we are animals too—is driven by fear and hunger and nothing else. Is that good? Is that bad? It's just reality. Sam obeys you because the whip and the bit give him pain, and he fears pain. Whip, pain, fear, go. Bit, pain, fear, stop.

"To avoid pain and to get some food, that's his incentive. You know what incentive is? A food reward. It's that simple. The more pain, the more he will obey, and learn his lesson. Then he gets the food. That's the way the world works, for all of us, humans *and* animals alike." Dad beamed at us and picked up "Field and Stream" again.

After bedtime I lay under my covers wide awake, thinking it didn't much matter if I was kind to animals or not. I could yank Sam's mouth and beat and starve him and it wouldn't make any difference. I just believed all that gushy oh-my-pony-loves-me stuff so I could get to ride. What Dad said was true. Sam was my slave.

Evvie and I hadn't said a word to each other since Dad said she was right. She and Robbie were curled up snoring together in her bed. I guessed owning and training a freedom-loving dog didn't count as slavery.

Could I put my nice new saddle on Sam and force him to carry me up hill and down dale? It had been rainy the whole month and the world was raw and dark and horrible; but maybe springtime would be even worse; because in April we would go Upstate, and I would ride Sam– or not ride him. If I didn't, what would happen to him? Where would he go? There aren't any orphanages for horses.

Next day it was fairly warm for March, and I decided to go talk to Mrs. Ackerl. I needed to be back in the old cozy Fox Hill world. After school I got on my bike and pedaled myself over. I found my teacher in the aisle tacking up a hunter. I wanted to throw myself into her arms and sob, but I just asked her was it true that a horse obeyed because of fear and pain.

"No," she said.

"A good rider seldom punishes the horse with pain," she said. "If the horse fears the spur or the bit, it does not go forward willingly, and if there is pain, it will balk or fight or run away. This is not only cruel. It is very dangerous."

Boy Jeez that was good news. One thing Sam did was stride out freely. Except for that one time.

"You must persuade the horse," said Mrs. Ackerl. "you must get him on your side. The horse should accept the bit and the work happily. Why shouldn't the horse enjoy its work? They love to move, to travel over the country."

Mrs. Ackerl's words sounded true, truer than Dad's. I didn't feel sick when she said them. She must be right.

Then Mrs. Ackerl told me more about bits.

"Some sensitive horses don't like the squeezing snaffle action," said my teacher. I confessed that sometimes he tossed his head.

"He tosses his head? Here's what we'll do. I'll loan you a Pelham bit, the curved bar bit with a little shank and double reins. Many horses go best in this bit."

I thanked Mrs. Ackerl when she gave me the bit and hugged me, and then she smiled at me with sad eyes.

"I've told a thousand little girls please to keep the heels down and please not to have a romance with their first horse," she said. "Some of them kept the heels down but all of them have the romance; so you have it too, with my blessing."

Halfway home the warm comfy feeling of Fox Hill wore off, and I began to wonder whether I liked Mrs. Ackerl's answer because it was true or because it was what I wanted to hear. She ran a riding stable for a living, so she could be fooling herself too.

I stopped and got off my bike and took Mrs. Ackerl's Pelham bit out of my jacket pocket. And stuck it in my mouth.

The metal bar was heavy and cold. I slid two fingers through the snaffle rings and yanked back, hard. The bit clanked against my teeth and pulled my lips back into a tight grin.

Now I knew how it felt to be a horse. It felt horrible.

The sun was going down. The wind picked up and blew bitter cold right through my jacket and made me shiver; tears came into my eyes. I kept holding the bit tight so it hurt my lips, and the cold from the steel seeped into my teeth.

I had jerked Sam's mouth with a piece of metal like this. I had hurt him, and he did what I wanted afterwards because he was afraid to be hurt again. If he hadn't been afraid he would have bucked me off and stomped on me. Maybe he should have.

Evvie had been right all along about slavery. She had loaned me her book on Harriet Tubman and said I needed to read it if I was ever going to understand. As I stood there wearing the bit, I remembered the chapter when Harriet Tubman's master hitched her to a loaded wagon and told her she could have her freedom if she could haul that wagon all the way to the gate.

Then all the cruel slave-owning masters stood around laughing and betting on how far Harriet Tubman could pull the load. When she made it to the gate she was nearly dead, but she had done it, she had won her freedom. Then the master laughed and said she was too strong a worker to let her go, so he guessed he'd just have to keep her after all.

Did they put an iron bit like this in Harriet Tubman's mouth when she hauled that load? Did the bit yank a grin onto her face, so she had to smile even when she heard that the terrible man had double-crossed her? Did Harriet Tubman grin and bear it?

I stood there and thought about all the things people did to animals to steal their freedom and make them knuckle under. Curb bits, gag bits, wire bits, check reins, tie-downs. Whips, spurs, chains, war bridles, electric prods, hobbles, blinders.

Who was I kidding, it was all cruel. They didn't love us, why should they? We tied them up, shut them in dark stalls, branded them, and tattooed them. We cut off their tails, we turned them into geldings, and stuck nails into their feet. The nicest thing we ever did was shoot them when they were too old and tired and lame to be of any use.

How could I ride any more? I had asked everybody I knew and did not trust their answers. Except. I didn't ask a horse.

I knew one who talked.

Sam Speaks

Be subject to one another –Ephesians 5:21

Ten days after I put the bit in my mouth, the Rossley family drove Upstate for the weekend to see the Pilchers– and Sam. I was determined to ask my horse what he thought about being ridden. I'd be asking him alone; when I showed the new bit to Evvie and told her what Mrs. Ackerl had said about it, she turned her back and walked away.

It was barely spring Upstate; there were patches of snow on the north sides of the hills at Pilcher's. The landscape had a cold hard look as if it was indifferent to all life. Would Sam remember me, or would he be cold and indifferent too?

Mom and Bea stayed in the kitchen, whooping and cackling as they caught each other up on all the gossip. Ed and Dad and we girls went out to the paddock to see Sam. When we opened the swing gate, the horse we had dreamed about and squabbled about all winter was standing with his pal Duke. They looked like other animals, like shaggy bears in their winter coats. When Sam saw us he upped his head, whickered, strolled right over and demanded a scratch.

Evvie hugged and kissed his head while I scratched his chest, then she scratched his poll while I buried my nose in his fluffy fur. Along with his sweet-rank horse smell, I smelled the scent of snow and winter wind that had got caught in his coat.

Ed and Dad watched us, chuckling, as we kissed our horse and pulled down his ears. When I eased the lead rope across his neck and buckled on his halter, Sam sniffed my neck and face just like last year. Neither Dad nor Ed made any comments about hunger or fear or whether there was any such thing as love. Not that I would have heard.

I led our big beloved teddy bear of a horse into Pilcher's dooryard to groom him and tack him up with the saddle and bit. I slid that Pelham into Sam's opened mouth and fastened the curb chain loose under his chin. Then I put my own saddle on his back and tightened up the elastic-billet girth, made special for a horse's comfort. Evvie had retreated to the stoop, but at least she was watching.

The sky was the color of lead and the trees were still bare, but the exciting smell of thawing soil came on the breeze into my nose. It made me want to get on and take right off at the gallop, but the fields were still too muddy to ride in; we were just going on the side of the paved road. I wasn't going to ride long anyway; Sam was so furry, I didn't want to make him sweat because it would take me the better part of forever to get him dry again.

I got on. As soon as I had gathered up the four reins and organized them between my fingers, Sam grunted, hummed and walked out. I slid the reins a notch shorter, and—I felt his mouth. I gasped and nearly yelled out, because I *really really felt it!* It was so different from before.

All in a flash I knew it wasn't just the new bit that was different. It was me. I had worn that bit inside my own mouth; now it felt as if Sam's mouth *was* my mouth. And I could tell Sam knew all about it, because he was turning himself over to me.

Not like you turn yourself over to the cops or something. It was more like when Robbie leaned up against my sister and then just let himself melt into her lap. I was melting too. I was turning myself over to Sam. I was shivering. Tears wet my face.

Sam was nodding his head saying *"yes, yes, it's all right, it's all right"* as if he felt what I was thinking, right through the reins. And I felt him too, in this different way. *It's all right, it's all right!* His mouth was smiling and my hands were touching it.

I could feel each of Sam's legs swinging out along the damp dirt shoulder and his back swaying from one side to the other. I asked him to move up to a slow trot. A minute later I dug my rear end into the saddle and closed my hands and legs, the signal to stop dead. He did.

And what do you know, his neck stayed relaxed and his head remained the way I hoped– ears at the top, nose at the bottom– not the other way around. "That's so *good*!" I dropped the reins and patted him. I wiped my eyes and nose on my jacket, picked up the reins, and we swung around and trotted back, posting, sitting, down to a walk, halt. I was sure everybody could see what had happened.

Evvie was staring from the stoop. I had never told her about how awful it was to wear a bit, but now it was all right and I couldn't tell her that either. She just had to see it.

"Take him down from a canter to trot to walk to halt," she said.

Halleluiah.

I swung around a third time, jogged back down the shoulder, swung around again, trotted, thought about cantering. Ta-da-DUM, ta-da-DUM, smooth as silk and pure heaven to ride. I started to cry again, *I loved this so much*! Then I remembered my tasks; I checked Sam to a trot. Then jog. Then another halt. Boom! Sam stopped on a dime. Head down.

I could see that Evvie wanted to get on.

"Wow," I said to her, "Did you see his head, how he didn't fret?" He had done much more than not fret, he had let me hold his whole body in my hands.

Evvie nodded but stayed where she was. I didn't ask her again, I just got off and looked at Sam. He was waggling his ears at me and jiggling the bit around in his mouth. Then he upped his head, looked beyond me to the snowy hills. Slowly, slowly he lifted his off-forefoot, stretched it out, and pawed the dirt.

"Let's go, let's Go, let's GO!"

Evvie leaned in Sam's direction but did not take a step.

Ronan Weighs In

Thy word is a lamp unto my feet –Psalm 119:105

After school let out in June, Mom and Evvie and I came home to the Farm, stopping at Pilcher's so I could ride Sam over. Sam knew he was going home too, and he just floated over the trail, his bare feet hardly making a sound. Tomorrow he'd get shod along with Rusty, and he wouldn't need any grain bucket with rocks in it either.

Jinnae rode Rusty up hollow next morning. She and I held both horses while they dozed in the shade of the shoeing tree and let Ronan nip and rasp and pound on them. Evvie hung back, watching us from the porch steps.

"Well," said the old farrier, straightening up and kneading his back, "Princie has decided to hold his feet up for me," Ronan pulled gently on Sam's ear. "Botha these hosses are a pleasure to work around. They got real quiet manners, unlike some I gotta do today. You gals don't wanna work 'em hard right off, ain't that so, Princie?"

Ronan smiled at us all, and Sam poked his nose into the old man's scrawny chest. I looked over at Evvie– *she was coming over*. She was going to talk. Evvie widened her eyes, took a deep breath and asked the question.

"Mr. O'Ryan, do you think it's cruel to make a horse carry you around?"

I held my breath.

"Well, sis," said Ronan, rubbing his chin and scratching Sam's poll at the same time, "hosses is joined up with people. Hosses ain't cows, they take an interest in people, like dogs do. What dogs like best is other dogs, and what hosses like best is other hosses, but they like us too, unless they been bad treated. Now I can tell that this hoss is real interested in you, ain't that so Princie?"

Evvie nodded. Evvie smiled. We helped Ronan pack up and we waved at him until his truck went into the woods. Evvie and I were back in the hoss business.

Jinnae had lots of news.

"Got drunk, told ya I would, first time ever, on Dad's apple cider," Jinnae said. "Stuck a piece of straw in the barrel and sucked it right up. Tasted awful. Got the runs from it, too. Woo-ee. Tried smoking too, don't see why folks bother.

"Monique had another kid, and this go she married the Daddy. They went to live in a trailer park over Fort Eddard way, and they joined up with this shout-n-pray Bible church. After they was saved, the church give them all this kitchen stuff and a bed and cribs and such, because they didn't have a pot to piss in.

"Wellsir. The Daddy he took to drinkin' again and lost his job with the Dee Pee Dubbya, and then he beat up Monique a buncha times, blacked both her eyes for her, and when Lu found out, she and Frenchy and John the Injun went over there and knocked the Daddy's teeth in and tossed him out the trailer and told him to get lost or else, and it was his trailer.

"Then what do you think? That old Bible church come and took back all the beds and pots and pans and dinette suit and all, so Monique and the kids moved back in with us."

"How come the church took away the beds?" Evvie wanted to know.

"Lu wanted to know too, she called up the big Mukamuk Bible Reverend, and he told Lu that the man is the head of the house, like God is the head of the Church, and God sez Monique had to do her husband's bidding, no matter what he done to her.

"And then Lu told Mr. Bible Reverend that Monique's husband was the no-good drunk and the ass-hole of the house, and God was the ass-hole of the church too, and Monique wasn't no slave and she didn't have to take any shit from either one. What do you say we take a ride over to Byron's big hill whatcha-call it?"

"Amon Hen," said Evvie.

"You girls go," I said. "I already rode Sam once. Evvie, you can try out that saddle, OK?"

Sam in Love

O, how I love thee! how I dote on thee! –Shakespeare

One morning early Jinnae came riding up, not on Rusty but on a big bay mare; and she asked us if we wanted to board her for money.

"These pals of Lu's own her, and they just got thrown off their place over Green Crick way and moved to a 'partment in town. We'd take her but her and Rusty don't get along. They say they'll pay ten bucks a month in the summer and twenty in the winter. They don't ride her none, so she's just like yours. Whaddya say?"

I couldn't believe it. This time last year I was sitting on pins and needles, going crazy from not having a horse while Dad thought about it and Ed finished his haying. And this year, just like that, another horse just strolls in off the street.

"We have to ask our Dad first," Evvie told Jinnae.

"We'll mention the board money, and besides it's a free horse."

"Plus shoes. Plus tack," said Jinnae.

Jinnae let us ride the mare around to try her out.

"This mare here is a push-button horse," she said.

"What kind of horse?" said Evvie.

"Push-button. Automatic, you know? Push the button and she goes, push the button and she stops; but she don't make you sing Hally-loo when you ride her."

The mare really was as boring as a horse could be. Mom had been saying how she would love a calm nag to ride out on every now and then, so she and Dad each tried her out too; they rode her in the hayfield and up the road. They didn't have any trouble with her.

"Her gaits are so smooth," said Mom. Those gaits were smooth because that mare was dead lazy and didn't pick her feet up any more than she had to.

Dad let the mare stay. So just like that Evvie and I had a horse apiece, and somebody was actually paying us to keep her. Evvie named her "Mrs. Lynde," after the good lady in "Anne of Green Gables" because she was "fat and clumsy and without a spark of imagination in her."

We liked her ok, but Sam loved her on sight. When we turned her out in the pasture he puffed up and strutted around in front of her, arching his neck like a stallion, which he wasn't. Sam kissed Mrs. Lynde's neck and withers with his tongue, and she nibbled Sam's crest. After all the necking stopped, the two horses them stood head to tail in the stall, swishing flies off each other.

Mrs. Lynde was just the opposite of Sam; we never used our heels on Sam, but we had to ding *her* every few strides or she would just slow down and stop. But lazy old Mrs. Lynde had a secret that our parents didn't need to know; she loved to race. She would poke her nose out, pin her ears back, and go like a bat out of hell trying to get to the front of the herd. She'd rage along till she passed Sam and Rusty, and then she'd forget they were there and slow down again.

Mrs. Lynde was shiny-clean. You practically didn't have to brush her. Sam on the other hand was a pig. He rolled in dust and mud; he always had burrs and twigs stuck in his mane and tail and grass stains on his white socks. The two horses went everywhere together, but Mrs. Lynde stayed in show–ring condition and Sam got dirty.

Her other main virtue was, she was easy to catch. She didn't enjoy being caught, but she would just stand there staring at us until the halter went over her nose. Then she gasped, rolled her eyes in surprise, took one backward step, and gave up.

On the other hand, after Mrs. Lynde arrived, Sam decided he would *not* be caught; I thought maybe he was showing off for his girlfriend. When we walked out to the pasture and caught Mrs. Lynde, Sam wheeled and ran away like Mr. Wild Horse, looking back at his beloved over his shoulder.

So we had to use grain, like we had at first, to lure Sam into catching range. Ed said a horse can only think of one thing at once, if it thinks at all. Sam would think about getting that scoop of sweet feed and forget all about us trying to catch him.

We caught Mrs. Lynde, hitched her up and gave her a handful of feed while Sam skulked around in the upper pasture. We put feed in Sam's tub, banged the scoop against a barn timber and called "SAAA-YUM!" This was our horses' dinner bell; Sam came bucketing back down the hill; he charged inside the stall, and we slammed the door shut on him.

The next day when Sam ran off again, and we used the same method, but our horse had done some thinking overnight. When we banged the scoop and called he charged down, trotted into the stall, snatched a mouthful of feed, wheeled, and bolted out again before we even got our hands on the door. He retreated to the middle of the pasture chewing his grain and waggling his ears at us.

"I happen to know that Sam is the world's smartest horse," I reported to Ed, "because he can think of two things at once, getting the grain and not getting caught."

Ed chuckled and rubbed his chin and said "That's about two more ideas than most humans can manage."

Now that Evvie and I each had a horse, we took longer rides, swapping steeds; whoever was on Sam had to get off and open all the gates, because the one riding Sam was having more fun and it was only fair she had to do more work. We and Jinnae rode to the top of Argue and down the other side; we went down the old railroad bed into Vermont. Jinnae taught us games like Fox and Hounds or tag. All the horses, especially Mrs. Lynde, loved to play tag; they would chase each other on their own. We rode wild and hard and had collisions and got dumped now and then. Once Mrs. Lynde got so excited she bit Rusty, which we decided to count as a tag.

The funny thing was, Mrs. Lynde's owners never paid us for her board. They had skipped town; lots of people were looking for them to collect on their bills, but we didn't care if they ever came back because we got a free horse and tack out of the deal. Dad and Mom decided she could stay forever to keep Sam company and take them for an occasional trail ride, because she was so mannerly and calm.

The Umbrella Affair

A righteous man regardeth the life of his beast: but
the tender mercies of the wicked are cruel. –Proverbs 12:10

In June we had a spell of weather; big black thunderstorms rolled over the mountain every day and sometimes twice. On really wet days we took car trips to tag sales or visiting or just "ridge-running," as Byron called it. Byron took us on excursions in his truck, to eat at his favorite diners, to look at sheep or pulling pony prospects, or to buy harness advertised for sale in the Penny Saver.

On one Byron trip we bought our own used Pelham bit and the double reins to go with it, and Dad returned Mrs. Ackerl's bit after one of his weekends on the farm; I wrote her a thank you note too and said my horse liked a Pelham and I was riding in a saddle every day.

Next weekend Dad and Mom and we girls went to a yard sale, and I bought an old book called "Diseases of the Horse, An Owner's Guide, Lavishly Illustrated." Evvie and I started reading the book together in the back seat going home.

"Don't read in the car," Mom said, "You'll get sick." Actually we were plenty sick already.

According to this book there were hundreds of horrible awful calamities that could happen to a horse. Equines were delicate creatures; their guts hardly ever worked right, their legs could snap like twigs, their tendons bow or spavin. Their feet were likely to crack, pick up gravel, or shrivel up altogether with laminitis.

By the time we got home, the book had taken over our minds. We worked our way through it as the thunder rumbled and lightning flickered outside our bedroom window. We became horrified in alphabetical order. We'd slosh out to the pasture to see if Sam or Mrs. Lynde had abscesses, bowed tendons, or colic. We dreaded encephalitis, founder and heaves. Not to mention strangles, stringhalt, and strongyles.

We worried most about Sam. Why had we never had the vet up to give our horse a check-up? We needed the vet. We begged Mom and Dad every day to call the vet before it was too late.

Our parents' tempers, already short because of the wet weather, took a nasty turn. Dad threatened to take out his deer rifle and put Sam out of his misery on the spot.

Unable to keep our fears to ourselves, we walked down the road to Byron's place in the pouring rain—we couldn't possibly ride Sam in his present state. Byron had doctored his horses back in The Old Days, and he would know just what to do.

Byron heard our tale and obliged us by driving us back to our place in his truck. He sloshed out into the pasture with us and looked Sam over, nose to tail. When he was through, Byron rubbed his neck, chuckled deep in his throat, and scratched Sam's neck.

"Boy Jeez," he said, "we might want to hold off a bit and see if he gets any worse."

We took his advice with a grain of salt. Byron loved horses, but he had only ever called in the vet for his cows, and not often even for them. If a milk cow got sick or lame, Byron said, a farmer usually called the Dead and Down Man to take her away for mink food. Or, if the cow was worth more than the vet bill, he might pay out the money, which, by the way, he didn't have, to fix her up.

Sometimes, Byron said, the poor sick cow lay suffering while the farmer hemmed and hawed, and as likely as not by the time the vet got the call it was too late to cure her.

"Damn vets, pardon my French," Byron would say. "Cow dying right under their nose and they're demanding cash on the barrel. It's enough to make a man strike his father."

But call the vet for horses? No animal that didn't bring in cash was worth doctoring. One time, Byron said, his best pulling pony stepped on a nail that was sticking through a piece of board in the barnyard. The pony hobbled around for a day stuck to the board with the nail sticking out the top of her foot, until Byron happened to notice it.

"I didn't call the vet," he said. "Vets charge you double for a horse what they charge for a cow, Boy Jeez. I poured turpentine into the puncture in her hoof. Foot got infected, and I had to sell her up to Canada for dog food."

The rains continued. To break the awful spell of "Diseases of the Horse," our parents suggested we go over to Colby Valley to call on the Pilchers, who were also going stir-crazy from not being able to cut their hay. We'd buy some fresh milk off them, and maybe the grownups would play whist. We would not however, mention the book or Sam's delicate health and that was an order.

Fine with me. Ed had also farmed with horses in his youth, but as far as Ed was concerned, horses were cows with mental problems. He didn't understand horses, and used the wrong farrier and told stories about the durn-fool things horses did whenever they got the chance. Evvie and I disagreed with his opinions, but we laughed at his stories anyway.

Duke was the Pilcher's only horse. He was 10 and had been retired for five years because Ed wouldn't let Wayne or anybody ride him. Ed had bought Duke cheap, in a moment of weakness, at an auction sale, and gave him to Wayne as a birthday present. Wayne took after his Dad, he didn't have any knack with horses, and Duke quickly discovered how easy and fun it was to dump Wayne in the dirt, and amused himself by doing it almost every time Wayne got on him.

Duke's final escapade took place on the tarmac of the Colby Valley Road. Wayne broke his arm falling on the pavement, and that was the end of riding on the Pilcher place. Duke, like so many farmers' horses, snoozed his life away under the old apple tree.

Wayne wasn't afraid to get back on Duke. Wayne wasn't afraid of anything as far as I could see. But Ed needed Wayne to work; he was going to turn whole operation over to him in a few years. So horse escapades and broken arms had no place in the Pilcher's plans to make a go of it in the dairy business.

Nevertheless, Ed thought it was real cute that we two girls still insisted on riding Sam and that we had not yet been bucked off, bitten, stomped, or kicked to death. So as we sat in the Pilcher's cozy kitchen eating Bea's famous prize winning pie and drinking creamy raw milk from that morning's milking, Ed grinned and asked me:

"Well, sis, how's old Sam?"

I forgot my orders.

"I dunno," I said, "We thought he had bog spavin, then we thought he had ear mites, then maybe he could have got heaves. I was worried he had caught laminitis and strangles."

"He caught a cold," Evvie said. "Standing out in all this rain."

Bea, hovering over the kitchen counter constructing another pie, shouted at us (It had dawned on me that she shouted because Ed was hard of hearing), "Why don'tcha go hold an umbrella over him then?"

The Pilchers and our parents roared with laughter. They laughed on and on. Tears rolled down their cheeks. They whooped and wheezed and beat their fists upon their knees.

"Hold—an—uh—huh-humBRELLA over him!!" they kept saying it and setting themselves off laughing again. They didn't understand. All farmers thought about was their durned cows. Mom and Dad couldn't see what it meant to love a horse. We took care of Sam, Sam took care of us. No dumping, no biting, no kicking. No yarning. No neglect. And we never. NEVER. Laughed at him. I kept explaining, trying to make these ignorant people see what I meant, and they just kept saying umbrella, umbrella, umbrella and laughing.

"Come on out to the barn and see my new calves," said Wayne suddenly, and Evvie and I jumped up and followed him and I slammed the door hard on the way out. It was pouring and mucky, but Wayne whispered to me he admired anybody who could stay on the top side of a horse, and don't mind the teasing, that's just their way of having fun.

We saw the little calves. They leaned against me and frantically sucked my fingers; they had been taken away from their mothers and tied to the wall in little pens "for veal" Wayne said.

"I don't like doing them this way, it's sort of cruel, but we need the income," muttered Wayne, and I could see he was sad about it, like Byron was about the pony with the nail in her foot. I didn't take up the slavery issue with Wayne, because if the cows were the Pilchers' slaves, the Pilchers were also the cows' slaves, working their fingers to the bone day and night. Besides the cows weren't pets like dogs and horses.

Then Wayne told us a bunch of corny hee-haw sort of jokes, and I could see he was trying to make us forget about being made fun of, so I laughed even though I didn't feel like laughing.

But on our drive home from Colby Valley Evvie and I got to hear about the umbrella all over again. Mom finally stopped, but Dad went on and on. Dad always liked to beat a joke to death.

For instance when Mom burned the food, or when she tried some awful new recipe from "Ladies Home Journal," he would always smack his lips and roll up his eyes and say,

"Joanie, you're a GREAT. GREAT. COOK. Better even than *My Mother!*" Just the opposite of what he said when we were at MomMom's, but just as mean. Mom never stuck up for herself, and she didn't ask him to quit teasing me. I guess she was glad she wasn't the one getting teased.

When we finally pulled into our dooryard, I said Evvie and I were going out to the barn. We had to give the horses their evening snack, check up on Wayne's heifers, and no, we didn't need an umbrella.

My sister and I waded through the wet grass, went into the barn, and slammed the door shut.

Evvie dug a scoop of sweet feed from the bin and splashed half into Sam's bucket and half into Mrs. Lynde's. She banged and called, "SAAAAAAAA-YUM!" She didn't call Mrs. Lynde's name because Mrs. Lynde didn't know it and never would.

Sam's whinny echoed against Argue Mountain sounding like a whole herd of horses. He thundered down the pasture slope and trotted into the run-in, followed by his faithful girlfriend, and bellied up to his tub. Sam's eyes were bright. He was not limping. Green gook was not oozing from his nose. Bea and the others were right, of course; our horse was practically bursting with good health. He stuck his face into the tub, sucked up a good mouthful, and contemplated us with serene affection as he chewed it up.

And spit it back out. In a little ball.

Sam looked into the distance, wrinkling his eyebrows thinking about it for a moment. Then put his nose in the tub again. Again he chewed, again he spat. Evvie's eyes bugged out as she turned to me and whispered in the voice she reserved for saying "ghosts;" she said, "*he needs to have his teeth floated.*"

"Diseases of the Horse" had hit pay dirt at last.

We knew that Horses' teeth grow all the time, but they get worn down by grinding grain and grass. Sometimes a tooth will wear down unevenly, leaving sharp edges that cut the horse's mouth as he chews. Then the horse doesn't chew properly and gets colic. Or he stops eating and starts losing weight and gets colic. But treatment is the easiest thing in the world. The vet files the tooth smooth. Floating Teeth! Simple.

Not so simple.

"How are we going to get them to call the vet?" I whispered back. At Fox Hill and in "A Horse of Your Own," horses got yearly dental care. In Bethel they didn't. Besides, Evvie and I had boxed ourselves in, and badly. Who would believe that there was *anything* wrong with Sam? We had rung the alarm bell too often. Nobody would believe our horse was sick if he were lying stone dead with his hooves in the air.

"Can't you float them?" Evvie whimpered.

"Me?" I thought about it.

We put our hands in Sam's mouth often enough, but only as far as the corners of his lips, never back to where the big grinding molars were. I would be scared to stick my hand in there. And what would I use as a file? Assuming, that is, that Sam would stand and let me fumble around inside his head. I couldn't do it.

"We've got to tell Mom and Dad," I said. "We've just got to make them understand that this time it's really real, and we need the vet and it won't get better by itself."

"They'll just laugh," sobbed my sister.

"We can convince them. We'll show them the picture in the book."

"The book? The BOOK? If you get out the book you know what they'll say," sobbed Evvie, big tears practically squirting out of her eyes.

I knew it. I heard it already, the dread word, the hoots of laughter. And while they were hooting away Sam would be suffering. I couldn't stand it. I wouldn't allow it. I had to confront my parents.

We squished back down the lane to the house. It had stopped raining, but it was cold and very dark. We went slow, thinking hard about a way to ask for help and not get an answer with the word "umbrella" in it.

"We need to call the vet, Sam's teeth are cutting his mouth and they need to be floated," was how I put it, as I crashed through the kitchen door.

Mom and Dad looked up from their coffee cups in surprise. Then my Dad's face lit up like a jack-o-lantern. Yes! here was another golden opportunity to say it one more time!

"Why don'tcha go hold an UMBRELLA over him then?" he crowed, laughing like a jackass.

"No, Dad, no," Evvie interrupted. "This time it's really true. Sam is making little balls out of his sweet feed and spitting them back out. He won't eat."

Dad's face got all red. He put on his whiny baby voice and sniveled, "Oooh, my poor wittle horsie is dying, oooh, let's wun and call up the vetewinawian!"

Evvie clenched her fists and matched her whine to his. "Dad, Dad, will you just please listen?"

Dad's face turned purple.

"NO! You listen to me, young lady," he said, squinting up his eyes at my sister, and poking his finger in her face. "And listen good. *No vets!* They cost money, which, by the way.... Dammit, there is NOTHING WRONG with that HORSE!"

"How do YOU know? *You* weren't out there, *you* didn't see him spit out his feed! All you ever care about is money! *You* don't know JACK SHIT about horses!"

That seemed to be me, screaming at my Dad. I didn't mean to. It felt like someone else was doing it, and I was just watching.

Dad rounded on me and slapped me good across the face and told me never to address him like that again. I just stood there looking at him. It couldn't feel my face, there was no sting to the slap like there usually was.

Dad glared back at me, with his hand cocked for another slap. Mom sprang up and said "shesjustalittlekidDaveshedoesn'tknowanybetter," so Dad yelled Ican'ttakethisanymoreJoan and sent both of us to our room for the night so they could fight in peace. I didn't care. All I wanted was to do right by my horse. Now Sam would suffer, lose flesh, sicken, get colic, writhe in unspeakable agonies, twist a gut, and probably die in front of our eyes, and I was helpless to do anything to save him. At midnight, when all hope seemed gone, Evvie sat up in bed and said,

"Byron."

The Vet Comes Up

Thou call'st me a dog before thou has a cause,
but since I am a dog, beware my fangs. –Shakespeare

Next morning we hiked down hollow to tell Byron about Sam's teeth. He left off fixing his pasture gate; just dropped the fence tool on the ground and went and got his truck.

"Nothing keeps them ponies in anyways, Boy Jeez," he said as he opened the door of the cab for us. On the way up hollow we told him about the umbrella and everything else. Byron nodded in silence. The horses were in. Byron haltered Sam and stood him in a corner of the run-in. He took hold of Sam's tongue and pulled it gently aside. He inserted a finger to feel the horse's molars.

"Boy Jeez, I can feel a burr. You girls hit it right this time," he chuckled.

"Can you fix him?"

"Boy Jeez, I never done teeth. That's a job for the vet. He got the right tools."

"Do you think the vet would let us do some work for him in trade for coming up and fixing Sam's teeth?" I asked.

"Well, Boy Jeezum, I dunno could be," said Byron, "But come to think of it, my show harness needs cleaning for next week's pull. Top of that, I been meaning to move some old boards out of the shed to make a stall for a new pony I picked up over to Kennedy's. I've got to take Her to the doctor after dinner, so maybe you could do my chores, and I'll pay you for the trouble."

So we drove back down and went to work soaping Byron's fancy show harness, buffing up the brass bosses and buckles with silver polish. Then we moved the boards, being careful of the big spikes sticking through them. We didn't want Byron to wander by and notice we were hobbling around with nails in our feet.

When we were done Byron gave us five bucks apiece. With our allowances and savings thrown in, we thought we could cover a vet bill. So when Mom and Dad were downstreet grocery shopping we called up Dr. Melton. He said his fee was twelve bucks to float teeth and he would be in the neighborhood today. We said come on up; Evvie retreated to her room for some reason, and I went and sat on the stoop to wait. My parents got home first, but the vet's truck was in their dust right behind.

"And who might that be turning in our lane?" Dad wanted to know.

"Oh, that'll be the *vet*," I said, upping my chin and turning my back on him to go meet Dr. Melton. Evvie didn't come down; she had a better sense of what was going to happen than I had, but I got to watch Dr. Melton put the speculum on Sam, back him into a corner, open his mouth up, and slide a narrow rasp way back in there.

Sam had a very surprised expression on his face while the rasping was going on, but he stood like a rock for several minutes until Dr. Melton was finished. He made no move to leave after the vet took the speculum off and turned him loose. I scratched my steed's forehead while the vet packed up.

"You made a sound diagnosis, young woman," Dr. Melton said to me.

"I—I've had been reading up on veterinary medicine."

"Good for you. You're a fine horsewoman and you're doing a good job with this big fella. He has perfect ground manners. He's a pleasure to work around."

"Thanks."

"Maybe you should consider going to vet school."

Dr. Melton smiled at me as we walked back down the lane together. "*Really?*"

"You have good powers of observation and a nice knack with animals. I'm sure you would do well," I paid Dr. Melton and he shook my hand, as if I was an adult.

I stood in the road smiling and waving as the vet drove off down hollow. I stood there until the road dust settled.

"How dare you," began Dad, "deliberately call the vet up here when I expressly told you not to?"

I smirked up my face and said "You did not *either* tell me not to call him, and besides we paid him ourselves. So there."

"And just where did you get the money?" Dad yelled.

"From Byron! We—"

"From Byron? You SNUCK down there BEHIND MY BACK and begged money from that poor old man?"

"Well I sure knew YOU wouldn't give it to me!"

"Waste my money for some imaginary illness of that goddamn stupid old nag? Not likely! Can't you do *anything right*? Why the hell is it you are always getting hysterical over that STUPID GODDAMN HORSE?"

"BECAUSE I LOVE HIM MORE THAN YOU!" I shrieked at the top of my voice. "YOU ROTTEN, STUPID GODDAMN, SELFISH HORSE-HATING MAN!"

Dad and I stared at each other. Then I was on the ground seeing stars.

Mom dashed out and got on her knees next to me and hugged me and started pleading with Dad.

"Dave, she's just a...."

Dad rounded on her, red in the face and shaking.

"You! This is all *your* fault! You always let this kid get away with murder. She deliberately defied me and continues to defy me. She is ruining this family! Get her packed, I want her out of here."

"Where can she go?" Mom sobbed.

"I don't care. To your sister's. I don't want anything to do with her, until she apologizes to me and learns to show me some respect."

He turned his back on Mom, got in the car, and turned over the engine.

I raged up to our room, taking the stairs two at a time and yanked my dresser drawers out onto the floor. Mom followed me up.

"If you'd only just say you're..."

"NO!" I was shaking all over as I stuffed some clothes and books in a pillowcase and stormed back outside. Dad had the car idling. He got out and for the last time demanded an apology.

"*I* don't have anything to apologize for, *you do,* you called my horse stupid, and said he had an imaginary disease, and so when are you going to apologize to *me*?"

"Don't you ever speak to me like that, or so help me God!" Dad grabbed my arm and tried to shove me into the car. I fought back, and he slapped me and yarned me around. I knew he was hurting me, but I felt nothing at all. I kept fighting and kicking and screaming the worst things I could think of at him. Cuss words I had kept private for years flooded out of my mouth. Mom was screaming and Evvie was howling and Robbie was barking and the world was spinning around upside down.

Dad crammed me into the car and drove off with me to the bus station in Briggsboro. I hunched up in the back seat, as far away from him as I could get, glaring out the window and listening to my heart pounding. Dad could punish me all he wanted, but I had done right. I had saved Sam. That was all that mattered.

About halfway there I calmed down enough to realize I was never going to see Sam again. Dad would probably sell him as part of my punishment. So I told my Dad I was sorry for saying all those terrible things, sorry I had disobeyed, sorry about everything. Dad turned the car around and drove back home. He never said he forgave me. Maybe because he knew I wasn't really sorry.

There Comes O'er the Valley a Shadow

Thou art become cruel to me: with thy strong hand
thou opposest thyself against me. –Job 30:20

"Do you see where all your permissiveness leads, do you see?" said Dad to Mom, before he even got out of the car. I got out with my pillowcase and ran right upstairs. But I heard it all.

"Ever since this whole horse business started, that kid has gotten even more sullen and disrespectful. Why did I ever let you talk me into this in the first place!"

Mom begged Dad to get out of the car and calm down… they didn't mean any harm Dave, they were worried about their… and did Ruthie apologize? Then can't you…for peace in the family…."

Evvie and I sat on my bed together. I swore that if Dad didn't accept my apology he was an Indian giver and I was going to take my apology back too, after all, he had been wrong and Evvie and I had been right about the teeth; and plus we had earned the vet money from Byron. But Evvie said she believed that informing Dad of these vital facts probably would not bring peace to the family.

Dad kept on at Mom for several days. Evvie and I stayed out of his way. He stomped around glaring and snorting and yelling when things weren't just the way he wanted, which was all the time. On about the fifth day, Mom stopped begging and pleading for peace in the family; she stopped talking to Dad altogether.

The rain finally stopped, the fields dried off, and Wayne and Ed came over to do the hay. We girls helped like last year. Bea came over too, and she and Mom got up the hay-makers' lunch in the kitchen, same as last year; but they didn't laugh and whoop. They talked hard and fast under their breath, and they hushed up quick if we girls came in the house. Dad went fishing.

Evvie and I worked in the fields for four hot days. Ed let me spell him on the tractor; Evvie and I could both toss bales, any color you wanted. We worked and sweated and itched and joked around with Wayne, and for a while there I almost forgot about how I had saved Sam and ruined everything else.

When the hay was all put up, I got to drive the tractor back to Colby, and Wayne drove me home and was nice to me. Next day Jinnae and Evvie and I helped Byron do his hay, and Byron treated the three of us to supper at Hamburger Heaven for three days running.

The Mom and Dad fight was still going on. We heard them arguing at night; we lay on the floor with our ears on the heat register listening as they raised their voices. Mom was using oaths, and she said something about "stuck up here at the butt end of a dirt road doing your goddamn laundry and cleaning your goddamn fish… see Paris before I die…when the hell do I get *my* vacation?"

"You've been on vacation your whole damn life." Said Dad.

Mom said something about wanting her "own car so at least she could …" and he yelled back "go right ahead, and where did she think she would get the money."

"Just you something something," she shot back, then something about "getting back to where there was music and people to talk to." Then they banged doors.

We just lay there on the floor awhile not daring to breathe.

"Are we going to go back downstate?" Evvie finally whispered to me.

"No," I said. Mom can go if she wants, I don't care; but Dad would never *never ever* leave The Farm."

The next day at breakfast, Mom said "I have an important announcement to make."

Silence.

"For the rest of the summer I am going to volunteer days at the town Library. I would like to get to know people in this community. Also, Bea has asked me if I would play the organ at her Church on Sundays this month, and sing and play for all the weddings and funerals that come up. For money."

Dad said nothing, and we said nothing. But Mom didn't ask us if we approved or not; and off she went to the village leaving her children to enjoy life on their beautiful farm, in the company of their favorite parent, Dad.

Dad seemed to be taking a much longer vacation than his usual two weeks. He went fishing a lot, and we rode around and waded in Mitchell's and berry-picked with Jinnae, but we couldn't avoid being home with him sometimes.

Dad looked all different. His skin looked too tight for his body. I could see veins sticking out on his neck and his forehead like they were about to bust.

Dad tromped around the house in silence. He commenced shooting animals on the place. Our pioneer hero Dad made us eat a woodchuck he had killed out in the haymeadow; the critter had stuck his cute little head out of his hole at the wrong time and Dad blew it off. Then Dad killed a red-tailed hawk, not to eat, just for pure cussedness. It was a friend to farmers because it caught rodents; and now it was dead. If it had babies they'd probably die too with nobody taking care of them.

For the first three days Mom worked, Bea or some of Mom's Library friends picked her up and drove her downstreet to the village. The fourth day Mom bought a banged-up old Ford pick-up from Cousin Billy. With her own money. Dad may have been hopping mad about Mom buying the truck, but since he was hopping mad all the time it was hard to tell.

Now Mom drove off every day in her own truck to town; some days she gave Injun John and Frenchy a lift downstreet to go shopping or to the post office to get their Social Security. Evvie and I got to stay at the butt end of the hollow and keep house and clean Dad's goddamn fish. On Saturday, when Mom practiced her organ music in the church, Dad drove us to the laundromat and left us there to do the goddamn laundry while he went fishing in the Otterkill.

Sundays when we had to go to church with Mom, Dad stayed home, blasting away at whatever innocent little animals still lived on The Farm. When Mom was home she and Dad didn't say boo to each other.

Evvie started to stay upstairs all day; so then it was just me doing the goddam housework. When Dad needed to yell at somebody it was just me too. Sometimes he hit me. It probably hurt but I couldn't really feel it. It hurt more when he told me that, incredible as it seemed, my cooking was *even worse than Mom's.*

"Can't you do ANYTHING RIGHT? LOOK at me when I talk to you!" he would yell.

I *couldn't* do anything right. I burned things and spilled things and broke things. I couldn't look at him when he yelled at me either, because when I saw his tight face and the veins I knew he still hated me about the teeth and the vet and ruining everything and he was going to hate me way past forever. But he grabbed me by the shoulders and made me look. Except that I went somewhere else inside my mind; I sort of blanked him out and I stared past him.

"You did that *on purpose*," he kept saying when I messed up. Maybe I *was* doing it on purpose, I don't know.

I hated him. I hated my Mom too for going off downstreet and having herself a time. And I guess I hated myself too, because after all I was the one who started it. Everything that happened since The Umbrella Affair was really my fault.

Evvie wouldn't even go riding, she just stayed in bed and read her books and sucked her thumb. When I nagged at her she clammed up and wouldn't talk to me.

Evvie peed her bed most nights. She got up in the middle of the night and wandered around still asleep. I know this for sure because I was awake in the middle of the night too.

I rode out alone with Sam and Robbie. I made a sack out of a pillow case, put a hoof pick, a brush, a sandwich, a water bottle, a couple of apples and some Milk Bones, tied the sack to the saddle and crossed into Vermont, wandering down the old logging roads or letting myself through rusty wire gates into forsaken upland pastures.

As soon as I got in the saddle the sky and the woods and meadows changed from grey to color and I could hear the birds singing and the brooks chuckling. I enjoyed faring into the wild with my faithful horse and dog; they were the best company, because I didn't have to worry about what they thought of me. They liked me. Ronan had said "Treat him good and he'll treat you good," which was true, but only with animals.

One day Robbie didn't come home with me. Sometimes if he missed Evvie he'd go home on his own, but this time there was no collie waiting when I returned.

I rode back over our cold trail, calling and calling until sunset. But there was no answering bark, no patter of feet scampering up the trail. When I got home again Dad laughed at me and said that Robbie probably got caught in a leghold trap, or some farmer shot him in their chicken house. Evvie didn't say anything, she was too sad even to cry. Now I had spoiled everything for her, too.

After that I wanted to stop riding and go upstairs and suck *my* thumb, but I was the one who lost our dog and I had to keep looking for him while there was any hope he was alive; otherwise Evvie would just die of a broken heart and it would be all my fault. Sam and I went on all the back lanes and roads, asking farmers if they had seen a stray collie. I'd look in ditches along the Macadam for a brown and white corpse crushed by a car. I would sit on Sam high up on the open hillsides, looking over the countryside for Robbie; or I'd get off, untack, and sit on a rock and chew off my fingernails while Sam grazed.

Coming home cross-lots I would let Sam gallop as fast as he wanted while I cried and cried and we didn't stop until we had to open a gate or cross a road, and by then Sam was all soaked with sweat and froth slicked up the reins and my face was smeared with tears and snot.

Finally Dad packed up and left to go back downstate. I climbed up into the mow and watched him loading his car from the hay door. He threw his fishing tackle and a suitcase into the trunk. He and Mom didn't say goodbye, they didn't talk at all or look at each other. Dad didn't come back the next weekend. Dad didn't come back for a long long time.

The Night Ride

Who can stay the bottles of heaven? –Job 38:37

July had been still and muggy, like the world was holding its breath. Then August let all the air whoosh out, and cool little winds rippled over the fields. Every day there were cloudless deep-blue skies. The old pastures and woods-edges bloomed out in goldenrod and foamy white Queen Anne's Lace and dusty-rose Joe-Pye-weed. Berries and apples swelled up. The sweetcorn came in; we bought some every day from Connor's stand, and it was the best I ever tasted.

The little animals scared off by Dad's shooting began to come back. Finches and blackbirds collected into flocks and sat twittering on the telephone wires. A family of coyotes had a raucous party yowling and yipping in the hollow below our house. Deer and their fawns capered again on the dewy meadows morning and evening. A great blue heron flew in and hung around the spring below the cornfield, snapping up frogs and dace with his yellow bill, tossing them in the air and gulping them down whole.

Wild turkeys grazed on the haymeadow. A dignified Tom with a blue head and a feather necktie stood on guard, while his wives and babies ate. The baby turkeys were curious as puppies, toddling around, cocking their heads to examine the new world around them. But when the flock turned and trotted back into the woods they scooted right after their parents.

Once last fall I saw an adult flock of turkeys flush from practically under Sam's feet. Sam froze in his tracks, but of course did not spook. The birds went almost straight up into their air, in spite of being so big. But turkeys with babies would never fly off and leave them; they all stuck together in a family.

I stayed outside most of the time, I couldn't stand being around Evvie. My sister had been curled up like a snail in her bed for a month, reading "The Hobbit" and then "The Lord of the Rings." When she finished book III, she just started "The Hobbit" again. She never said anything because her thumb was in her mouth all the time. I didn't like being around Mom either. She looked angry and sad all the time. At me.

Even though Jinnae was in Wyoming again with her sister my wanderings with Sam weren't so lonesome now. I met some other girl riders; the Holden sisters, Germaine and Katie on their fat Appaloosas; and Annaliese Mueller, the village doctor's daughter, who rode a big skewbald ride-drive pony called Speedy Boy, who knew all sorts of circus tricks, like rearing up and walking on his hind legs. I told them all to keep their eyes peeled for my lost dog, and they said they would.

We swapped horses; Annaliese loved to ride Sam and he would do anything for her. I appreciated Speedy's smooth gaits, pretty spots and cute little ears. His mouth was hard as iron, though, and stopping was not his best thing. The Holdens wouldn't ride Sam, they said he was "too wild." They stuck with their own ponies or old Mrs. Lynde.

Germaine and Katie invited me to their house once. They said their Dad needed to meet me, because he had to approve of all their friends. The Holdens lived in a big old farmhouse on the other side of town so I had to ride a long poke on the side of the Macadam to get there but Sam didn't mind the traffic going by. Germaine and Katie and I sat in their kitchen drinking lemonade and they explained about their Dad, who was a retired Army Sergeant.

"He's so-o—o strict with us," giggled Germaine. "He yells at us like we we're in the Army, and when he says jump, we jump, or *else*."

I nodded sadly saying I was familiar with this sort of Dad.

"He's downstreet at the Agway, but when he gets back, you can see for yourself," said Katie. Just then a truck pulled in, and I froze. The kitchen door slammed against the wall, and there was Sergeant Holden standing there bellowing:

"Whe-e-e-re's my girls?"

Mr. Sergeant Holden charged right at us roaring like a wild animal and I backed up fast and knocked over my chair. He grabbed his daughters around the neck and started hugging and kissing them and growling, calling them "punkin" and "sweet pea." When he left off hugging he patted them each on the can.

He just shook hands with *me*, though, and asked me some questions about my folks and where I was from and I answered as best I could. But all the time I felt like I was going to puke.

I didn't want to be at Katie and Germaine's any more. Those girls, all they did was giggle and squeal and talk about boys and hair-dos. Plus they were terrible riders, sloshing around in their saddles and letting their fat lazy horses eat on the trail. I left pretty early, so I could get home before dark, I told them.

"Come on back soon," they said.

"Maybe. Sam doesn't like the Macadam, it's hard on his legs."

Hot weather came again, and sometimes we would all meet at the old slate-quarry swimming hole in Trace Hollow. Mom and Sergeant Holden and Ed had ordered us to never to swim in there because somebody or other had maybe drowned there a hundred years ago. After they said "no swimming," the place drew us like a magnet. We'd turn the horses loose in a brushy old pasture, strip to our undies and splash around in the water for hours or sunbathe on the raft that somebody had put in there. The Quarry was so much fun that I could sometimes forget about Dad and Mom fighting and Evvie not talking, and me ruining everything and then losing Robbie. I figured he must have been long dead by now.

One day Annaliese and I had the Quarry all to ourselves. Our conversation was more earnest when the Holdens weren't around. Annaliese took me seriously even though I was younger. We discussed books, horses, the Meaning of Life. I wanted to tell her about my parents fighting and Dad leaving, but I didn't.

Annaliese was tall and had long palomino-colored hair that she wore in a braid down her back. I wanted to be just like her, so I started wearing my hair in a braid too. I loved just lying on the raft with her. I loved the little white-gold hairs shining on her arms, and I loved how she smelled, like spring-water and sunshine and hay. We talked and dabbled our hands in the water all afternoon, until it suddenly got dark; big black storm clouds started blowing in over us.

"Weather's coming, we'd better get on home," she said.

We climbed out of the quarry and into our jeans and boots, caught our horses, threw the tack on them, waved, wheeled, and lit out in opposite directions. I walked Sam for a while to get him warmed up again, but as the rain started to patter on the leaves overhead, we cantered up the Trace Hollow trail. The air beneath the trees went all thick and green; it felt like I was riding in an undersea cave.

It was thundering when we turned onto the Lame Buck road. We trotted up it, the rain blowing right in our faces; I was wet to the skin in two shakes. Lightning started to flash, making people's white roadside mailboxes seem to jump out at us a perfect excuse for any ordinary horse to pull a spook and bolt for the barn. Sam never twitched as the thunder growled and the green daylight faded.

"*Hast thou given the horse strength? Hast thou clothed his neck with thunder?*" I yelled; that was my favorite part of the Bible and it seemed to fit right then.

As we swung around the final turn before the big hay-meadows at the end of Lame Buck Road there was a crackling noise and lightning hissed near us…in the glare I saw a dark horse and a white-cloaked rider standing in the street. Sam's head jerked up, but he kept trotting towards this horrible white thing, with its cloak whipping and crackling in the wind. It was the ghost of Armand Pelletier, come to get me at last…

The ghost raised its hand, and Armand became Evvie in a plastic poncho, riding Mrs. Lynde. As we passed by that stolid beast whinnied, half-reared, wheeled and fell in abreast of us as the heavens opened with another blast of thunder and a squall of pelting hail.

"I got scared, I came to find you, the bar gate is down!" Evvie yelled.

Sam understood, and broke into a hard gallop. This was Mrs. Lynde's finest hour. She snorted as she ran with her face alongside my knee and a mad look in her eye. We pounded up the old dirt track through the dead center of that open field with bits of ice bouncing off us.

Sam changed leads and cut hard left onto the trail home. Wet leaves swapped me in the face; I yelled but it was more like an Apache war whoop. Sam flattened out and hurtled full speed into the blind dark of

Mirkwood.

I closed my eyes, I couldn't see anyhow; I grabbed mane and ducked against Sam's neck to avoid any low branches. Byron told me once that horses see like cats in the dark, so I just turned myself over to Sam; he bounded down over the steep ledges without slackening his pace. I heard Evvie laughing and whooping behind me, "HYAAAAAH!" and Sam went even faster still as he hit level ground.

I knew we were crossing the down gate-bars because Sam's body lifted into a jump. We came out in the orchard; rain and hail hit us like buck shot again. Sam galloped on, splashing through the fresh puddles, gathering himself and leaping up the ledges on the pasture side. As lighting tore the sky and showed me the fields and barn below, my horse rocketed down the steep pasture slope.

"YEEEAAAAAAAH!" I grabbed mane and held on for dear life, ready to bail out if Sam decided to run into the stall. In the lighter dark I could see water shining– the barnyard was flooded. I yelled "WHOA" just as Sam sat down and slid to a stop. Mrs. Lynde skidded beside us, snorting and shaking her head from side to side.

Evvie and I led the horses through the yard into the barn, untacked them, threw burlap feedsacks on their steaming backs, and poured their nightly snack into the tubs. The rain had stopped. I looked at Evvie. She was shivering and her lips were blue. But she was laughing, and so was I.

We heard the sound of Mom's truck chugging up hollow and we ran for the house. It was her late evening at the Library. Mom pulled into the drive as we came stumbling and whooping through the big puddles in the lane. The rain had stopped and the clouds were blowing away south.

"Hey, Mom, guess what!" I called to her

"What? Oh my Lord Ruthie, Evvie, you're wringing wet!" said Mom. "Did you get caught out in that storm?"

"Rode right through it, both of us, from over Lame Buck way."

"You did WHAT? You rode through that open field in the middle of an electrical storm? Are you trying to get yourselves KILLED?"

Mom's face began to pucker up. We braced ourselves for the tears and the pleading to be more careful. But Mom stopped halfway to a full pucker. She looked at me and then at Evvie and back to me then Evvie again. And she grinned.

"Well I'll be! You are the craziest couple of wild Injuns in the COUNTY!" Mom giggled. Then she stamped her foot right in a mud-puddle, slapped her thigh and laughed, like a loon;

"YahHaHaHOOOIE!"

"We galloped through Mirkwood, and we couldn't see where we were going." Evvie declared.

"In the pitch dark WOODS? GALLOPING?" Mom bawled like a calf and bugged her eyes out.

"All out," I said.

Right at that moment a big yellow August moon came out from behind the Mountain. Mom howled at the moon and commenced hopping down the drive, splashing up yellow moonlit water from the wheel ruts, and slapping the hindquarters of her truck.

"They're RIDing in the rain, jes' RIDing in the RAIN..."

So we started in singing too and followed her, stomping in puddles. We grabbed each other's shoulders and jumped up and down in a big puddle in the middle of the road singing "YA,YA,YA,YAH!"

We danced downstreet screaming out more songs, like "On the Sunny Side of the Street," and "Ghost Riders in the Sky," until we were sung out; then we went home. The well and the pump and the water heater were all in a good mood for once, so we all got to have hot baths. Then we climbed into our jammies.

"What we need is hot toddies, which is tea with hooch in it," Mom said. "It's about time you sinners were properly introduced to the redemptive powers of booze."

"We already drank hard cider at Willett's!" Evvie said.

"And we picked wild mushrooms and ate them!" I yelled.

"Anything else you want to confess?" howled Mom.

"I thought I saw the ghost again but it was Evvie!"

While we drank the toddies we told Mom about Frenchy and Injun John poaching deer and the Willetts being drunk and us stealing stuff from the haunted house; we got so excited we knocked teacups off the table and Mom didn't care, and she laughed and laughed and then suddenly she got real serious and said,

"All I ask of you two is, Next time there's a thunderstorm, get your crazy little butts under cover and stay there! I don't want to see piles of dead children and horses littering up my Scenic View!"

Was Mom drunk? I didn't think so. But she seemed so different. She yelled out loud and didn't cry and she finished all her sentences.

I went to bed but I couldn't sleep right away; I lay there listening to the lazy drip of raindrops off leaves, smelling the clean fresh smells of the wet grass and road.

"Evvie! Evvie, you asleep yet?"

"Yes."

"Evvie, we could be dead right now."

"But we aren't."

"Were you scared ever?"

"No. Those horses never put a foot wrong."

"I rode blind, I just gave Sam his head and let him take off."

"Mrs. Lynde never had so much fun in her whole life. Did you hear her snorting? Did you see her shaking her head?"

"Did you hear Mom snorting? You know what?"

"Yes."

"What then?"

"We never had so much fun in our whole life. Lately, I mean."

"Jumping ledges, riding down that steep hill in the dark."

"Let's do it again. I mean, *I mean,* let's take a real long ride," said my sister, who hadn't been near a horse for weeks. "Let's go somewhere. The last big farewell summer ride."

"Let's go to Colby valley. We can camp out on Ed's big hill. Annaliese and Jinnae can come if she's home. We'll watch meteors again."

I lay awake, listening to the sweet night sounds. One big ride could finish off this whole rotten summer just right. But then I began to think about why the summer had been rotten, and what it would be like to leave here and go downstate where Dad was. I started to shiver and I couldn't get warm again.

On Our Own

*For I am poor and needy, and my heart
is wounded within me. –Psalm 109:22*

After The Night of the Puddles Mom told me how much she really loved it on the Farm, especially now that she had her friends and her town jobs, and had found a way of being of service to the community. I told her I was worried all the time that it was my bad behavior over the umbrella and the teeth and the vet that had made Dad so angry. I told her I felt horrible because I had lost Robbie. Mom said that none of it was my fault and not to worry any more, everything would work out.

"All right, Ruthie and Evvie," our Mom began. "I need to ask you some things."

It was almost Labor Day and Evvie and I and the Holdens and Jinnae and Annaliese had done our big overnight ride to Colby. All the Pilchers and Mom too, had joined us up on the big pasture hill, jouncing up the dirt track in Bea's pickup. We had watched the falling stars and sat around our camp fire singing and laughing and telling stories til all hours, while our steeds grazed among the cows.

But nobody had said a word or heard any word from Dad or even *about* Dad for three weeks. That Sunday Mom was supposed to play her last church service before we had to pack and leave for downstate.

She arranged for us to have dinner in the village with the McMahon's; because, she said, she needed to have a talk with the minister. She talked to him the whole afternoon and into the evening.

It was dark by the time we got home. We patched together a cold supper and ate it in silence around our own kitchen table. Mom drew in a deep breath. I held mine and stared at the table.

That table was from Carney's, and its white enamel top had big bluish gouges chipped out of it. I wondered who had owned it before us. Maybe some broke farm family had sat around this table not all that many years ago and made their decision to sell out and try their luck in the city.

Were they sad or excited? Did the farmer Mom cry? Did the farmer Dad reach across this table to pat her trembling hand and say "There now, honey, everything will all be ok if we all stick together?" Did the kids huddle close around their parents, big-eyed and quiet? Did they make it ok wherever they went?

Mom finally sighed and said,

"How would you girls like to live up here for a whole year?"

I could see Mom was trying to not be the old helpless Mom who cried whenever anybody said boo. I watched her trying to be the new Mom, the one who drove a pickup truck and led the choir of the Bethel Presbyterian Church to new heights every Sunday. The one who whooped and stomped in puddles.

"You mean, go to school here and everything?" said Evvie.

"Sure," Mom said in a too-cheery voice. "Wouldn't you like to spend Thanksgiving and Christmas here? Imagine how lovely the mountains will be under the snow."

Mom always thought of The Farm and the hollow as some pretty-pretty picture postcard, and it annoyed me. She was always gushing about "the scenic view," as if she was holding it in her hand and looking at it, like some flatlander tourist. I felt as if I, Ruthie, lived inside that postcard, walking, riding, haymaking; a little figure of me inside the picture, part of it, not standing outside viewing it. But right then I saw that Mom was living inside a different postcard, which was a country village, where neighbors helped each other.

Evvie said "But what about our house, and school? What about our friends? What about going to MomMom and PopPop's for Thanksgiving and Christmas?"

Not to mention what about Dad? *Where was Dad?*

"Think about it a minute," said Mom.

I looked hard at those blue gouges on the edges of our table, in the center of our little tin-roof lean-to kitchen. This house was hardly even a house. MomMom had called it a "camp." She wouldn't have been wrong if she had called it a "shack." It was ok in summer, but would it be warm enough in winter?

Our well was none too good either, and when you used too much water at once it ran out; then air got into the pump and it could burn itself out in two shakes. This had happened a few times this summer, and we had to pee in the woods and take baths and do dishes in brook water. This was fun in a Swiss Family Robinson summer sort of way but I didn't want to be peeing in the woods in a in a February blizzard at 20 below zero.

"Well, I want to stay here," Mom said. "The town has asked me to run the library. And I have the church job, plus extra for weddings and funerals. And I'll give people piano and singing lessons," Mom paused. "We'll get some help from... from Dad, too. It'll be fun staying up in the country around the seasons."

I kept looking down. I was afraid to ask what did she mean, "*Help from Dad?*" Where WAS Dad?

"Where's Dad?" said Evvie. She was crying. Our mother's face began to crumple up too, in the Old Mom way. But she did not cry.

"He's been. Well. Transferred. To another city," said Mom. "His dad, PopPop, tried his best to make them keep him in the Company's New York office, but they, they– they needed him– in Ohio for a while."

"How can we stay here?" Evvie whimpered. "We don't have any winter stuff! We don't have radiators!"

"We have an oil furnace and we'll get a wood stove too, it's quite economical, Ed says. It will be quite an adventure!" Mom chirped and smiled at us. "Things have a way of working out."

"Mom, don't worry, we can handle it!" I heard myself say, imitating her fake-happy voice. "And maybe if we're real real lucky Dad will never come back!"

Mom burst into tears, and cried big windsucking sobs with her head down on the table, and could not stop.

"SHUT THE HELL UP JOAN!" I screamed at her. She went right on bawling. I sat there glaring at my Mom and my sister crying. And there was nobody to say "There now, honey, we'll see this through if we all stick together," and no strong hand to reach across the table pat those trembling hands.

On Labor Day Ed and Bea and Wayne came over. Bea gave us some fresh baked sticky buns and asked how we were doing. We told her about our night ride; she said we were crazy kids but nobody could say we were sissies, and we sure knew how to handle a horse, which was something she never could do.

Then she and Ed sat with Mom in the kitchen and Wayne took us out to the barn, to talk business, he said.

"Lookit," he said, after we all climbed up to the mow and pulled up some bales to sit on. "I'd like to winter over my heifers at your place this year. Could you take care of 'em, see they don't get out, and feed 'em out some hay twice a day? Tell you what. I'll out 'n out give you the hay for your horses, no charge, if you do my heifers, fair trade?"

"Sure, Wayne, anything, just ask, we can do it," we burst out together.

"Ok, he said. "Deal." We shook on it.

"You girls gonna help me get the hay in next June?" Wayne asked. "No running off to play when things get tough, right?" He looked hard at me; I grinned back. I didn't mind when Wayne teased me now. He liked me and he knew I could do farm work; drive a tractor, mow a straight line, heave bales onto a stack.

Come to think of it, my sister and I had grown some. We were a pair of innocent Flatlanders two summers ago. Now we were tough and strong; we could work. We knew how to read the sky for approaching weather, how to feel the hay and know when it was ready to mow or bale; how to tell if an animal was sick or lame or in trouble. We were country kids, Woodchucks, ready for anything. Wayne had said so.

Dear Old Bethel School Days

I have been a stranger in a strange land. –Exodus 2:22

So next day we went downstreet to the Bethel school and signed up. I was in eighth grade, Evvie in sixth. Afterwards we went with Mom to pick up a woodstove and some firewood from Steve Murphy. That stove looked way too small to keep us warm if you asked me. But Mom had asked Steve.

Our cousins Downstate sent us a box of new-looking school clothes they had outgrown. Mom said she was a little ashamed we were "Living on Charity." I thought being poor was kind of romantic, like the books about spunky orphans, "Anne" and "Daddy Long Legs."

I was kind of like of an orphan now. But Boy Jeez, I had me a pony.

I wasn't too nervous to be in a new school; I figured Evvie and I, being country girls now, would fit in just fine with the farmers' kids.

Except. I hadn't counted on the Westford twins, Daphne and Delilah whom, after two whole summers, we still had not met.

Daphne was in my class but she was much older than the rest of us. She came strutting in the room like school was a joke to her. Daphne was a big handsome girl with curly blonde hair and pale china-blue eyes. She glared at me like I had killed her grandma, and plunked down in the seat right behind me, muttering under her breath and clicking a cigarette lighter. When the teacher was writing on the board, Daphne set my binder notebook on fire.

The binder was on the rack under my seat so it took a while before I noticed the smoke. I screeched and knocked over my desk, jumped on the binder and stomped the flames out while Daphne cackled and pointed at me and the other kids laughed.

When the teacher finally noticed and demanded to know what was going on back there, Daphne widened her eyes and shrugged her shoulders. The teacher sent me to the principal's office. As I left I heard Daphne say out loud what she had been muttering:

"Thinks she's Somebody."

The principal asked me what had happened. I ratted on Daphne and she got detention.

At lunch the Holden girls took me aside and warned me not to have anything to do with a "certain element," especially the Westfords. This element was known by a special name that the Holdens were not allowed to say but they would say it just this once.

"Trailer Trash," Germaine hissed in my ear. "They have no self respect. They pick fights, they drink, and they'll let Boys do anything, anything they want to them," said Katie. *"That* element has babies without being married and goes on Welfare. Dad says we can't talk to them and or even talk *about* them."

The next morning Delilah Westford showed up at school. She looked just like her sister only meaner. She came walking over to me before we went in, and nary a word did she speak. She just knocked me down. I got up and charged her. Delilah wind-milled her arms, growling and cussing while she socked me and socked me and socked me.

I kicked at her and tried to grab her hair, but mostly I ducked and covered. Delilah's fists never let up. My nose burst out bleeding, and the kids yelled that the teachers were coming. I hesitated one instant and Delilah head-butted me, and I went down like a shot, with stars and flash-bulbs popping inside my eyeballs.

I went back to the principal's office for the second time in two days, which was also the second time in my whole life. Delilah went there too, but she seemed to be used to it. She gave the principal a big cheery grin, and he gave us a stern lecture and detention. I promised him, sincerely and with my whole heart, that I would never do anything like this again.

Delilah didn't promise anything.

After detention that afternoon the twins got onto the late bus with me; there was just the three of us. Daphne jammed me over against the window and Delilah sat behind me. Each twin had a cigarette tucked behind her ear. They stuck their faces in close to my face and bared their sharp yellow teeth.

"We know all about you, you little piece a shit. We seen you riding your trash nag on our land. That's private property. We catch you and your old plug in our pasture again and we'll punch your lights out, see?" Daphne clicked her lighter under my nose.

"Stoppit!" I squealed, jerking away from the flame. Daphne un-clicked her lighter and grinned, her eyes all weird and white.

"Anyhow," I whimpered, "Byron—your Dad—gave me permission to ride in there, so I'm *not* trespassing."

"By-ron, By-ron, she calls him! Well ain't that sweet. You keep the hell away from him too, you hear?" Delilah, darted her big hard hand out and grabbed my braid, jerking it as she talked. "Or you'll be real.(jerk) Real.(jerk) SORRY."

When the bus stopped at their place they swung off and lit up. They stood together right in the center of the street breathing smoke and glaring at me as the bus went up hollow. Even from a hundred yards away they were the scariest girls I had ever seen.

When I got off two miles later I was still shaking and puckered up for a serious cry when Mom got home. But Mom had beaten me to it on both counts. She was already home, and already crying.

She stopped bawling for a second when she saw what a beat-up mess of a daughter had appeared at the door. When I told her a few kids were picking on me and I fought them and got a black eye, she collapsed again, leaking tears and dabbing her– not my– eyes with a dish towel. I talked all gruff and tough and said don't you worry about me.

"Can't you just... get along... with people?" whimpered Mom, waving her hand in a limp helpless sort of way. "Can't you just try to fit in?"

"Oh I get it, it's all MY fault!" I howled at her.

I stomped off to the barn with the cry still stuck inside me. I threw hay bales at the cows, cussing them as they skittered out of my way. I waved the grain scoop in the horses' faces until they threw up their chins and backed away from their tubs.

The Westford twins had not lived much in Mitchell Hollow for a few years, but now they had a reason to return to their parents' house– the same reason that kept them coming to school every day even though they would not answer in class or do any work. That reason was– making life miserable for me.

They recruited other members of That Element including their cousin Thomas Jefferson—alias TJ—Westford, to torment us. Whatever the Westfords lacked in scholastic aptitude, they sure made up for in leadership ability. Girls I didn't know hissed bad names at me in class, threw food at me at lunch and tripped me as I walked up to the blackboard.

The boys were worse. I never met boys like this before. They were dirt mean. TJ and his pals crowded up against me in the hall laughing and jeering and putting their hands where they didn't belong.

"TJ and them other boys is a buncha gelders," said Jinnae. "I wouldn't piss on them boys if they was on fire."

"What's 'gelders' anyhow?" I asked her.

"Pig has a litter," said Jinnae, "the best ones they let breed, and the no-good ugly runty ones they cut so they can't get babies."

"So?" I said.

"So-o-o," said Jinnae rolling her eyes. "If you're dumb and ugly and good for nothin' you should ought to be cut to keep you from getting more just like you. But they don't ever do it to people. Should, though.

"All gelders do in this life is get in trouble, or get girls in trouble," said Jinnae. "Church tries to get 'em to come to Youth Program, but they already got a youth program all their own.

"TJ's cruel to horses," said Jinnae. "Used to would ride with him and try to show him how to do, but he don't care. Yarned one of Byron's ponies till its mouth bled. Byron won't let him ride no more. Don't let them Westfords get your goat."

But they did get it; I screamed and cussed at the gelders; I fought a couple of trailer trash girls, but I never won. I thought too much about the blood, eyeballs, and teeth flying; always mine, never theirs. I landed in the principal's office regularly.

The Westford twins sat back and grinned from afar at the work their deputies were doing, but they never missed a chance to follow me down the hall chanting "She-Thinks-She's-Somebody." Thinking you were Somebody was the worst sin anybody could commit at Bethel Public

School. Even the principal thought so. When I was sent to the office again he asked,

"Do you think you are Somebody Special in this school Young Lady?" I froze up and stared at him... The principal told me Nobody was above the rules of good conduct in this institution and he was not going to make any exception for me.

The Holdens stopped being my friends. They said sorry, their Dad didn't want them associating with girls who fought in school. Annaliese stuck by me; we rode together on the weekends. One day when the maple trees were glowing like banked coals of every red and yellow color, we went up Argue. Annaliese had tied sleigh bells to the horses' bridles, so the varmint hunters wouldn't shoot us by mistake. The sound of those silver bells in the clear cool air opened up my heart; I told Annaliese the whole story about Sam and the vet and Dad leaving, and my troubles at school.

"The kids here, they hate anybody different," Annaliese told me. Annaliese spoke with a little accent. Her Mom and Dad had been born in Switzerland. "They hated me too. Then they got used to me."

"But how am I so different than them?" I asked her.

"You weren't born here, that's all," she answered. "What does your Mom say about your fights in school?"

"She blames me for everything that happens."

"Maybe so, maybe not."

I got home in the chilly blue dusk, and Mom was waiting for me in the kitchen.

"Ruthie, the principal called me today."

"What about?"

"About losing your temper in school. He asked me...."

"So did you tell him *it's all my fault?*"

"Ruthie, take a deep breath. I told him we were trying to fit into our new life here. And he said it was normal for new students to get some rough handling, but the teasing usually stops on its own. He asked me to help you deal with the situation."

"Maybe you should try crying and telling them I'm just a little kid and I don't know any better! That's how *you* deal with situations! It works great."

Mom and I stared at each other a long hard minute.

"If you could just not..."

"I need to fight! *You* never stick up for me, *nobody* sticks up for me but me myself and I!"

"Fighting back will only make it…"

"Not if you win! Sam fought Rufus Bates and made him quit hurting him! Sam couldn't stand it any more so he ran old Rufus right off this farm."

"But you didn't– but Sam doesn't fight Ronan."

"Ronan doesn't pick fights with horses. Besides, if Sam *hadn't* fought Rufus his whole spirit would of been broken and plus he wouldn't have Ronan now!"

"Well…well. There's something in that…" Mom looked down at the table for a good while. "Look, Ruthie. Ronan didn't come up here and pick a fight. Ronan found another, better way to deal with Sam. What you– and I– need now is to be like Ronan and find another way to keep the bullies of this world from– jerking? Yanking? What is it you and Evvie call it?"

"Yarning us around."

"We need to find another way. Not their way. A better way."

"But Mom, I don't know what that is."

"I don't know either," Mom sighed. "How's Byron doing? I haven't seen him much this fall."

"Oh. He doesn't care about us any more."

"His wife is in the hospital again. You should ride down and pay him a call, he'll think you've forgotten about him."

I never visited Byron any more, nor did he bother to drive up-Hollow to see us, I noticed. Every so often we'd pass each other in the aisle at the A&P, and the twins were always with him, glaring at me. He'd look sheepish and nod and mutter "how do," but he always kept on walking with Daphne and Delilah, and I kept moving right along too.

One day I bumped into him by himself at the Post Office and he said Boy Jeez he was sorry he hadn't been up to see me but She was poorly again and his daughters had come to nurse Her and keep house for him and he was driving Her over to St. Peter's Hospital Albany for treatments several times a week. I said yeah, sure, see you sometime maybe.

My Day of Rest

On Sundays we all went to church. I liked it there because I loved singing in the choir and saying the grand-sounding words from the Bible. Plus, people at church smiled at me and told me I was such a good little singer. Even some of the kids who ragged on me in school smiled and said how do.

Mom taught Evvie and me a duet for church, that we also sang for a couple funerals. It always made people tear up and blubber and give us extra money. It went

Loving Shepherd of the sheep
Keep thy Lamb in safety, keep.
Nothing can thy might withstand
None can take me from thy hand.

I really loved this song which was a kid version of the twenty-third Psalm. I loved whenever the minister talked about God as being the Good Shepherd. I didn't like it when he called God The Father; I just kept seeing Dad.

But the Good Shepherd. The one takes care of his sheep in the green pastures. The one who seeks after the lost ones and heals the sick ones and leads them beside the still waters, that God I could picture in my mind. Byron had sheep.

I prayed to God, just for fun, not that I thought he would ever answer, to take his rod and staff to comfort *me* and give mine enemies a hard time, but it's not likely you would catch God patrolling the halls of a school. Fighting off the Trailer Trash and Gelders seemed to be my problem.

The minister had another point of view. He would get up in the pulpit and say sweet comfy things about how we should do like God and all love one another because God loved everybody the same. He claimed we were all Somebody in the eyes of the Lord. Even unto Trailer Trash. Even unto Gelders. Even unto the least of these.

I sat all safe in the choir loft sort of believing it all, because the organ was going and the choir was singing and the sunlight came in through the colored windows. God was with us and in God's opinion we were Somebody. And all us Somebodies had charity, and we loved our neighbors as ourselves.

Except when Monday rolled around, God went off home and people went right back to treating each other like dirt. The nice kids like Germaine and Katie hated the Trailer Trash and the Gelders, who hated them back. And pretty much everybody hated me.

So what was the sense of going to church and pretending to be all lovey dovey for a few hours every Sunday? Either some people were damn fools or some people were out-and-out lying. Or both.

Did Trailer Trash and Gelders count as Somebody or not? When the principal asked me if I thought I was Somebody was he saying that God didn't care about me? Maybe God preferred the Rufus Method over the Ronan Method as a way to force his people to knuckle under. Where did God actually stand on this point? God had a whole lot to answer for it seemed to me.

Nobody

The Westfords and their gang didn't bother Evvie that much, because she had Jinnae in her class sticking up for her, and nobody ever messed with Jinnae. The first month of school Evvie got off the bus at Willett's with Jinnae so they could do their homework together at Willett's big oak table. But one day she rode all the way up Hollow with me.

"Why aren't you studying with Jinnae today?" I asked her.

"Jinnae can't read," Evvie said.

I felt my guts squirm around. I remembered that I had called Jinnae an "illiterate hillbilly" that day when she wouldn't go near the haunted house. Well, turned out I was right and she really *was* an illiterate hillbilly. "How'd she get into the sixth grade then? Why isn't she back in the first grade?"

"She lied about her age too," Evvie said. "She's thirteen. They kept her repeating first grade, and she never learned reading, so now they just pass her forward to get her out of school. The teacher just lets her wander around drawing pictures or doing puzzles or taking care of the terrarium and stuff."

"Did you ask her how come she can't read?"

"Yeah. She just said 'I'm dumb I guess.'"

"So that's why she never knew the stories or the names of people in the books we lent her. Boy Jeez that's horrible, not being able to read. Are you gonna tell Mom?"

Evvie did tell her, and Mom came up with a good idea.

"Well, Evvie," Mom said, "Why don't you offer to help teach your friend how to read?"

So my sister got off the bus at Willett's again and taught reading to Jinnae. Then she hiked the three miles up hollow home in the late-October twilights. Evvie told me she read aloud to Jinnae from our all-time favorite books; "The Hobbit," "The Swiss Family Robinson," "Anne of Green Gables" "Charlotte's Web," "Five Children and It," trying to tempt her into learning to read them all by herself.

She cut colored construction paper letters for Jinnae to learn off by heart. A is for Alfalfa, B is for Bossie, C is for Crow, D is for–"Dumb," Jinnae would say. Evvie said it was hard to get Jinnae to sit still, so sometimes they walked up and down street spelling, cat, rat, bat, hat.

"Nothing takes with her," Evvie told me one night after we had gotten into our beds. "Jinnae's not dumb, she knows all sorts of neat things, and she can draw horses and play ball and fish and ride, and she beats me at checkers now...." Evvie's voice trailed off. I thought she was asleep. Then she said:

"She's going with T.J. Westford,"

"*What?* She *hates* T.J. Westford even more than I do!"

"I asked her not to go with T.J.," Evvie went on. "'You know how mean he is,' I told her. And Jinnae just said 'Well heck, I gotta have some fun sometime in this life, you know? What else 'm I gonna do? So I said 'What does your Mom say? And she said 'Oh Lu don't care what I do.'"

Evvie went to Jinnae's a few more times, then one day she just stopped going. My sister had this a dull shocked look like a sick animal. She wouldn't talk about Jinnae, she was best friends with Lindsey McMahon now, was all she would ever say.

Then Evvie stopped going to school. Every morning she complained of a pain in her stomach. She really looked sick so Mom let Evvie stay home alone.

I could barely look at Jinnae any more in the halls or on the bus, and Jinnae wouldn't look at me. She wore black raccoon eye-shadow rings around her eyes like her sister Monique, and she hung all over T.J. and puffed on a cigarette and talked too loud. Jinnae had gone bad and nobody cared. Nobody thought she was Somebody, except my sister.

The Valley of Shadow

Lu Willett asked me to board Rusty up to our place till she could decide whether to sell him or not, because Jinnae wasn't taking care of him any more, so I said sure. I tried to ride him up-hollow, but he dumped me because he was mad and missed Jinnae. So I walked him up, turned him out with the others and let him be.

Evvie may have been too sick to go to school but she always recovered in time for choir practice on Thursday nights. Then she was sick again on Friday morning, OK on Saturday and definitely perky on Sunday. I told Mom I thought Evvie was just lazy and trying to get out of going to school and doing chores, which, by the way, I had to do. I pointed out to Mom that my sister was gobbling up mountains of food when she was alone all day in the house; whole jars of peanut butter, quarts of milk, entire loaves of bread. No wonder her stomach hurts, she's such a pig, I said. Mom didn't say anything.

Winter came on early; the shadow of the Mountain was on our house all morning. The beginning of November it snowed. Every gray morning I trudged out to the barn, fed out hay, checked Wayne's heifers and gave the horses their scoop of sweet feed. Then I changed into school clothes and rode the bus to school with the twins and Jinnae. Even when the sun came up the world stayed gray. Food didn't taste good to me, and I didn't notice if I was hot or cold.

Sometimes I'd go out to the barn and sit there with Sam, picking the burrs out of his mane and tail. I thought maybe I would go for a ride, but there was always a reason why I couldn't. It was cold. It was icy and he didn't have cleats, or even shoes. Sam might buck and throw me on the hard ground. How would I get him dry again if he got all sweaty. So I never did ride.

I didn't see the gold leaves hanging on to the silver-gray beeches in Lothlorien after all the other leaves had dropped, or the pale beams of sun slanting through the skeletons of the maples and poplars, or the deer slipping shyly through the brush trying to hide from the hunters.

I didn't notice the frost sparkling on the grass in the morning, or first sprinklings of snow on the leaf litter in the woods that we used to call "sugar-on-Wheaties." I didn't raise up my nose to catch the smell of a snowstorm coming down the wind, or cock an ear to hear the sigh of snowflakes brushing past the dry beech leaves. I could have been hibernating in a chuck hole, for all I noticed.

In Rama Was There a Voice Heard

The one and only thing that stood out in my mind happened November 10. I was catching a cold, so Mom had picked me up early from school. She wanted to stop a minute at Connor's to deliver a new Braille book from the Library to Grandma. Mom told me to wait in the truck. "No sense exposing the old lady to your bugs," she said.

I was snuffling in the cab when I heard a high pitched shriek from the outbuildings beyond the house. My ears may not have been attuned to the sighing of snowflakes in the beechen boughs, but they knew the scream of a horse in an instant—a horse in terrible, terrible pain. I screamed too, ran toward the house and wrenched open the kitchen door.

"There's a horse out back there and somebody's hurting it! Make them STOP!" I screeched at Mom and Ma Connor and the blind Grandma. They were sitting near the wood-stove, calmly drinking coffee and eating donuts.

"Can't you *hear* it? *They're hurting a horse!*"

"Naw," said Ma Connor. "It's the pig."

"What are they doing to it?" I yelled at her.

"They're after killing that pig," said Ma calmly. "They aren't hurting it any."

"But it's SCREAMING!" I screamed. I was shaking all over.

"Pigs always scream," said Grandma. "Pigs is the only animal except people that knows when they're gonna die. It does sound sort of like a horse, don't it?" she mused. "Only a horse kinda makes ruffles on his squeals, he whickers, like." And she dipped her donut in her coffee and took a bite.

I heard the pop of a rifle, and the screams stopped.

Ma Connor sighed and shook her head.

"You never quite get used to it. My Boys are good Christians and pig-killing time just tears them up. You know, they raised this particular pig on a bottle and kept it as a pet. Seemed like he screamed worse than the others, because he was like one of the family, and he realized he'd been double-crossed. The Boys feel it."

"Uh-huh," I said, not in agreement, but because I had hit the floor as I fainted. I wasn't unconscious, it just felt as if my head had come off and was rolling around Ma Connor's kitchen.

"Poor kid's fainted," said Ma. She and Mom gathered me up and wiped my face with a clammy dishcloth.

"She's burning up with fever," said Mom, just like they say in books. "I'd better get her home." Just like they say in books.

"I'm in a book," I said to Mom.

Ma went to call the boys to carry me, but then she remembered that they were probably both up to their elbows in their dear pet pig's blood and thought better of it. So she and Mom scooped me up in the Fireman's Carry and put me into the truck.

I spent two days in bed with a fever, sweating and thrashing around. I couldn't get the screams of the Connor pig out of my head. Crying out with all its soul against the cruel joke played on it by those Good Christians who had nursed it like a baby and fussed with it and then turned on it and said NO, you are *not* a part of this family after all; you are NOBODY, bye-bye, and blew its brains out.

But finally the fever went back down and the pig screams stopped. I wobbled on my legs when I got out of bed but in a few days I was ready to return to my beloved school. On my first day back, though, I could barely concentrate on what the teachers were saying. At lunch break I was leaning my head against my locker wondering if I should go to the nurse's office, when T.J. and the Westford twins surrounded me.

"Honeybunch, where you been? We missed ya!"

I turned to face them but I was too weak to slap their hands off or to yell any cusses. They poked and pinched and leered and jeered at me; they were like vultures and rats, all over me.

All of a sudden they all three stopped what they were doing and pulled back off me as if they had hit an electric fence. Their faces looked stupid and scared. There was this awful high loud noise in the hallway, like a horse in terrible terrible pain; and I was making it. And I kept right on making it until a teacher ran up and hustled me down the hall toward the principal's office.

One minute I was sitting on that familiar hard chair outside the principal's office, and the next minute I was in my bed at home and Mom was standing there holding a bottle of ginger ale, a sack of pretzels and "The Complete Adventures of Sherlock Holmes."

"You fell asleep, Ruthie." She said. "The nurse says you dozed off outside the principal's office. The first kid in history."

"Did I get detention?"

"No, I think it's all OK. Your teacher said you were screaming bloody murder in the hall."

"I dunno. I think I screamed like…like that pig."

"The Connor's pig? The one that was killed the day you got sick?"

"Yeah. It was crying because it thought it was a regular member of the family and then it found out it was just a stupid pig and nobody really loved it after all."

Mom sat down on my bed without saying a word, held my hand and looked hard out the window a long long time, until I dozed off again.

Keep thy lamb in safety, keep.

The Westfords stopped bothering me. They wouldn't so much as look at me in the hall and they never touched me again. Daphne and Delilah dropped out of school on their 16th birthday. A rumor went around they were both knocked up by the same guy, and that guy was Barry Connor, the youngest son of the prosperous and pig-murdering Connor clan. But then everybody forgot about it.

It was easier at school now, but I couldn't talk to many kids, I felt so tired. After school I would come home, do homework, and feed the stock, almost glad that the day was as gray outside as I was inside. Sam and Mrs. Lynde and Rusty, the shining steeds of two summers past, were just part of the herd of big dirty animals I had to feed out hay to, in the icy muck of the barnyard.

Sometimes I sat there and just looked at Sam, and he looked back at me. I didn't pat him or anything. Then one dark afternoon I looked at him and the gray feeling turned into something else.

"If it wasn't for you..." I said to him. He pricked his ears. "If it wasn't for you and your *damn teeth*."

I was crying now because I was going to say if it wasn't for you and your damn teeth I'd be Downstate and our family would be all together. I walked out of the barn and slammed the door.

After five most nights Mom would come home and she and I would open cans and toss some sort of supper together. Evvie came down and sat with us at the table and crammed more food on top of what she snuck up to her room during the day.

"I wish I could get her go back to school," said Mom one Sunday evening, "but she is so sick every Monday morning."

"Can't you just *make* her go?" I yelled. "Boy Jeez why can't you just not feed her unless she goes or something? She's getting all fat! She's getting away with murder! Why should she get to do what *she* wants and leave the all the chores to me?" I said.

"I've just given up," Mom said. "You can try to persuade her if you want to," sighed Mom. "I can't even get her to see Dr. Mueller."

I went upstairs.

"Evelyn," I began, "you listen to me."

"Lemme alone," said my sister, her eyes on her book.

"Are you just going to lie up here forever? For your information I am doing all the barn work and the house work AND my school work, and *you* only show up when it's time to eat! You're a selfish fat pig, and you've been on vacation your *whole damn life*."

My sister gently closed "The Two Towers," then rose up off her bed and bellowed back in my face

"Don't you yarn me around!"

"You need some yarning if you ask me!"

"I'm not talking to you ever again!"

"Well good then! I don't care!"

I stomped back downstairs and reported to Mom that she was spoiling Evvie and Mom said she's just a little kid and yelling only made it worse. And I said I hate you and Mom started crying.

Happy Holidays

The year dragged on. We had Thanksgiving at the Pilchers, who did all they could to cheer us up. But the cold and grayness was on us all and we could only shake it off for short periods of time, like when Wayne clowned around or Bea told us some juicy bit of church gossip while she piled mountains of fresh whipped cream on top of her famous Wellington County Fair Blue Ribbon pumpkin pie.

After dinner we sat around the woodstove in the parlor and Ed started in with a few of his worthless-nutty-horse stories, and when he finished I was mad as a snake.

"Why is it always *horses* that are so dumb?" I snapped at him. "I've heard tell that *tractors* are dumber than horses! *I've* heard tell that they could roll over on you and kill you."

Everything in the room stopped dead. Ed shot me a startled look, like he was seeing a ghost, and then his face crumpled up and he covered his eyes with his hand. Nobody breathed.

After a long minute Ed cleared his throat. "Well, sis, how *is* old Sam?" and I just said OK, I guess.

At Christmas we were supposed to go downstate to MomMom and PopPop's and see Dad, but at the last minute there had been a change of plans and Dad was not coming, so we weren't going either. I lay by the hot-air vent eaves-dropping on Mom's long, angry phone conversations with Bea. Dad wouldn't do something PopPop wanted, and PopPop was mad at him, and something about the mortgage on the house.

So we ended up back at Pilchers for Christmas. Actually it was sort of fun. We gave Bea macramé hangers for her potted begonias, and Bea gave Mom macramé hangers for *her* potted begonias, which had been *Bea's* cuttings of potted begonias last summer, and we all laughed about it till we cried.

We also gave each other new decks of cards, a used Scrabble set from the church bazaar, and books and home made cookies for stocking-stuffers; I got a red and white crocheted potholder shaped like miniature Sam with a clothespin dressed up as me stuck on it.

At dinner Ed told tall hunting tales, and we all hee-hawed and shouted and helped ourselves to thick slices of Flossie, who had been Wayne's 4-H pig, now enjoying a return engagement as the Christmas ham. The Pilchers raised their cider glasses to Flossie's memory, and everybody but me laughed heartlessly at her fate.

I couldn't join in because the betrayal of the Connor's pig came into my mind again, and my tongue clove to the roof of my mouth. But Mom reached under the table and held my hand and the black thoughts didn't stay too long. Then I ate some of the ham.

After we gathered around the woodstove to digest, Bea told the story about her and Ed growing up before the Electric came to Colby Valley, which didn't happen until after the Second World War. She told us how Ed was so handsome and gallant, how he courted her and proposed to her by moon-and-lantern-light.

"Speaking of days gone by, have you girls ever seen an all white deer when you ride up on Argue Mountain?" said Ed.

No, we hadn't, we thought just the deer tails were white.

"Deer around here will sometimes throw an albino fawn," said Ed. "Snow white all over. The Canucks say the white deer are the ghosts of French people who ran sheep up there before they all died from the Ague. 'Argue Mountain' is a mis-spelling of the old name, 'Ague Mountain,' you know. When I was young it was a cause for excitement all over the state if somebody bagged an albino buck.

"There was a big one on that Mountain that nobody ever got," Ed continued. "Maybe he's still there. Every few years a hunter will swear he saw the old fella, but nobody ever gets a clear shot. The Canucks say he's the head ghost and nobody can kill him. It's my belief that when these hunters—even the local men who have to hunt for food—when they see that animal they get buck fever so bad they seize up. Red-eyed he was. Eight points, and a rack the color of ivory."

"Did you ever see the White Buck?" asked Evvie.

"Eyuh," said Ed. He stopped talking for a minute. "I was on Argue, it was getting on for dusk, and that White Buck stepped out in front of me, just like he had been waiting for me to come along. I was that close. Never even raised my rifle, I just looked him in the eye and he looked me in the eye. We stood there a long while, then the Buck walked back into the brush and disappeared. I can still picture him. It was the most beautiful thing I ever saw. I came out of the woods empty handed but I didn't care. He must be long dead by now, so I guess it was sort of dumb of me to ask you if you'd seen him."

"Maybe he has a son that color," Evvie said. "Maybe there's still a White Buck of Argue Mountain."

"I sure would like to see him," I said.

"You know, I had a lot of sadness in my life that day," said Ed. "Bea and I had lost a child."

"Oh, I'm so sorry," said Mom, taking Bea's hand. "I didn't know."

"After that day things lightened up. I took an interest in life again. And next summer Wayne came along, and that was a gift. Somehow I always sort of connect seeing the White Buck to being blessed with another son."

We all sat there quiet awhile, with our heads bowed, just breathing. Then Evvie and I sang "Loving Shepherd" for Ed and Wayne who had not heard us do it, and I saw Ed wiping his eyes after. Then Mom announced that the Wellington County 4-H wanted to hire her as a program administrator.

"My gosh Joan, you'll be running the whole county soon!" said Ed. I took a good look at Ed for once; he was a little stooped and his hands were twisted up from arthritis, but Ed was still a handsome man. He had a leathery face, a big square jaw and chestnut-brown eyes that were still bright and wet as he smiled at my Mom.

Bea shouted that "it was about time somebody with brains and talent came along to redd-up the mess the men had made out of Wellington County."

I looked at her too, like I had just met her. Beatrice Pilcher was not beautiful at all. She had no front teeth and one eyebrow had a big scar through it from when a cow had kicked her. She did her share of heavy barn work, kept the farm books and cooked for the men and grew begonias and sold sweet corn and tomatoes and gladiolus from her roadside stand. Bea was homely and tough and stubborn and loud mouthed, but Bea could have passed for a heavenly angel right then.

"Well, I guess we'd better go milk," said Ed.

Wayne stood up and put his hands on his Dad's shoulders and said "Aw, Dad, it's Christmas, I'll do it. Ruthie and Evvie can help me out. Whaddya say, girls?"

Wayne was not handsome; he took after his mother. His nose ended in a big red knob, and his beady brown eyes lay too close together and his front teeth too far apart. His face was always red and the beginnings of a belly hung over his belt buckle. But he was just so good.

I knew for a long time that I loved Wayne. But when Ed smiled up at Wayne and Wayne smiled down at Ed, I saw real love. I knew then how God had looked smiling at his son Jesus, when they kicked back in their heavenly thrones on Sunday nights, with the Holy Spirit bringing them coffee and a nice piece of pie.

We bundled up and headed for the barn. It was really cold, too cold for snow, but I was warm inside, but wanting to cry at the same time because I was bursting with love. Wayne let the cows in and showed us how to clean the milking equipment, how to attach the four cups to the cow's teats without getting kicked or lashed by a tail. Evvie put the feed out in the central trough, and Wayne and I milked. It was cozy and Christmasy to be with Wayne in a barn among the big warm bossies.

We were leaning across the back of the next-to-last cow when Wayne said in a low confidential voice, "Ruthie, I got something important to ask you." My heart bolted like a wild horse.

"I'm gonna get married this spring," said Wayne. "I'm gonna marry Laura Mitchell over to Shiloh. She's got her college degree, but she wants to farm. Dad's gonna retire and give me the place. Whaddya think of that?"

I backed way from Wayne, backed away from the warm cow, until I hit the cold iron pipes that made the wall of the stall.

I knew I should say congratulations but I couldn't talk.

"You okay there Ruthie?"

"Sure. I wisht I would get a farm and herd handed to me some day."

"Naw, Ruthie. You're a good little Woodchuck, but this life ain't for you. You'll go off to school."

"Laura went off to school," I shot back at him.

"Yeah, but she took a 2-year degree in ag management, Ruthie. She's a farmer's kid like me. You, you're going to study music, like your Mom. That's what I thought when I heard you girls singing tonight. You ain't gonna spend your life like a Woodchuck mucking out the barn and baling hay."

"What's wrong with that? *You* do it."

"Nothin wrong with it, it's the life I'm made for. Dad taught me since I was two. I'm big and strong and dumb and I love doing it."

"You're not dumb. And plus, how do you know it's the life you're made for?"

"Can you imagine me going to music school, Ruthie? Or studying French poetry or some fancy thing like that?"

"I-I—" There was no answer but no. I couldn't imagine that.

"So, getting back to business," said Wayne, "will you girls sing at the wedding?"

"I-I-I dunno."

"Well you ask Evvie, and let me know, OK? I'd sure like if you did."

We finished up and we walked out of the barn. I slammed the door.

Christmas night driving home from Pilcher's, the stars shivered over the bare fields. I didn't want to go back to our house. Pilcher's felt more like home than ours did; it was so cozy and full of good smells and laughing, and love. Our place was cold and small and dark. The well didn't have enough water for baths, so we shared the same tubful and poured in boiling water from the tea kettle to keep it sort of warm. Our walls didn't have any insulation, and all the window frames let in big drafts. We had to put rags and newspapers around the frames, then tack up clear plastic for storm windows on the inside, but the when the wind blew down Argue Mountain it sucked the heat right out of the house.

We turned into our lonely dooryard, got out of the truck and filed into the dark kitchen. Mom turned on the light-

"AAAAAAAHHHH!" We all screeched at once.

It was flies. Not just a few of them buzzing around, but *thousands of big fat ugly flies*, piled up on the window sills, falling off onto the counters, onto the floor, crawling around everywhere.

"What the hell is *happening*? Where did they *come* from?" yelled

Mom, "Oh Jesus H. God, what a horrible smell! Get the brooms! Get the dustpans! Get the Vacuum Cleaner!"

The flies were buzzing and crawling in every room. We started vacuuming them up over and over again. We filled a bag, dumped it outside, then filled another. The strange sickly sweet smell of them stayed in the air, making us want to gag.

Finally we got all those fat stinky flies out. Our teeth were chattering and we were sweating and shivering and gagging all at the same time. Mom looked pale and on the verge of tears.

"Girls, you swab down everything with Pine Sol, I'm calling Bea." Mom lunged for the phone but she didn't pick it up.

"No, dammit, I'm *not* calling Bea. Tomorrow is soon enough to—to hear her tell me that what we had was *flies*." Mom said. So we all washed down the floor and the counters and window sills.

When we were through we collapsed at the table. Nobody said anything. Then the phone rang.

"Hello? Oh, JEEZ, *Bea*!" Mom almost shrieked, then she bit her lip and held the phone a little out from her ear. We could hear Bea shouting from Colby Valley. Mom put the phone back to her ear and replied in a normal voice,

"Yes, thanks, we got home ok. No, no, no, everything's fine…well, Merry Christmas again to you too. Oh, by the way Bea, I was meaning to ask you… did you ever have a lot of—of—well, flies—come into your house in the winter? Well, yes, there were a few. We swept them up. Pine Sol, yes we did. No, it's OK. All right then, see you in church Sunday and I'll remember to bring that book for you. No trouble, thanks again, Merry Christmas…g'bye."

Mom came back over to the table and plunked down again.

"Cluster flies," Mom said. "Cluster flies. They crawl into the walls of the house and live there." We all shuddered and stared at the walls.

"Well by Jeez," sighed our Mom. "We got more insulation in this house than we thought."

We went to bed, and once I was under the covers I thought about Wayne. Nobody loved me; I was a tiny speck, totally alone in the cold hard world.

No. I was not alone. I put my ear to the wall and heard the buzzing of the next batch of flies. I would never be really alone again.

Fire and Ice

For behold, the Lord will come with fire, and with his chariots
like a whirlwind.... –Isaiah 66:15

The day after Christmas the serious part of the winter set in. The thermometer went down to twelve below, and that was during the day. The New Year was gray and even colder; some nights our loft room felt like it had no roof or walls, and Evvie and I snuggled in one bed with all our clothes on. Sometimes we both slept with Mom.

It snowed, then rained, and then froze up even colder, so my eyeballs ached when I went out to the barn. I knew it was going to be winter for the rest of my life, every day the same: bitter, dark and pitiless.

Then something really bad happened. The last night of January we had gone to bed but couldn't sleep. The night was almost as bright as day; a full moon floated high in our southern window, shining down on the crusty snow, slick and hard as a china plate. Every icicle hanging from the eaves over our bedroom window had slices of moon frozen inside it. The whole world looked blank as if God had erased it. Evvie nudged me under the covers and sat up.

"Do you hear it?" she whispered.

Bells. Sirens, coming up hollow. No, coming up Connor Hollow. We got out of bed and ran to our north window, the one that looked towards the Connor place. The window-pane was covered with frost-flowers. On the inside. We rubbed little holes in the frost, and just as we got our eyes to the holes, we heard an enormous "WHUMP!" saw big orange flames shot up above the trees.

"It's Connor's barn!" I yelled. "There goes the hay-mow!"

As we pulled jeans and sweaters over our long johns, we heard the sound of engines; they were coming up our hollow now, and we could see them pulling into our fields, our drive, our barn lane. Cars, trucks, even motorcycles.

Engines were killed, doors slammed, and black silhouettes stumbled and staggered on the frozen snow. Nobody talked or yelled, they just headed for Lovers' Lane, their breath puffing out in clouds. All the Woodchucks knew that Lovers' Lane connected with Connor Hollow. They probably realized there would be firetrucks and maybe ambulances clogging the lower hollow, so they drove up Mitchell's instead.

We tore downstairs. Mom was dressed putting on her checked hunting jacket and watch cap. We yarned on our outdoor gear and joined the crowd. Big strong guys were kicking their heels through the ice crust, breaking a trail for the women and children who panted along behind them to see Connor's barn burn down.

We all floundered through the lane until we got to the steep slope where the fence line was. The big guys got the wire gate loose and opened it up, and everybody coasted down that hill on their cans.

As we fetched up on the level ice of the crick bottom in Connor's pasture we could see the whole farmstead and fields lit up by the hundred-foot flames roaring out of the barn. The firemen had put intake hoses into Mitchell's and were starting their pumps, but they were hosing down the Connor's house to keep the sparks from catching on the roof; there was nothing they could do about the barn once the fire had gotten into the mow. We stood on the far side of the creek, and all around us the ice glowed orange streaked with yellow gleams from the fire-truck headlights. We didn't shiver. It wasn't cold.

Neighbors and strangers were all around us, but I couldn't tell one from the other. Mom had gone up to the house, in search of Ma and Grandma Connor. Firemen, black shadows against the orange flames, labored to save the other outbuildings. Everybody stood on the ice until the moon set. Nobody could stop looking.

"There she goes!" The barn walls fell into the foundation and the crews put out the last spark. The sky turned pinky gray. And the talk started.

"Maybe it was rats chewing the lectric wires."

"Maybe Connor done it himself for the insurance money."

"My wife heard the Connors talking in the Agway about building a big metal barn and keeping their herd confined year-round. Big Plans they got. Think they're Somebody."

"Have the cops gone up Argue to question the old man?"

"Who could get up there on this ice? He'll keep. Him and his half-breed pal."

"The old man only done it the one time. Doesn't make firebuggin' a habit. My money is on them that stands to gain."

Mom found us around dawn, and we toiled back up Lovers' Lane behind the stragglers. People were hanging around our place, just talking it all over. Byron and his daughters were sitting on the tail-gate of their truck in our dooryard. As we passed them and said good morning, Daphne popped her lighter, lit a cigarette, rolled her pale eyes and grinned at me, baring her pointy shark's teeth, like she and I were sharing some private joke. I thought about my notebook and her lighter, ducked my head and hurried up the porch stairs.

Next day the police arrested Pierre "Frenchy" Paris, "on suspicion of arson." They didn't have to go up Argue to get him; Frenchy and Injun John were sleeping off a drunk at Willett's. The day after that, Ed and Bea Pilcher bailed both old men out of jail and invited them to stay in Bea's Dad's hunting camp over Colby way. Nobody could make a case that Frenchy had burned Connors' barn, and besides Grandma Connor said she knew it was not them, and she had Second Sight, so all charges were immediately dropped.

"So that's water under the bridge," said Bea.

The Road to Damascus

Saul, Saul, why persecuteth thou me? –Acts 9:4

It was April 2, my fourteenth birthday, but everybody seemed to have forgotten; I was still hoping for some sort of surprise party, but when I got home from school Mom sat Evvie and me down around the bare kitchen table. She told us that Dad was going to stay permanently in the west somewhere and he would be selling our downstate house and sending us half the money and furniture.

"Oh, yeah, great, our furniture won't fit in this shack," I muttered to nobody, because nobody was listening. Then I realized we would probably sell most of it over to Carney's.

Evvie asked Mom if she and Dad were getting divorced and Mom said probably. We all sat silent and stiff, a long time.

Then Evvie asked, "Is he going to marry that girl from the ski trip?"

Mom looked as if someone had shot her. "I don't know."

My sister got up and left the table and walked out without another word.

"You come back here *right now*, dammit!" I bellowed at her. "You haven't been *excused*! You can't just go hide upstairs for the rest of your life!"

My sister kept going.

Mom was flopping over and leaking tears onto the kitchen table again, as usual. Evvie was probably reading "The Hobbit" for the 100th time in the loft and stuffing her fat thumb in her fat face.

"YOU FORGOT MY BIRTHDAY!" I yelled at Mom. She just kept crying, so I got up and ripped my coat off its peg. I needed to get away from these crybabies, just go somewhere off this damn Farm. I could get on Sam and gallop away. With the wind in our hair. I slammed the door and stomped down the lane.

The horses were in the barn. I closed the run-in door and grabbed my tack. I tossed the reins over Sam's head when he came over to me; the horse jerked his head up and twisted it away.

"*Quit* it!" I grabbed the bridge of his nose and tried to pull it down, but he backed away from me into Mrs. Lynde who squealed and kicked.

"STAND!" I went right after him and pushed him into a corner. I grabbed his foretop and pushed on his head between the ears. Stupid nag wouldn't put his head down. I slapped him in the face.

"Damn you dumb old horse! Mind me!" I forced my fingers into his mouth and made him open up. The cold bit clanked as I hauled it over his teeth. I got the crownpiece over his ears somehow then went for the saddle while all three horses shifted around and snorted behind me. What in hell was eating them?

Sam flinched when I tossed the saddle on his back, and danced around while I was trying to grab the girth and pull it under his belly. He lashed his tail and tossed his head when I jerked it good and tight.

"Lay OFF, willya! That's the same hole as always, whyncha stop blowing yourself up you stupid ass horse!" I kneed him in the ribs. "Stop groaning, I didn't HURT YOU! Mind me now or I'll REALLY hurt you, and then you'll see how you like it!"

When I opened the stall door and tried to lead him through the barn-yard muck, he balked, bracing his heels against the doorsill. I yarned on him good, til he finally gave in and slithered through the mud and onto drier land. I hauled him over to a good mounting place; but when I gathered my reins and put my left foot in the stirrup, the dumb shit swung his haunches away right, so I had to hop around after him with my foot still up in the iron.

"Dammit STAND!" When I got my foot back down and went to tighten up his outside rein to stop his whirling, he backed up. I hit him and yelled at him and he backed up further, sinking back on his hocks, offering to rear and wheel.

"Can't you do ANYTHING RIGHT? You selfish, ugly, stupid STUPID GODDAMN HORSE!!" I let the reins slip long and booted him in his belly, hard. Then I kicked him harder. He grunted, whirled jerked free and ran to the upper pasture, breaking the reins and dislodging the saddle. I ran after him, screaming at him,

"Come back *come back* COME BACK!!"

When I got to the upper pasture he was trotting back and forth along the fence, high-headed and snorting.

"Damn You! *Damn You*! DAMN YOU!" I picked up rocks from the ground and hurled them at him. When one rock hit him in the flank he bolted right past me back toward the barn, kicking and stumbling as the saddle came off entirely.

I fell down kicking and pounding the ground, yowling after the horse. I grabbed up a flake of shale rock and began chopping at my arms and wrists with it, until blood and mud and tears and nose goo mixed together in a horrible sticky mess on my hands and face and arms and jacket. I puked and rubbed my face in my own sick.

I lay there with the chill wet seeping into my clothes, until the terrible pounding in the sides of my head eased off. I heard somebody breathing near my neck. Sam had come back. He was right there with me, he'd been there a long time. He was standing almost on top of me, snuffling me.

I got up very slowly and then I reached out and put my arms around his neck. I put my face into my horse's mane.

There were burrs matted in his hair. Sam was filthy. Where was his mane comb? I needed to groom him, I needed to take care of him. I started whispering to Sam, I was going to tell him everything about school and God and Jinnae and Wayne and Evvie and Mom and Dad, but all that came out of my mouth was

"It's all right, It's all right, It's all right." Over and over. It's all right. I reached my arm over and eased the bridle over his ears and off his head, and dropped it on the ground. He stood like a stone.

I got on his back, I don't remember how. Maybe he put me there. Sam stood square and didn't move. I lay down along his wither and closed my hands around his dirty, burdocky scraggly, neglected mane, and I kissed it. I closed my eyes. The heat from him seeped into my hands and legs.

Time went by. The sun sank behind the hills and the wind came up sharp, carrying the smell of thawing earth. Sam moved gently across the pasture, carrying me, searching for grass, eating a little. Then he stopped again, lifted his head and pricked his ears toward the woods, holding his breath, not chewing even. I sat up and listened too.

A distant milking machine. Cows mooing. A truck shifting gears in Connor hollow. The wind whispering in the tree branches. A man's voice comforting his cattle in the ancient way.

"S'baaass, S'baass."

In the spring woods, a chorus of high, silvery notes. The sweetness and the sadness in them shot through my heart like an arrow. Anybody could tell you it was the spring peepers. But what Sam and I heard was the music of the spheres.

Revelation

Behold I am vile; what shall I answer thee? –Job 40:4

"Is that Byron's truck coming upstreet?" said Mom. Somehow or other we had all commenced talking the way our neighbors did. It was "street" not "road," and "chesterfield" not "sofa," "commence" not "start," "eyuh," not "yes." Now even Mom said "Boy Jeez" and other oaths when she needed to vent her feelings.

We also knew the sound of every engine in three hollows, from Connor's baler to Glenn's old Farmall H tractor. Byron's truck was having gear trouble it sounded like, grinding and groaning its way uphollow towards our place.

"We haven't seen him but once all winter," said Mom.

"What's he doing driving up here at 11 o'clock at night?" I said.

Mom got up, locked the doors and reached for the shotgun in the gun rack on the wall. Then she switched off the living room light.

"Why are you getting the gun? You can't shoot!" I said.

"Sure I can. This is my shotgun. I shot skeet in college," said Mom.

Evvie came crashing down the stairs and announced "Byron's on a drunk and he's in our dooryard.!"

People had told us that Byron went off on occasional toots and got really roaring. Usually he did this before he went coon-hunting with the Bethel Coon and Cat Club, an organization Evvie and I regarded with loathing and disgust.

Coon-hunting involved keeping a Coon Dog chained up short most of its miserable life and only turning it loose on moonlit nights when you and your pals had gathered and gotten stinking staggering drunk. Then you would all follow the dog, crashing through the woods falling off ledges and tangling yourselves up in bob wire and other damn fool things, until the dog treed a coon or a wildcat. Then the biggest drunkest fool of all would climb the tree, knock the poor animal to the ground, and all the other fools would whack it to death with clubs, have another round of drinks and try to find their way home.

But this was not a moonlit night. It was, in fact, raining and muddy out, so when Byron lit down from his truck he slipped in a mud-puddle and slid under the chassis. He roared and cussed and floundered around in the drive, then started singing or sobbing and crawling across the dooryard towards the front porch steps. Byron flopped up the steps on all fours like a seal, and managed to stand up and lean his head against the glass part of the door. Which he then pounded with a heavy farmer's fist.

"Joanie! Joanie!" roared Byron. "Come on out here. You're so lonely by y'rshelf up the end of this holler and Boy Sheesh, I come to something something something you up!"

I couldn't move. I knew that old Byron was no saint, but he used to be so kind to me and Evvie; we had done hay and horses together and gone ridge-running together, until his precious Daphne and Delilah came home and ruined everything.

But this man on our stoop scared me. Byron was as strong as an ox, strong enough to walk right through that door. But he didn't have to, because Mom went and opened it. She stood in the doorway asking him if he was ok and would he like a lift home. Evvie, who was huddled up behind me, gasped, let out a little squeak and dropped straight to the floor where she lay twitching all over.

"Joanie, Joanie, lemme be your handyman" roared Byron. But even as he lunged forward in Mom's general direction he noticed that she was cradling the shotgun in the crook of her arm. She looked very professional. He stopped his lunge, bracing himself with both hands against the door posts, coming almost nose to nose with Mom.

Mom did not flinch. He must have stunk on ice, but she didn't even blink. Byron pushed himself back and muttered something under his breath. He rubbed the back of his neck as he did when he was thinking about horses. He mumbled something else but his false teeth weren't in so I couldn't get much of what he was saying.

"Get in the truck, Byron, I'll take you down to your place," said Mom, lowering the gun, putting her hand under Byron's muddy elbow, marching him down the steps and helping him into to the cab of his truck. I remembered for no reason that Byron always called the cab "My Office." Mom and the shotgun got into My Office on the driver's side, turned over the engine, and with a scream of unwilling gears, she set the truck on the street.

As I stood there gawking after the disappearing lights of Byron's truck, I became aware that Evvie still lay squeaking and shaking right under my feet. I knelt down next to her.

"It's okay," I told her. "Mom is just driving him home, she'll be right back." Evvie continued to make squeaking noises and she continued to lie there and shake. I crouched lower and looked in her face, and what I saw made my hair stand on end.

"*What's the matter with you*?" I croaked, grabbing her by her shoulders. She was stiff as a board all over. Was she taking a fit? I tried to sound hearty and tough to reassure her that everything was ok, but the words came out of my mouth as a whisper. "Byron didn't hurt us, he was so drunk he couldn't find turds in the outhouse. Mom took care of *him*."

Evvie grabbed my arms and held on to me hard. She pulled herself to sitting.

"Not *him*," squeaked my sister "*Not him*." Her mouth was working up and down and her eyes were wide open and not looking at anything.

"What? *What*?" I whispered. "Not him? Who? Did somebody come after you? Was it the twins? Was it T.J.? What are you saying right now?"

Evvie was shaking worse than ever. Her mouth was all the way open, like she was screaming, but her scream came out as a tiny whisper. "Mom." "Mom."

"MOM'S NOT HERE! TELL ME EVVIE, WHO WAS IT?" I yelled, or it seemed to me I yelled. But I was whispering too.

Evvie's head shook and Evvie's lips moved again but no sound came out of them at all. But I saw.

Not Mom. She wasn't saying Mom. Bob. Bob Willett.

Jinnae's Dad? Bob Willett, Esq. Prop.? Bob Willett was practically a moron, with his silly wall-eyed face, and jerky wobbly head. Bob Willett mostly went around alone, he was usually down street in the bar, or sometimes he hung around the school grounds, just humming in his whiny kid voice and looking goofy and friendly. Lu treated him like he wasn't there, and Monique ignored him too. At Jinnae's-

Then I sat down too, all of a sudden and grabbed my sister again, hugging her tight. I couldn't breathe. The ghost in the corn. Bob Willett had followed us home. Waited for us. Chased us. Making that whiny humming noise.

Monique with a baby at fourteen. Jinnae saying *"They don't do it to people. Should, though."* Jinnae, running around with the meanest Gelder in town. What else could she do, she had said. I didn't want to think about it but and I knew it all already, right in the pit of my stomach.

Bob Willett. Bob Willett had done something terrible to Evvie. Oh holy Jeez, was she pregnant? Was that why she was eating all the time? Oh Jesus God. What kind of place was this? The kids were dirt mean, the farmers were cruel to animals, and the parents…

I started to cry too, and black thoughts came shooting through my brain and out my mouth.

"Oh Damn Hell Jesus God. I hate it here, I hate it here. Everybody's crazy and mean and evil. They do whatever they want and get away with it. Where is God all this time? What the holy hell is God waiting for anyway, for *something really bad* to happen?"

Mom pulled Byron's truck into the dooryard. About five minutes had passed but it seemed like forty days and forty nights.

Mom came in, leaned the shotgun in the corner; she saw us huddled on the floor and opened her mouth to speak but I screamed at her.

"I WANT TO GO HOME, I WANT TO GO HOME RIGHT NOW!" Mom kneeled down and hugged Evvie and me while we both cried.

Mom did not cry. She held us until we stopped sobbing and then she talked to us.

"Ruthie, Evvie, it's OK. Byron meant no harm to anyone. He was just drunk and confused. His daughters took him in and gave him coffee and a talking-to, and ran him a bath."

"He does not *deserve* coffee and a bath," I screeched at her. "Byron Westford should lie out in the goddamn rain in a goddamn ditch all night and catch the pneumonia and die, and I would go and dance a jig on his grave."

"No, Ruthie." Said Mom. "You wouldn't really want that. He's still a good friend of yours. He's our good neighbor. He has his troubles in life too. He can't help it if he gets drunk now and again."

"You always make excuses for everybody bad! Just like Dad said you do!"

I wanted to go right on and tell Mom all about our other good friend and neighbor Bob Willett, who couldn't help it either, when he chased after little girls, and ask Mom if she had an excuse for him, but I couldn't get the words out.

"I hate *everybody* up here, they are all ignorant drunken *criminals* and they all stink to high heaven," I said.

"The Pilchers don't stink," said Mom, "and the Connors, and the Muellers, and the McMahons, and the people in the Presbyterian Church don't stink."

I was opening my mouth to say Oh yeah, the Pilchers and the Connors are *killers*, but Evvie was talking.

"Mom." said Evvie, "Can we make an appointment with Dr. Mueller? Maybe she can fix my stomach."

"OK," said Mom. Then we all sat there quiet a while.

We sat together by the wood stove until the coals died down and we started to drowse. It was two in the morning when Mom tucked us in and said that everything would be all right now. After she turned out our lights Evvie came and got in bed with me.

"Can I sleep here? I don't like it when I'm alone," she whispered. My sister snuggled up against me and I wrapped my arm around her.

"I'll watch out for you," I said. "That varmint messes with you again and I'll call the cops, or Mom will shoot him."

We lay there for a time.

"What." I whispered. "What did he do to you anyway? Didn't you yell or fight back, didn't you tell Jinnae and Lu? Or Mom and me? Why did you keep everything so secret?"

Evvie didn't move, but I could feel her go all tense and her breath started coming in little whuffs and gasps.

"Why are you so mad at me?" she whimpered.

"I'm NOT MAD...I JUST DON'T..."

I snatched my arm away from around my sister, rolled over and turned my face to the wall. Evvie ootched away from me and curled up, shaking and sucking her thumb.

I guessed I *was* mad, I was mad as a snake, because my sister's spirit was broken because I was blaming her for what Bob did because all men were bad because Dad was right when he said the Strong Preyed upon the Weak and that's just the way things were because there was no such thing as love. So I stared at that wall till the dawn light turned it grey.

When it was light outside, I heard somebody walking upstreet; it was Byron, come to get his truck. He had on a clean shirt. His teeth were in. He climbed right into "My Office" and turned over the engine.

Idling the engine was what real Woodchucks did when they drove up for a casual call, just to let you know that they were paying a short visit and weren't going to traipse into your house, because then you were duty bound to offer them food. We sometimes sat and jawed for hours with neighbors, them sitting in their pick-ups, us sitting on our picnic table. Mom and Evvie and I threw on some clothes and went out and sat there now; and Byron hung his elbow out the open window, and ducked his head.

"I come up to tell you I'm sorry," Byron muttered.

Silence.

I opened my mouth to tell him exactly what I thought of him scaring us like that but what came out was,

"That's OK."

There was another long pause where we listened to each other breathe.

"I like m' liquor," Byron smiled, but it was not a happy smile. "I been drinking since I was ten-twelve year old. Drink gets me nothing but trouble, always did." Byron paused a while, and his shiny blue eyes looked out into our pasture to where Mrs. Lynde and Rusty and Sam were grazing.

"He used to take and beat us with the horse harness. The buckle end. We'd harvest the oats and he wouldn't let us take any drink of water till we was through, dust so thick in our gullet we couldn't talk. He'd get drunk, he'd whup us, and Mother too. I thought that was the way of things.

"I got married and I beat Her round the barn like he done and did the same by the girls and my boy to make 'em mind. Boy run off as soon as he was of an age, and the girls turned against me and done what they wanted anyways. What they wanted most was to get my goat and they got it good. I used to yarn my horses around and beat 'em. I teased the cows with the lectric, when I was mean drunk, and I'd laugh to see 'em hump their backs up and run to get away from me.

"Not one of them ever did what I wanted them to, and they hated me b'sides. Except them ponies. Time I got them, I learned my lesson. I treated 'em kind and they would pull any load I asked, or Boy Jeez they'd try. Except for the ponies, it's too late to change things. She– my wife, my kids, …they just remember how I did them all them times. They hate me good and proper, and I don't blame them. I try to show 'em I'm sorry but it's too late."

"Maybe not," said Mom, "maybe not." She smiled at him and he smiled shyly back at the nice lady who only last night had offered to blow his head off. We didn't say anything at all. I had never heard a grown man talk this way before, saying things from his life, right out loud. I sat frozen to the bench staring at him, heart pounding, eyes wanting to cry, hardly breathing.

"I'm goin' back to them A.A. meetin's again," said Byron, looking my Mom right in the eyes. They both smiled.

I was not mad any more. I didn't hate Byron. Maybe what he said was just a lame excuse. Maybe he handed the same sob story to everybody the day after he went on a toot. But I didn't really care. I didn't think "this guy is nothing but a lying stupid dirty drunken Woodchuck." No. I saw he really was a good man.

On Monday Evvie went to Dr. Mueller's with Mom. I didn't tell Mom about what bad things she might find out when they got there. When I got home from school my sister and my mother were sitting around having coffee and donuts. Evvie was talking a blue streak, making plans for going back to school, going riding this summer, doing volunteer work at the Library. Mom on the other hand, looked as if she'd been rode hard and put up wet. She was gray in the face but not crying. I told my sister I was sorry for being an idiot and not understanding anything and for yelling at her and she said that's OK.

About a week after Evvie went to the doctor, Byron came up in the truck again. He was sober. Evvie and I went out to meet him. I wasn't nervous or embarrassed. It felt the same as always.

"Got sumpm in the truck," he said. He put the ramp down and unloaded two of his big mean hammer-headed pulling ponies, already in harness. And a plow.

"Thought you might like a garden patch this year," said Byron "You and me can plow it and then you ladies can plant it up."

Byron picked the spot where he said the garden used to be when the Goodenows lived here. We hitched the ponies, and Byron clucked to them and they jerked the plow forward and began un-zipping the turf. The turned earth smelled really exciting. Like Spring.

Evvie and I watched Byron plowing; then he let us try. I turned over a shallow crookedy furrow and practiced swinging around at the row ends. The ponies stopped when I said "Ho," then side-passed around the plow to double back. Evvie did some and Byron helped her keep the plow in the ground.

"Boy Jeez, them ponies go good for you," said Byron, "Tell you what, we can teach your big old red hoss to go in harness too. I got some horse harness stuck away somewhere. He should learn how to draw."

"You mean teach him to draw a plow or a wagon?" I asked.

"Well, boy Jeez, both things. We'll start him with a stone sledge." Byron gazed out at the pasture and rubbed his neck, the way he did. "Now I think of it, I know where we could lay hands on a old cutter."

"What's a cutter?"

"Boy Jeez, a cutter would be a one-hoss sleigh."

Right away I saw myself in an old-fashioned picture postcard. Next Christmas. The hills and fields frosted with sparkly snow. Smoke coming out our chimney. The sky that skim-milk color that means more snow coming. Sam in light harness pulling a red-painted sleigh. Bells jingling. Us in red tassel caps singing carols and visiting our good neighbors and giving them Christmas cookies we baked ourselves. I could hardly wait.

Bring Hither the Fatted Calf

He was lost, and is found. –Luke 15:24

Spring came practically overnight. The shad bushes bloomed along the old fence lines; maple flowers burst out red in the woods; pinxterbushes blossomed near the springs. Our Farm shone and sang and smelled and bloomed out like nothing I had ever seen before.

Wayne's heifers frolicked and bucked in the greened-up pasture. The horses chased each other around; rearing up and wrestling, tossing their heads at each other, or ducking down on one knee, pretending to bite each other's legs.

Orioles whistled in the elm trees, the red-wings sang conk-er-ee in the bogs, the oven-birds called for their teachers at the meadow edges. Wrens pealed out their party-streamer melodies, thrushes played their flutes in the deep woods, flocks of bluebirds and goldfinch sat and gossiped on the phone wires; and hawks made their wheezy whistling calls, soaring high over Argue.

Bees fumbled in the scented blooms in the old orchard, and all the apple trees that had snuck off by themselves into the woods, made little hazy-pink clouds among the other trees. The green smell of the grass and sweet fern and spruce made me want to howl with happiness; it was so, so…well….green.

I was in the paddock currying out the last of Sam's winter fur, which floated away on the green breeze. The birds could pick the orange tufts up and use them for a nest maybe. I tacked up; I was riding over Colby way, because Bea said she wanted to talk to me about Wayne's wedding arrangements and some other stuff, she wouldn't say what. In two hours I would be there, prancing down Colby Valley Road, sitting proudly on my noble steed, his new hair coat shining in the sun.

Sam was fidgety and raring to go, but he stood politely as I hauled myself into the saddle from the off-side. I was training myself to mount from both sides, because it was a handy thing to know in case you were injured or in a tight place sometime.

"What side of the horse does a true horse-person mount from?" I quizzed myself; "the uphill side." Sam didn't mind my getting on from the right side at all, but I was pretty clumsy doing it.

The day was perfect for a trail ride. It was warm, and fluffy little–lamb clouds floated in a baby-blue sky. I rode in under the orchard trees and pink flower petals spilled down all over Sam and me.

"Here comes the bride," I sang, "for lo the winter is passed, the flowers appear on the earth, and the voice of the turkey is heard in the land, gobble gobble gobble." I loved Bible talk, because it could sound magnificent one minute and homely and countrified the next. There was a Bible quote for every occasion, or almost.

We went at Sam's easy rolling canter through the big field at the end of Lame Buck, then walked lightly on the dirt road between sunny fields. Then we turned off the road went "up in through" the woodsy old wagon tracks to Trace Hollow and Colby.

The trees arched over our heads and made a lacy lattice-work of tender shoots and new goldy-green leaves; new green grass carpeted our feet. There was Armand's house. I waved how do. I wasn't afraid of the ghost now. There was no such thing as ghosts.

We turned out of the woods onto the Colby Valley Road; it ran straight between orchards and haymeadows shining like it was the first day of the world. I could see Ed and Bea sitting in lawn chairs in their dooryard almost a mile away. Sam and I collected ourselves and pranced down the middle of that road and the Pilchers laughed and whooped to see us.

We swept into the drive, and stopped dead square, right from the trot. Ed and Bea applauded. I let the reins drop, vaulted off and untacked, saying how do; Ed turned Sam out with Duke and I went and set with

Bea in the kitchen.

"Well, Ruthie" said Bea, after the pie was et, and the milk drunk and the wedding arrangements thoroughly discussed, "how would you like to spend some time living over here, helping us out for a month or so?"

She used her regular speaking voice, not shouting, because Ed had taken the truck and gone over Granville way to see about leasing a Hereford bull for Wayne's heifers. It was time for them have their first calves, and Ed wanted a small-sized bull to pasture-breed them over at our Farm, so the calves would not be too big for the young cows to carry or to birth.

"You mean, like help you out while Wayne goes on his honeymoon?" I giggled. Wayne and Laura were taking a luxurious three-day honeymoon at Lake Bomoseen. Fishing, playing canasta, planning their future; along with spooning and snuggling. I pictured them in bed together wearing their coveralls and big rubber barn boots. Pasture breeding. Made me feel sort of goofy, but not jealous or sad any more.

"Ed and I could use some muscle around here, sure. Your Mom asked if you could board here for a bit."

"Why, is she sick of my ugly back-talking ways?" I grinned. I knew Mom was proud of me. I had settled down and was doing good at school. The Trailer Trash and the Gelders had lost interest in me since the Westford twins dropped out.

"Your Mom wants some time alone I guess," said Bea. "Evvie is all set to stay in town with the McMahons. The thing is, Ruthie, your Dad wants to come back."

Silence. I just stared at her.

"Ruthie," Bea went on, and it seemed she was very far away in the room. "It's hard to understand about your Mom and Dad. But we got to try."

She paused and gathered up her words behind tight-pressed lips. I could see she was trying to not just spew her opinions around like she usually did.

"I know you don't like your Dad very much. And just between you and me and the gate post, I don't like him very much either. Seems like he acts as if the world never quite measures up to his expectations. Ed has hunted with him for years and he don't understand him either, but men can get on when they go hunting. They don't talk all that much.

They didn't like him. They didn't like him.

"I always loved your Mom," Bea was saying. "Everybody does. She's the reason why people stay neighborly with your family. She runs the church music and the library and the 4-H and does a great job, everybody likes working with her. She makes 'em all feel special somehow. She could run for alderman or the State Legislature if she cared to and she'd win in a landslide. But I gotta tell you Ruthie, I think your Dad is a real unhappy person, a lost person, and maybe it's kind of a good sign he wants to come on back."

I just sat there like I was turned to stone.

"OK Ruthie, I can see you're a little surprised. Now I'm gonna tell you the whole story of what happened this past year, and I want you to just listen all the way through."

Silence. Bea pursed her lips again.

"Ruthie, last summer your Dad got fired from his job."

I felt my stomach flip over. I kept staring at Bea.

"He didn't tell your Mom for a long time. I believe he was so ashamed and scared and didn't know what to do. Your grand-dad got him that job with the Company when your Dad graduated college. It's the only job he has ever had. He's never really been out on his own."

"Now your grand-dad was a big man in the Company, as you know. But your Dad was not liked there. And plus, he could never tell his dad, only your Mom, but he hated working there. But he stayed there because he had your Mom and you two girls to support, and maybe he was afraid to go against his dad and find other work. So he went every day to a job he hated so that you could have a nice house downstate and get a summer place up here. He told *that* to your Mom, told her plenty, whenever he thought she was getting too sassy."

Bea let that last bit out before she could stop it and she looked sorry. Then she pressed her lips together, shook her head, took a breath, and continued the story.

"When your Dad got fired, your grandpa pulled some strings in the Company and got them to take him back again, but at a much lower salary, out in the Midwest. They treated him like a Nobody there. He still hated the work, and soon he was fired again. So then he had to sell the downstate house and live with his parents. And I guess they fought up and down all the time, them trying to make him knuckle under and go back to work at the Company, him saying he wouldn't.

"Finally he told them he wanted to start a wood-working business making custom bows and arrows and trout rods and gunstocks, like he has always did for fun. Ed's got a fancy gunstock your Dad made him as a present, for giving him the tip when the Goodenow place came on the market. People would pay good money for work like that."

"But your grandpa didn't care. He was good and mad at your Dad after everything he had done for him, and I guess he was some ashamed too. Your Dad is an Ivy League graduate, and I'm sure your grandpa laid out big money for his education. When he told his dad he wanted to work with his hands for a living, his dad kind of disowned him. He threw him of the house, and took back some money he had loaned him too. Your grandpa's from Europe, somewhere, ain't he? Maybe he thinks working with your hands is low class or something. Heaven knows what he'd think of us."

Bea got up, punched down the bread, put a cake in the oven, and let me chew on that cud for a while.

"So." She said, pouring us each another cup of coffee, and settling down at the table again. "There are other sides to this story than the one you knew. Your dad's been at his sister's, working on his designs, and making a few pieces to show, and putting ads into "Field and Stream" and "Outdoor Life," and such. And he says he wants to get back with your Mom and try to work things out. Probably he'll be a darn sight happier doing what he likes and living in the country. So maybe he won't act so rank and offer to yarn you around so much."

We sat there for a time, until the scent of the baking cake filled the room. Devil's food.

"Well, Ruthie, what are you thinking?" Bea sat down next to me and reached out to pat my hand.

"I don't want him to come back," I muttered.

"I know you don't, honey, and frankly, neither do I. But your Mom is willing to give him another chance. Can you understand that?"

"No. I can't."

"Well, Ruthie," Bea sighed and looked out the window toward the barn. In an hour we would get the cows in and milk. "Let me tell you a story you may not know about my family.

"When Ed and I were first married, people around here dug up an old rumor that Ed's family had gotten all their land by underhand means. People didn't like that Ed would hold all of Colby Valley after he married me and took over my dad's farm. "He thinks he's Somebody now," they said. Friends stopped calling. People wouldn't speak to us in church.

"I knew folks were just coveting our good fortune, which is breaking a Commandment. But I couldn't stand it that they found fault with us. I told them just what I thought about them and their old story. Ed and I were young and in love and full of ambition; we should have been happy, but people around here made sure we tasted the gall of bitterness, and I came to hate my neighbors.

"We 'trod the winepress alone, and of the people there was none with us.'" As the Bible says. We worked hard and did real well, and eventually the talk stopped. But when. When our son. Died. The rumors started up again. People said losing our son was God's judgment for profiting from a crime. They said we were cursed.

"Then more trouble came; we had a cowman living here then, a distant relative of Ed's we were sort of helping out. His wife and daughter fell down the well at the old house in Trace and drowned. They didn't find their bodies for months. The man went sort of crazy and got drunk and accused Ed of murdering all his relatives, and then he set our dairy barn on fire. He wasn't really competent to stand trial but I insisted on pressing charges, and at his hearing he stood up and talked wild and cursed us, and that made things worse. You know who I mean, don't you?"

I nodded.

"Folks usually pitch in and help a farmer after a barn burns, but nobody offered us a hand to rebuild. The bank wouldn't give us a loan. They called in loans we had outstanding. The whole town gloated and turned its back, and then it was my turn to go crazy.

"I cursed and scolded folks every chance I got. I wrote 'em nasty letters. I offered to fight 'em in the street. I stood up in church service and dressed 'em down and marched out, I thought for good. 'Can a man take fire in his bosom and not be burned?' As the Bible says. The hate I had for my neighbors just poisoned my soul.

"And plus I had to witness Ed nearly dying. 'His heart was wounded within him.' As the Bible says. He talked wild about giving up the farm to atone for whatever his people were supposed to have done generations ago. He'd go out hunting alone– nobody would go with him– and I never knew if he'd come back. I thought. I thought he might. Shoot himself out there.

"Then one day. That day he mentioned."

Bea got up suddenly and took the cake out of the oven, put it on the counter and looked down at it steaming there for a long minute. She sat down next to me and wiped her eyes.

"That day– he just changed. It's my belief he had an epiphany. You know what that is?"

I nodded.

"Well Ed had one; he found strength, and he gave me the strength to ask for forgiveness, and to forgive those who trespassed against us, as we are commanded to do. Those same folks who I thought I could gladly kill if I got the chance. And we all let by-gones be by-gones.

"Ruthie, I learned the hard road, and I know for a fact that you got to let go the old hurts and forgive; forgive even the unforgivable. We all sin and are sinned against. Wasn't there ever a time when you did something terrible to somebody and now you wish you could take it back?" asked Bea.

There was. The day Mom said Dad was never coming back. I hurt Sam. I hit him, cussed at him and called him stupid, just like Dad had done to me. Sam ran off, but he came back and stood beside me and let me fall upon his neck, like in the parable of the Prodigal Son. He forgave me, he forgave me, and bare me up lest I dash my foot against a stone. He carried me over field and pasture to hear the peepers singing.

I started to cry really hard, and Bea patted my hair and told me I was a good kid, and she wisht she had a daughter like me.

"Bea?" I said when the tears and sobbing stopped.

"What, Honey?'

"Will you teach me how to cook?"

Cana

Wayne's wedding came off really well. I sang "If Thou art Near" by Bach, and Evvie and I did "Loving Shepherd," and Mom played organ. I can't say that Wayne and Laura were a lovely couple, because they were both big and chunky and plainer than your shoe. But they were such good people.

After the minister married them we threw rice and oats and sweet feed and rolls of toilet paper at them and then followed them over to Pilchers' and had ourselves a party. There was a huge table piled with all kinds of food, which I had helped make. Cousin Billy's teenage nephew Jean-Claude from Quebec played fiddle for the dancing. He told me I could really sing and that he wanted to kiss me, so I kissed *him* right smack on the mouth and he asked me to write him letters.

The day after the day after that, Dad was supposed to come back to Mitchell Hollow. Two weeks after that I was going to ride Sam back home. I ignored this fact as best I could. I was working hard helping the Pilchers and their extra hired men with the new calves and the milking and then the haymaking. I also helped Bea cook the gigantic meals the men ate three times a day.

We made waffles with ham, syrup, jelly, honey, coffee, eggs and biscuits for breakfast. Lunch could be meat loaf or chicken, potatoes, carrots and peas, pie and cobbler. The big crockery pitcher of new milk stood at the ready at all times. For dinner we made pork chops or steaks, boiled potatoes, green beans, bread, gravy, cake, canned fruit and whipped cream. Maybe I didn't want to marry a farmer after all, you just could not keep them filled up.

One day in a free hour I rode Sam up to the top of Ed's hill pasture and into his wood lot. We wandered along the deer trails and stood looking over Colby Valley, with its green pastures and still waters shimmering in the midsummer sun. We stopped by the ring of rocks where we had made last summer's campfire, and I got off and let Sam graze and sat there a long time.

Bea and I stayed away from our regular Church, "to give your mother some peace." We went to the Congregational Church over Shiloh way. Bea said the Congregationals were too liberal minded but church was church so we went.

It was good to go; I could sit quiet in the pews next to Bea and meditate on the Life Hereafter (not the actual Kingdom of God, but the life Here, After Dad Came Back). I thought about how I was going to go home and practice charity, like Bea.

I needed to stock up on charity before I could face Dad. I did believe– on Sunday anyway, with the Bible words and the organ and the colored lights—that things really could be different. Now that I knew the story about Dad's troubles maybe I could open my heart and forgive him for being so mean.

Sitting in the pew I suddenly felt all sort of womanly. Maybe I could cook him some nice meals and make it all up to him somehow. I knew I was growing up. I would be a real woman soon. I had kissed a boy and I was going to write him letters.

The Prodigal Returns

And, re-assembling our afflicted powers, consult how
we may henceforth most offend. –John Milton

My ride back to The Farm started off well enough. The woods were cool under dark green leaves. But I didn't wave at Armand's house; it looked haunted again. Sam walked with long eager strides through the Lame Buck Field and Mirkwood, where Evvie and I had whooped and galloped full-tilt through the storm. But when I got on again after closing the bar gate at the beginning of our land, Sam tensed up. He commenced to jig in his old irritating way, shaking the brains out of my head and the calm out of my soul. I started thinking about what was really going to happen when we arrived.

What would Dad do? Would he see me from afar off and run to me and fall on my neck and apologize for the rotten things he had done last year? Would I bust out crying then? Would I say Dad, it's all right it's all right I love you and I forgive you?

Sam and I jigged and jounced through the orchard and halted at that place in the pasture where you can see the whole farm. Dad was there. He was carrying equipment and stuff into the shed behind the house that would be his workshop. Mom and Evvie were helping him.

I had enough jouncing so I slid down and untacked Sam right there. Sam neighed like the trumpets of God, calling for Rusty and Mrs. Lynde.

They whinnied back; Sam shook his head and charged down the pasture slope as they came busting out of the barn. The three animals greeted each other, prancing around tails up, half-rearing, squealing, nuzzling, sniffing snoots.

I trudged down the hill where my horse had galloped, and put up the tack. My entire family had stopped what they were doing when Sam trumpeted; now they stood in a line in the dooryard watching me walk down the barn lane. No busting across street nor squealing or nuzzling nor falling on necks from any of *them*.

I swung my legs in my big boots and stuck a piece of grass in my mouth but my stomach was flipping around inside me, and my arms and legs felt like sticks. I extended a hand to my Dad and squeaked "Hi."

And Dad shook my hand and said Hi, it was good to be back here. He remarked about how pretty the spring had been, how nice our new garden was coming along, how lush the hay looked. He stated he was looking forward to fishing, and getting his workshop all set up and going into production. I said that's great, I am sure lots of sportsmen would want to buy his beautiful hand-made things.

My Mom just stood there watching, her head cocked a little, her arms folded on her breast. I couldn't imagine her crying or begging for peace in the family any more. Dad actually looked smaller than her. I realized something.

Mom was Boss! The head of the household! The one who had held our family together and paid the bills and scrounged the truck and the firewood and the stove and the second-hand clothes, and swept up the flies and escorted the drunks away from our door while Dad was busy running away.

At the same moment I realized *Mom was Boss*, I believe I sniggered.

Dad turned red. He winced and narrowed his eyes.

"Hm. Things are going to be different around here this time. We are going to forget everything that happened," he said. "I expect us to start over and live as a normal, happy family; and I can tell you now I am not going to put up with the sort of sullen and rebellious behavior you have exhibited in the past. Do you hear me?"

"No I don't," I said, grinning and cocking my head and glaring at him right in the eye.

"You listen to me, you'd better come right down of your High Horse, Young Lady."

"Still can't hear you," I chirped, turning on my heel, and showing him my back. I marched out to the barn. Sam had finished frolicking, so I scrambled up onto his bare back and sat stiff and tall as he stood head-to-tail with his long-lost love, Mrs. Lynde.

I sat there all the afternoon. The horses wandered off to graze in the upper pasture. They strolled over to the spring and drank. I got off and drank with them. I could hear a big Discussion going on inside the house—Mom sounding firm and urgent, Dad carping and whining. Evvie sat on the stoop dipping into a bag of chips, knocking back a soda and watching me with Dad's binoculars.

As the sun started setting Evvie came down the lane waving a white paper napkin. She trudged over to me on Sam and said "Are you going to go back to Pilchers?"

"Sure," I snapped. "Forever. *They* think I'm swell. Who needs this jerk coming waltzing in here like he expects a medal for finding his way home? Suddenly it's all *my* fault, the way he acted. If only I had been a nicer little girl, maybe he wouldn't of left, and maybe he could see his way to forgiving me some day next year."

"He's sorry for getting you upset," said Evvie.

"Oh REALLY? Where is he then? Is he out here in this pasture begging my pardon for being a jerk? Oh *no*, I see that it's *you*, Evelyn, my *sister*, who has come all the way out here to bring me these glad tidings."

"You talk like he talks," said Evvie and she turned tail and walked away.

When it was dark, I slid off Sam. My feet had gone to sleep; when they hit the turf a thousand needles shot up my legs. I went inside house and told my Dad I was sorry I sassed him. Dad said that he was sorry if he upset me, too.

The Welcome Home Party

Unquiet meals make ill digestions. –Shakespeare

Dad settled in to work in the shop. He stayed out there most of the time. But when he came into our house he traipsed saw dust into the kitchen. He used up all our hot water and then he left his grimy towels and dusty work clothes on the bathroom floor. He ate big helpings of our food: chicken & dumplings, stuffed peppers with sauce, pork and gravy, apple Betty, all the receipts Bea had taught me. But. He never mentioned whether he liked it or not.

He didn't say grace with us and he never talked during meals, he just ate. When it was just Mom and Evvie and me, we always used to laugh and tell each other how our day had gone. Now it was like nobody had anything to say.

Dad didn't offer to yell nor hit any more, but he fumed and sulked, just to let us know that things weren't the way he wanted. The way he looked at us I could tell he didn't like that I was so scrawny and Tomboyish, or Evvie was so fat, or that we talked like illiterate hillbillies. He was all nicey-nice to Mom though, and she seemed to enjoy Dad sucking up to her.

After we had survived two weeks like this, Mom decided it might be safe to exhibit us in public. She decided to throw a party; she invited the Pilchers and the McMahons, who had taken us girls in for a month at their place so poor Dad would not have to put up with his children while he was romancing Mom.

Dad was going to grill up a big steak. Mom asked me to make cherry pie, and I said I'd do a big potato salad from scratch, like Bea had taught me. We were all going to pretend to be a normal family celebrating Dad's return from his long long vacation.

Bea and Ed and the MacMahons and Linsey all arrived together in Bea's truck, all slicked up for our party. Ed had on a checked shortsleeve shirt and stiff new jeans, Bea had on a white sundress. I had never seen Bea wear a dress when she wasn't in church. She had on white open-toed wedge sandals too, and pearl clip earrings with matching necklace. Bea and Ed were officially retired, so they could put on the dog and not have to rush back home for milking; Wayne and Laura were handling that now.

The food was tasty, and thank God my pie came out almost as good as Bea's. Dad's steak cooked up real fine, and we had slaw and three-bean salad and Bea had brought a jar of her prize winning pickled beets, and pretty soon we were all laughing and chit-chatting.

Boy Jeez we were even having fun; joshing the Pilchers about their new life of ease, and they were joshing us back about our huge herd of three horses. Nobody brought up the subject of *where the hell was Dave* while his family struggled through the winter in a rickety shack with drunk guys pounding on the door and one daughter got beat up and the other daughter got molested, things like that.

Ed had moved on to bragging about how good Mom had done administrating the 4-H, and how she had whupped the Methodist choir into ship shape and recruited a flock of new volunteers at the Library. Then he repeated his prediction that she could run for State Rep and win in a landslide.

"I don't approve of career women," said Dad, butting in on Ed. "A woman should act like a woman, and know that her job is running the home, not taking away some man's job."

"Hey you Big Jerk, *We* were running the home, acting like women, and *where* may I ask, were *you*?" I opening my yap to say this, but I shut it again.

"' For the man is not of the woman, but the woman for the man," Dad quoted, raising his fork heaven-ward. "The head of the woman is the man.' Shakespeare said that."

Bea, who knew her New Testament cold, opened *her* yap and closed it again because Dad was glaring right at her.

"I don't approve of 'working gals.' As they call them. Too loud, too aggressive."

Deadly silence all up and down the festive board. Dad went braying on.

"The women I had to work with in the Company, who managed to claw their way up to managerial positions were really unattractive. Every last one of them was frustrated and bitter."

Mom said in a tight sort of tone that "women weren't the only frustrated and bitter ones at the Company."

Dad laughed at her, and changed the subject to those deluded women who dared to go into music or art, and how inferior to men they always were, and how women had never created anything worthwhile in the history of the world. Mom and Mrs. MacMahon, who played organ at the Presbyterian church, looked down and chewed their lips.

"Just name me *one* famous woman composer!" Dad brayed, and pointed his fork at Bea. "I ask you, did a woman write Beethoven's Symphonies?"

Bea, who looked as if she was chomping on a mouthful of horseshoe nails, shouted back that "although she was not an expert in the music field, it seemed to her that a fair number of men hadn't written Beethoven's Symphonies either."

I caught Evvie's eye. It was wild and showing white like a spooking horse. Mom was hiding her mouth behind a napkin. Ed and Mr. MacMahon were looking at their plates.

Dad was laughing too loud and bleating away about aggressive, mannish "horsey women." He swung around and put his arm around Mom.

"Which reminds me, Joanie, when is Ruth going to get over *her* horsey phase. Don't you agree she's a little too old for that?"

"First I'm too young now I'm too old," I didn't say.

Dad chuckled in my direction.

"Ruth, Isn't it about time to start curling your hair and wearing lipstick? When are you going to stop riding and start chasing the boys, heh heh?"

"Oh, *heh, heh,*" I said, "I guess I won't get around to doing *that* until

I'm really *truly* desperate, like Mom was when she came chasing after *you*."

I saw Dad wince. Mom told me to quit it, but I wasn't going to stop because– because I couldn't.

"But, MO-O-OM, Dad *always* says he married you because he felt so sorry for you, but he reeeeally should have married that other girl, that *better* girl on skis, the one that *MomMom* liked."

"Pfah!" whuffed Dad, rolling his eyes. "What. I. Meant. Was…pfah. That she could make an effort to look a *little* more attractive. She should fix her hair in a more becoming way for instance. She looks like she lives in the barn."

Bea, who until very recently, had lived in a barn every day of her life, shot a murderous look at Ed. Ed coughed and stirred in his seat, and the McMahons swiped their mouths. Mom told Dad to leave me alone for heaven sakes, but it was too late.

"But really Joanie," bawled Dad, "she could do something with her hair. Frankly though, with her looks, her best bet is to learn to cook."

Bea popped up and hauled Ed out of his seat. The MacMahons put their napkins on their plates.

And me? I did something with my hair. I cut if off. I just took the bloody carving knife off the table and sawed off my braid and took and mushed it into the half-empty bowl of potato salad that I had made all by myself. I swilled it around in the mayonnaise and onions and pickle chunks, around and around and around.

"HAPPY NOW? HAPPY NOW? HAPPY NOW?" shouted a voice, all high and hysterical. My voice.

Dad stared at me. I stared back. Dad flinched. He looked down and shook his head. Then Dad got up from the table, stomped over to his city car, got in and drove off, crashing the gears.

Well, I guess the party was over.

That night Dad locked himself in his shop and hit things with a hammer, and Mom, having washed the wad of hairy mayonnaise out of the salad bowl, turned the bowl over my head and evened up my remaining hair with the shears.

"Boy Jeez, what do I have to do to make him happy, cut off my arm?" I complained to Mom.

"Do you want to make him happy?" she said.

I thought about that while Mom bobbed my hair.

I didn't tell Mom, but I had decided what I wanted. I wanted Dad to leave. So I commenced trying to get his goat. I never answered him or obeyed him when he spoke to me. I just LOOKED. "Look at me when I'm talking to you," he used to say. So now it was me looking at him, wasn't it? I'd stare him right down, and he would flinch and turn away. I was going to be Boss of him, and we'd see how he liked it.

I won every time, Dad couldn't look at me. But it didn't take him too long to figure out that all he had to do to beat me at this game was never meet my eye, because I couldn't stare down a person who wouldn't stare back.

Meanwhile, Dad tightened up the house, put in insulation and expanded the downstairs bedroom. He had a deeper well dug so he could finally have enough bathwater with maybe some left over for Evvie and me and Mom. So it was Dad's house again. He stomped around his house with his chin out, the Lord of all He Surveyed, as long as he didn't survey me. Dad looked past me, around me, over me, and through me. He talked to everybody but me, and acted like I wasn't living in his house, like I had just disappeared.

I found myself sort of missing last summer, because when Dad was yarning me around I knew I was at least *there*. Now I was invisible and I was losing. I had to get his goat some other way, make him hate me and hit me so he would leave and I would win.

I burned things and spilled things and broke things like last year, but now I did it on purpose. I knocked over lamps and chairs. I dropped skillets of hot grease and glasses of milk and platters of hot food. I set potholders and dish towels on fire when I was cooking. I left the tap running so the pump would suck air and burn out.

"THAT KID OF YOURS did that *deliberately*!!" Dad would whine. "Joan, she deliberately..."

"Oh, no," I would whimper, "It was jus' a widdle accident, weally, I'm SO SOWWY!"

Why was I talking babytalk like that? *I was mocking my Dad.*

When Dad used to make fun of us when we were younger, he talked babytalk. Now when he was romancing Mom he started with the goo-goo ga-ga in her ear. He called her "Mommie." His widdle voice would get all high and he'd say "Duz duz duz oo wuv me, Mommie?" begging for a widdle pat behind the ears from his Big Boss. I guess Dad, not Mom, was the desperate one this time around.

Mom would always smile and say yes dear and give him a peck on the cheek; she was just encouraging Dad to behave like a kid. But he was a grown man; I was a kid. And Mom was *not his Mommie,* she was *MY MOMMIE.* So I commenced to talk baby talk too.

When I said "I'm so SOWWY" when I broke things, Dad would stomp out to the shop or drive off downstreet so he wouldn't have to notice me. I could get him mad as a snake any time I wanted, but I could never make him happy. Shoot, might's well do what I did best.

Mom got me alone and asked me stop it please.

"Why *should* I? Give me one good reason!"

"Please, Ruthie, for me," she said. "Maybe things would calm down if we could all be a little– a little forbearing. Making fun of your father doesn't help anything."

"Then why the hell does he do it to *me*?"

"Don't use that lan— He…he doesn't even realize that he—it's just an old habit he needs to...."

"Well I just guess he realizes it now!"

"Please Ruthie, somebody has to realize that all this sniping just makes it worse. I don't care which one of you stops it first. Don't you want to win the race and be that one?"

No. I did not want. I knew that Big Boss Mom had made Dad promise never to hit us anymore, so if I could get him to look at me and hit me, he'd break his promise, and I would win and she'd tell him to go away and never come back. But whenever he got mad enough to kill me he'd go downstreet or hide out in his shop and stay there.

At least I had him pinned down pretty good; so it was my house again. But it was so hard to draw a breath indoors. So whenever I felt like letting Dad out of his shop I rode out on Sam. I let my horse do whatever he wanted, walk, trot, gallop, sleep, graze with his bit on, I didn't care. But leaving the house turned out to be not a good idea because while I was out my sister double-crossed me. She stopped eating and reading and started hanging around with Dad.

She went and helped him out in the shop. One weekend she traveled with him to a sports show. When they got back Dad was talking baby talk to *her* too, calling her by her old nick-names, Boo-Boo, Woozzums

Daddy's Widdle Gurl, and my dumb shit of a sister nestled up against him soaking it all up just like Mom.

Evvie and I went to bed that night without any word spoke between us. I couldn't sleep, I just thrashed around and twisted myself up in the sheets, thinking up nasty horrible things to do to Wuzzums Daddy's Widdle Twaitor, until I finally dozed off.

At dawn I popped awake because I had had this terrible dream. I saw Daphne and Delilah Westford and me standing together with our arms around each other. I saw clear as day why they had hated me so much. Why Daphne had set me on fire and Delilah had beat me up. Why Daphne had grinned at me in my dooryard last winter.

They didn't hate me because I thought I was Somebody. Or because I cantered Sam through their stupid pasture.

It was Byron.

The twins may have hated their Dad for being drunk and yarning them around, but they still were shitfire jealous. Seeing Byron palling around with a new pair of girls, such sweet good girls, must have sent them half crazy; that's why Daphne set my book on fire in school. I sat up in bed whuffing hard.

Because I also knew, just as if I had done it myself, that the twins had gotten even with Byron for beating them by burning his house down. And maybe they got even with Barry Connor for getting them both pregnant and not offering to marry either one– or both– by burning his folks' barn down. Daphne had grinned at me and lit that cigarette that night, like I was supposed to get some joke between her and me. Well, now I got it.

I went and crawled in bed with Evvie and told her about the dream and that I just now understood why the Westfords had it in for me, and that I was mad and jealous of her and Dad just like they were with us and Byron.

"I still don't understand why you made up with Dad after he was so dirt mean," I said. "How can you stand to hang around with him?"

"I dunno I just need to," Evvie said.

So my sister and my Mom and Dad became a happy normal family. Dad called his sweet good daughter BooBoo. He called his lovely wife Mommie.

Me, he didn't call at all.

The County Fair came, and Evvie shaved the bots off Sam's legs but left his beard and fetlock hair on, and asked Byron to truck him to the fairgrounds with his ponies. Evvie rode Sam in the gymkhana and people laughed at him until he and Evvie won the Sit-a-Buck class riding bareback in a halter. Sit-a-Buck is when they put a dollar bill under your can and you have to ride at all three gaits and sit tight trying to keep that dollar there. The one who sits the buck the longest wins all the dollar bills that got loose, so Evvie got fifteen dollars. Dad congratulated her and told her she was not a bad little rider.

I won second place in the bake-off, for an apple pie. Nobody congratulated me, but I didn't care.

Sitting

"Lead me to the rock that is higher than I." –Psalm 62:6

I commenced sitting on Sam every day when I got home from school. I wasn't tacking up, I wasn't going anywhere; but I hated being in the house, I couldn't suck in a free breath in there.

Sam let me live on his back, he just wore me like a blanket while he went about the business of being a horse. Sometimes I brought a schoolbook and sat on him backwards, studying with the book propped on his hip bones. But usually I just sat. And watched. I watched what Sam watched.

We watched the leaves of the birch grove above the orchard turn pale gold, quivering against the blue, blue sky, then swirling around us as they fell. We watched the turkey family taking a dust bath together, chortling and shuffling their wings in the dirt. We saw coyotes frolicking with their pups in the upper pasture, all in one wriggling, giggling, tail-wagging jumble.

I watched the other horses too, how they got along. Sam was Boss. Then Mrs. Lynde, then Rusty. Sometimes when they weren't snoozing or grazing, they would tease each other. Sam would sneak his head over close to Mrs. Lynde and gently nip her. She would squeal, kick a little and swing her head around threatening to nip back, but she daren't because Sam was Boss; so she'd go and nip Rusty. He would squeal and lash his tail around. Rusty was bottom horse; so the nipping always went one, two, stop.

One time, Rusty, having gotten bit, sidled over to where I was sitting and took a bead on my leg as it hung down Sam's side. I saw him half-shutting his eyes and thinking "Dammit there must be somebody around here *I* get to bite!"

I glared daggers at him and said, "Don't you ever, ever, *ever.* " Rusty flinched, ducked his head and backed right off.

So I was Boss of Rusty, sort of. I didn't want to be Boss; I wasn't going to order a horse around ever again, not even Sam. So I just sat there. Not going anywhere.

Rusty wasn't content being bottom horse though, so next day he made a surprise attack on Mrs. Lynde and gave her a serious chomp; she screamed and flattened her ears, whirled her fat behind around and kicked him with both heels right in the ribs, ka-BOOM-"ugh!" Rusty staggered around trying to catch his breath, and Mrs. Lynde kept glaring at him with her ears pinned back all the while; then she turned tail and ignored him. Rusty was kicked out of the family.

After twenty minutes of being all alone in the world, Rusty tip-toed back up to Mrs. Lynde, reaching out his head and making kissing motions with his mouth.

"I'm sorry, let's be friends again," he said. And what do you think Mrs. Lynde did; she *nuzzled* him. That cranky old mare started nibbling little noogies along Rusty's crest, and he sighed and closed his eyes. Rusty was happy to be back in the family, even though he was still bottom horse.

Not long after that Jinnae and T.J. took Rusty over town to T.J.'s Dad's barn. We heard at school that Jinnae had finally given in and let T.J. ride Rusty and that Rusty dumped him, and when he tried to get back on Rusty kicked him and busted his leg for him, and after T.J. came back from the hospital he went out to the barn on his crutches and shot Rusty dead with his deer rifle.

The day after that I was sitting on Sam in the birch grove overlooking the orchard and I saw Bob Willett, Esq., Prop, knocking the last of the late-season apples off the trees with a long stick and putting them in a feed sack. Bob Willett, the slimiest snake that ever crawled, who had followed us home and chased us in the corn, who hurt Evvie, who made Jinnae go bad and Rusty get killed; and now here he was stealing my apples.

Sam pricked up his ears and whickered, and Bob jerked his head around. As I glared down on him, Bob looked up at me with eyes as blank and sweet as a new born calf. He smiled and waved how do.

It was me, not Bob, who flinched and looked away. He was the lowest-down most evil-doing person I ever met. But after I looked in his dumb innocent calf eyes I saw that although Bob Willet was not a little kid, Bob Willett really didn't know any better.

I sat on my high horse on a ledge going nowhere watching Bob dragging his sack of apples downslope. The woods were dead quiet except for Bob; he was humming to himself.

Sliding

Dear Jean-Claude,

Merry Christmas and Happy New Year. This Christmas I am sort of lonely because we just stayed home. We didn't have guests or go visiting on Thanksgiving either. Ed and Bea invited us over to Colby but Mom said no thanks because my Dad and Bea do not get along these days. The Pilchers never come over here any more.

We did do some neat stuff though. My sister and I learned to cross-country ski on skis we got at the church swap. Mom said it would be nice if we all gave each other hand-made gifts this year, the way they did in the "Little House" books by Laura Ingalls Wilder. What she didn't say was, we have no money for bought gifts this year. Anyhow she taught Evvie and me to crochet and we made hats and matching mittens for our parents and each other. Mom and I did a turkey with all the trimmings and I made a venison mince meat pie which was pretty tasty if I do say so, but nobody mentioned it, so I wisht I had been at Pilchers' where they appreciate good cooking. Yours truly, Ruth Rossley. P.S. Are you coming to visit this summer? I could ride Sam over Colby way and see you.

Dad planned to go downstate the week between Christmas and New Year's, on business or something, who cared. All I knew was I would rejoice to see the back of him.

Mom said. "Let's invite some of your friends over this Saturday for sliding and skiing." Then I really rejoiced, because ever since the famous welcome-home-Dad party last July, none of our friends had come calling except Byron once in a blue moon, when he could sneak away from all his women folk.

We invited Annaliese Mueller, Linsey McMahon and even the Holden girls. Mrs. Holden worked for Mom and the Library and I guess she had told her husband that no daughter of that marvelous Mrs. Rossley could be a member of That Element, so we were all friends again. Annaliese had her own truck, and she offered to pick up Linsey on her way over. We told everybody to bring sleds and skis, and we would provide the refreshments, a bonfire and the hill.

A dry light snow fell Friday night, and Evvie and I rejoiced a third time, because the pasture hill would be perfect for sliding. In the crisp bright morning, Mom went to town to practice on the organ and buy refreshments; and Evvie and I scraped the snow off a level ledge above the pasture, and stacked up apple-wood for our bon-fire. Sam and Mrs. Lynde pricked their ears at us, but stayed in the barnyard eating hay.

Our company arrived around two. Annaliese looked beautiful in a red tassel ski hat with a matching sweater. She waved the breast-plate from Speedy's driving harness over her head as she climbed the hill.

"What's that for?" I said.

"If we get too tired of ski-running we can hitch Sam up and let him pull us around,"

"You mean like—waterskiing?"

"Ja, Eyuh, one rides, one slides. You have to try it, it's fun!"

"Sam doesn't know how to pull yet!"

"He'll learn it in two minutes!"

Katie and Germaine dragged their big four-man toboggan up to the ledge, and commenced to pack snow on the uphill side of the stone pasture wall to make a jump; Mrs. Holden and Mom stood around the fire gabbing about the Library; I made a special effort to be polite to her and inquired how was Mr. Holden.

"Get on the toboggan, we'll all test the jump!" Six girls piled on, starting upslope of the fire. We picked up speed and went over the ramp and into the air screeching like banshees; the sled shot down the hill and past the barn so fast we had to bail out to avoid crashing into the fence. The horses bolted, just for fun, bucking and kicking up sprays of snow.

After we slid a few dozen times, we put on skis and glided down into the orchard, past the old apple trees hung with a few left-over apples with withered gnome faces and snow caps. We poled up the giant-step ledges through Mirkwood where the criss-crossed branches made silver crocheted lace against a navy blue sky. Curtains of snow floated down on us as the branches waved in the breeze, so the whole air glittered and winked. We went all the way through the Lame Buck field, then turned back in our tracks through woods, orchard, and right down the pasture hill. Finally we caught Sam and put the breastplate on him and tied ropes to the tugs and made him pull us one by one, trotting around the Upper Pasture..

"Evvie, let go the ropes when you fall down, I don't wanna plow with you!"

"Whoa, hey Annaliese, take your skis off before you get on my horse!" I was so busy enjoying myself I forgot I was never going to ride Sam again.

The Moms were smiling, we girls were laughing, Sam was humming happily to himself as he hauled us around, and the whole hillside turned from silver to gold in the afternoon sunlight.

I blanketed Sam and walked him in the orchard to cool him down, and our guests stood singing and stomping around the fire drinking mugs of hot chocolate, toasting marshmallows and making Pigs-in-a-Blanket, which is wieners wrapped in Bisquik dough.

The sun commenced to set behind red and purple clouds and the blue hill-shadows slid east towards us over pink snow. Our Farm looked like one of those old Currier & Ives scenes, with titles like "Winter Frolics," or something; and I got that old cozy feeling of being inside the picture, sitting on Sam with the bonfire smoke rising, and Evvie and Linsey skiing down the hill kicking up puffs of rose colored snow and blue snow as they shot from the light into the shadow.

A car was coming up hollow. Dad's car. The headlights, two cones of yellow in the blue air, turned into the dooryard. Dad got out, slammed the car door hard and stood looking up at us, standing frozen on the hill looking down at him. Dad commenced walking down the lane. The sun went down and the air and the snow went gray.

Dad came up the hill, scuffling through all our ski and sled tracks. He went right up to Mom and stood in front of her. He didn't look at anybody else, and he didn't say, "Oh, *hello* there, how are you, nice to see you, my, it looks like you're all having *such fun.*" He didn't say anything. He just stared at Mom and she looked back at him.

The silence was getting embarrassing, so Mom spoke up.

"Well, well. I guess it's getting close to supper time, I'd better go and get my husband something to eat, so... well, I guess we should call it a day. Thanks so much for coming...."

In two seconds everybody picked up their sleds and skis and hurried off home with barely a good-bye and they'd probably never come back; my charming Dad made it so clear he didn't want them here.

The Rossley family stood alone on the hill in the dark.

I looked down on Dad from up on Sam's back, and wished he was dead.

We all just stood there, waiting for somebody to apologize, explain, shit, scream or go blind. Finally Dad went over and stomped the fire out and dumped the last of the cocoa on it; then he kicked more snow over the ashes. Mom moved next to him and slipped her arm through his and kissed him on the cheek. She said something to him real soft that sounded like,

"You didn't get it, did you?"

He shrugged off her arm and strode off down the hill without speaking to her. She tagged along behind him. I didn't hear her say

"*Did it possibly occur to you that you just single-handedly ruined your children's party? Would you perhaps like to apologize now?*" Because she would never have the grit to say it.

I knew they would probably talk that night, though. Maybe Mom would point out how rude he was, maybe she would even find the grit to throw him out. I stayed awake, lying flat on the grate listening as shoes hit the floor and drawers and doors banged shut. Now they commenced talking soft and fast, back and forth.

It got real quiet. Then I heard these terrible sobs. Shit. Now Dad was making her cry. I had never heard Mom cry like that before, not even at the table last April. The sobs burst out half yelping and half choking, like a yard dog I saw get run over once.

What was he saying to her? Was he threatening to leave her again? I wished like crazy he would do it; and I hated him for doing it, and I hated her for boo-hoo-hooing about it.

What did Mom want Dad for? He treated her, the only person on earth who still liked him at all, like dirt. He had acted as if our snow party was some big personal insult to him, as if we had snuck behind his back and stolen that good time out from under him. Jerk.

As the sobs got softer I heard Mom's voice talking gently at the same time. I stopped breathing and lay frozen there on the floor. Because the person crying wasn't my Mom.

It was my Dad.

Spontaneous Combustion

Way Down Yonder by Myself: Couldn't hear nobody pray.
–Negro Spiritual

"Boy Jeez, sometimes I don't know whether I found a length of rope or lost a cow." Byron said that to me one day when he was hung over after going on one of his Coon & Cat toots. I didn't know what he meant at the time, but now I did.

After the night I heard Dad sobbing, I didn't know what to think. By rights I should have rejoiced to see the slump of his shoulders and that whupped-dog look in his eye. But I didn't.

I still tried to get his goat. I didn't want to any more, but I couldn't stop. If Dad had been a horse I could have put my hand on his neck and said Ho Princie it's all right. But he was Dad. Except he wasn't evil like I thought. He was weak and pathetic. I felt sorry for him and was mad at him at the same time; but mostly I despised him. And that was worse.

The Sunday after New Years, driving to church with Mom, I was so miserable my bones hurt and I clenched my hands and ground my teeth to keep all the bad feelings from bursting out. But I heard myself asking her out of the blue,

"Mom, does God put curses on people?"

Mom said "I think people put their own curses on themselves, don't you?"

"Like when they do evil and they know better but they keep doing it and then they feel awful?" I wasn't planning to say this; the words just spurted out on their own.

"That is our minister's definition of hell, Ruthie. Life right here on earth, but separated from grace."

"So why doesn't God swoop down and make folks stop being bad if he cares about them so much?"

"Some people in church would say that he did."

"Yeah, just one lousy time, way long ago, and all his neighbors double-crossed him!"

"You don't need to yell Ruthie, I'm right here."

"If God really cared," I yelled, "he should swoop down every few days and restore our souls before we do evil. And he should catch evil-doers right in the act and smite them, they way you train an animal."

"Is that the way you trained Sam?" said Mom.

"Sam isn't an evil doer."

"Rufus Bates thought he was."

I remembered the words of Rufus, how he said, this horse is a killer, and how Rufus smote Sam, and how really swell that had worked out. I was thinking about somebody else who smote and yarned her horse, with the same excellent results. I remembered the words of Ronan O'Ryan, how *he* said "Treat 'em good and they'll treat you good."

"Well, you're right about Sam," Mom said "People are the ones that do evil, that's why we humans go to church on Sunday and Sam gets the day off. The minister would say that God gives the human race some fine general guidelines to live by, and then he steps back and lets us make our own choices for good or ill."

"Well I think he has stepped back too durn far. How can we be sure he's even paying *attention* any more? If God doesn't smite the evil doers, don't the righteous people have a duty to step in and do it for him?"

"You mean like Robin Hood?" Mom asked. "Or more like the Nazis and the Ku Klux Klan or the righteous people who shunned Ed and Bea? Ruthie, I think the minister would say you have got a good idea turned inside out.

"You know what he would say, that God is patient and understanding, like a loving—like a loving shepherd, who cares for his sheep even when they are straying and misbehaving. And we, the people who are trying to be good, are supposed to follow his example. We want to be slow to anger and not take revenge or try to be a law unto ourselves. Don't you think?"

"But Mom, it doesn't *work*. Everybody just *pretends* that it works. They say the words but then they do the evil anyway."

"We just have to keep trying. It takes a long time to learn grace. If God was constantly swooping down and smiting we'd only behave ourselves out of fear. We'd be no better than slaves. We need to make a knowing choice to be good. And that is not so easy to do."

"Well, so then why doesn't God at least rescue the good people who are suffering at the hands of their enemies?"

"Oh my." she said, "that's one of the Mysteries of Life we have to solve. It's hard to see where the justice is sometimes. If we could see it, we'd all be saints I guess."

"I still think it's pretty lousy of God not to offer a helping hand to the sore oppressed. Why did Ed and Bea have to suffer? Why did Byron or Frenchy have to suffer? Why do…It wouldn't kill God to help them out a little."

"Well, maybe he offers that helping hand more than we think," Mom said. "Maybe we just don't reach out and take it. Maybe God is there hoping we notice him when somebody does a good deed, or helps their neighbor or forgives their trespasses. Maybe God is there when we find something or somebody to love, and it changes us, you know?"

Then she said, very quickly "If God came down and told you to stop fighting with your Dad, would you do it?"

"Only if *he* apologizes *first,*" I shot back at her. Mom didn't say anything else, she was probably wondering if I wanted *God* to apologize first or *Dad* to apologize first. I didn't know either at that point. I had begun to feel really awful inside.

I couldn't sing when the choir warmed up before service. My throat was so tight no notes came out, so I went downstairs and sat in the pews. But when the service started I looked at all those people folding their hands praying for peace *and* praying to get even with their enemies on the same hook, all bleating like sheep, and I thought I would scream except I couldn't. I couldn't breathe. So I got up and went outside.

I went and sat in this little tool shed over near the old graveyard, where they kept the lawn mower and watering hoses and spades and stuff. It wasn't the church but it was still on holy ground; maybe the reception would be better away from the racket of all those hypocrites blatting and baa'ing together.

"Forgive us our baa baa as we forgive those who baa baa." They weren't repenting, they were just pretending to. On Sundays the pastor said "let us pray" and they all said "Baa, baa, we're God's little lambs," and on Monday they would yell "baa, baa, she thinks she's Somebody," "Baa, baa, let's set her on fire."

I bent over and stared at the floor. I clasped my hands tight together between my knees. I tried to say the words but nothing came out. I tried to think them but my head was full of noise. Maybe God heard what I meant anyway. I wanted him to send me a sign, that I should do it. Forgive him. Let bygones be bygones.

I sat there listening for an answer. Dead quiet. Nothing happened. They had even stopped bleating in the church. Not even a bird sang outside.

"*I thought so*," said a little tight voice. The only noise in the world.

The church doors swung open and a big happy hymn poured out all relieved and pleased with itself. It wasn't hard to sneak around the church and into the side door and join up with the sheep going out the front. The people already in the yard were yelling something, and suddenly everybody was crowding towards the door.

"Somebody call the....!" the minister yelled in his big sermon voice. Through the windows people saw that the tool shed was on fire and burning fast. Men rushed over to try and save the stuff, but other men held them back because the gas can for the power mower was in there too.

Then a big fireball went up and a roar, "WHUMP!" just like Connor's haymow, and the building collapsed, and black cinders rained down on the upturned faces of the assembled flock, who cried "baa, baa" in their dismay. The minister said comforting words to quiet them down and the firemen arrived and sprayed their little hoses on the ashes but they were much too late to do anything about it at all.

Doth He Not Leave the Ninety and Nine?

He that entereth not by the door into the sheepfold, but climbeth up some other way, the same is a thief and a robber. –John 10:1

Dear Jean-Claude,

Happy Birthday. There is a thaw here and no snow. My Dad has gone crazy and will not talk to anybody except to say he wishes I had never been born and to criticize my cooking. He won't let me have friends over after school, he cusses us out and won't let us have a fire in the stove and slaps my Mom around with a gun barrel if she says boo. I hide up in the woods because I don't want to be in the house alone with him, there is no telling what he might do. The only thing interesting happening here is there is a thief in the neighborhood. Here is a clipping from the paper about it, and as you can see I am in the story.

BURGLARIES PLAGUE OUTLYING FARMS

By Evan Letique, Town Crier Staff

Last week Bethel residents reported a series of minor burglaries, and the police were called in to investigate the disappearance of small items from an outbuilding on Shiloh road and in both Connor and Mitchell Hollows. In an exclusive interview Barry Connor told this reporter that he did not think the robbery was tied to the Connor's dairy barn fire last winter.

"Nothing big was taken," Connor averred, "Somebody broke into the shed and took some butchering knives and a block and tackle. Good thing this year's pig was already kilt."

Mr. Connor continued, "People in this town should be concerned for the safety of their stock and machinery." The young farmer added that "he personally was installing floodlights in his barnyards."

Mr. T.J. Westford, who drives a grader for the Bethel Highway Department, reported that someone had broken into his father's shed and stolen his deer rifle, plus a valuable tooled-leather horse bridle that he said was a gift from his girlfriend.

Mr. David Rossley, woodworker and retired businessman from New York City, reported that a fishing creel and trout-fly case and several other small but irreplaceable items from his woodworking shop had been removed or tampered with.

Mr. Rossley offered the opinion that juvenile delinquents from the village had burglarized him while he was away displaying his custom-made gun stocks and laminated hickory-wood deer-hunting bows at a sports show. "I believe the police should round up all the idle young people who have dropped out of school and question them closely," Mr. Rossley said.

The police also took statements from other members of the Rossley family. Ruth Rossley, a sophomore in Bethel High School, said she had seen a suspicious looking person lurking in their hollow. Her description—a white male, short, slight, dark haired, and wearing a John Deere cap—fit a resident of Mitchell Hollow, Mr. Bob Willett. Mr. Willett was subsequently interrogated by the Bethel police, but was soon released on his own recognizance."

After the January thaw the freezing wind came. Sam did not have to carry his usual guest, poor little Ruthie, because she could not sit still any more and besides she decided it was dumb to spend that much time sitting on an old horse going nowhere.

During those dark days a ghost might have been seen wandering in the woods in the shadow of Argue mountain, but the ghost was invisible even in broad daylight. If it got too cold out she knew where to go to get out of the wind. Into barns and sheds or gullies. The ghost built little campfires and squatted over them, throwing sticks and other small but irreplaceable items into the flames. But the ghost never could get warm.

This ghost was standing in one of her secret places in the woods, a deep gully in Mirkwood. She was poking the last embers of one of her little fires and talking to herself. A heavy gray sky sagged above her and some big flakes of snow commenced to float down. The ghost knew her feet were cold but she was used to it and she didn't really feel them any more.

Soft steps in leaf-litter; the ghost jumped like a rabbit and whipped around. The tree trunks made black bars in front of the gully mouth, and something moved behind them. A sudden flash of white became the lop-sided blaze of a big furry horse. The horse poked his nose into the gully mouth and whickered, waggling his ears at the ghost inside, because he could see her. Why had Sam left his hay rack and warm barn to come all the way up here?

Sam walked right into the gully. He put his head against the ghost's chest and gave her a little nudge. Her hands were frozen and stiff in her pockets and she couldn't feel them.

But then I reached out my hands and hugged Sam's face. Then I pulled his ears sidewise a little. Sam sighed and lowered his head snuffling around the ashes of my fire. I grabbed his mane, stood on a rock and hauled myself back up on him.

Sam had to back out of the narrow gully; then he turned his face toward home, following the little deer trails. The snow fell harder, the big flakes spinning around and around like wagon wheels, and the world went white. When we came into the orchard I could see the grey shapes of two spike bucks standing under the trees. They upped their heads and swiveled furry ears at us. Sam stopped and pricked his ears too.

Out of the birch grove on our left stepped another ghost. A ghost deer, all white, almost invisible among the white birches, with the white snow whirling around him. It was the White Buck of Argue Mountain.

Sam snorted, and the Buck stopped in mid-stride, his foreleg in the air, his head raised and turned toward us. The Buck had ivory white antlers and red eyes; and those eyes looked at me and Sam and we looked back. Minutes went by and none of us twitched a muscle.

At last the great Buck lowered his head and moved to join his sons, and the three animals turned their heads toward the mountain ledges; they walked away slowly as deer do in hard weather, saving every drop of strength. The snow closed its curtains behind them as they slipped into the woods. Sam lowered his head and glided through the orchard to the pasture. He and I went down to the barn through the swirling whiteness. Everything was washed whiter than snow. A Blank Page. A sign.

Hell Freezes Over

*"Remembering mine affliction, and my misery, the wormwood
and the gall." –Lamentations of Jeremiah 3:19*

I commenced sitting on Sam again, because he loved me and kept
me warm. He goeth into the mountains and seeketh me out when I went
astray. He pulled me out of the pit and carried me gently in his bosom.

I'd sit there on his back in the barn, listening to him and Mrs. Lynde
chewing hay and breathing, and the mice running around living their
lives in the mow above my head, and I would try to hear the peepers or
picture the White Buck in my mind.

At five I'd slide off Sam and go in the house to cook supper, and
we'd have another silent family feast, where you'd think the food was
going to freeze solid on the plates. Then I'd go do my homework, get in
bed and get up and go to school. But really I didn't know where I went
or what I was doing, except in the barn.

One night Mom was at a 4-H meeting and I was getting a late supper.
I made Macaroni and Cheese Casserole without cooking the macaroni
first. I threw in some spice that might have been oregano or it might
have been mint, and scraped some old and maybe moldy Velveeta out of
a jar in the back of the fridge. I shoved the whole thing the oven and it
was only a little burnt when Mom got home.

Dad slumped in from the shop, heaved himself into his chair and poked his fork into his mouth before we finished saying grace. We said it through anyway. When we looked up after "Amen," he was squinting at Mom and his face was twisted up in a mean grin.

"Joanie, Joanie, this is just like old times. This dish is a *triumph*! My Mother's cooking could *never* come up to this. I've said it before, but I say it now with a whole new meaning; Joanie, you are a great. Great. Cook!" And he snorted and threw down his napkin and stood up. I stood up too.

"Hey, wait a minute. *I* cooked this," I said to him.

Dad winced and looked at me, right at me, in the eyes. I looked right back, with my heart thumping because I could see he was thinking about apologizing, and I knew I was thinking about apologizing too.

"I could throw it out, and start over," I whispered. Dad's face twitched and changed expression a few times. Nobody breathed. Then the grin came back and stuck there on his face.

"Well, well, well, following in your mother's footsteps I see," said Dad with a chuckle. "Let me guess... did you put kindling in this? Or, could it be-yes! Hay! Hay, hay, from the barn where you seem to be living these days? Is that the secret ingredient that makes this inedible slop so memorable?"

"Hey," I said, "Why don't you just go back home to your big fat ugly *Mommie* and get her to cook for you? Or won't she let you in the *door*?"

My Dad turned pale as ashes. He was shaking all over. Then he started to screech, like a girl.

"You FILTHY BITCH! You dirty whore, you Goddamn SLUT, don't you EVER—ever—how dare you, how..."

I crashed over my chair and made the pig noise and threw the food and plate and the fork and spoon at him and then I ran out to the barn and up into the mow and cried and cried.

Because this time Dad was not trying to win a round in our little secret war. He was not trying to Show Me Who was Boss. What he said to me came right up out of his heart before he could stop it. What he said to me was true.

Mom came out and called me down after a while. I suppose she had to clean the food up first. She wanted to take me for a drive, just to get me away somewhere. I sat slouched over against the car window, staring out at nothing. Mom just drove for a long time.

"Ruthie," she said finally, "are you really living in the barn?"

"Yeah. So?"

"Oh God, I'm so... isn't it...too cold? Wouldn't you rather come to the Library or the Grange building with me afternoons and do your homework?"

"I sit on Sam to keep warm. I study out there while it's light. I like it there." I said.

"I'm sorry I can't be home to make things easier for you. I feel terrible that this feud between Dad and you goes on and on like this. I really had no idea...What can I do?"

"WHY DON'T YOU JUST PUNISH ME AND GET IT OVER WITH!" I bawled at her. "You *always* take *Dad's* side! You are always with him and against me!"

"Your Dad says just the opposite, he says I always side with you. And tonight... I know you were trying to stick up for me– in your own way– and I'm grateful to you for doing that. But I don't want to take sides in this, I'm on both your sides. I just want to help you get over this bad patch. I'm really sorry I haven't been able to help you. Would you like to go talk to the minister about it?"

"NO!" I screeched at the top of my voice, banging the side of my head on the window.

Mom gave me a little sidelong look and breathed in quick, as if she was going to say something– or else she had just put two and two together and gotten Fire. My heart raced, my head ached and my throat closed up again, but I just sat there saying nothing.

That night in bed I thought of killing Dad. With the shotgun that Mom almost shot Byron with. I could just squeeze both triggers and blow him to Kingdom Come like a woodchuck. Blood splatttering, bones splintering, teeth and eyeballs flying through the air. I would feel good again. I thought of setting fire to the shop and burning him and all his precious wooden things that he loved so much, to a black smoking crisp. And then gnawing on the bones.

I couldn't stop these thoughts from coming into my mind, and I knew I was far worse than the dirtiest name Dad could called me. Worse than he could possibly imagine. I was dirt and deserved to be treated like dirt.

For a while I went to the Library or the 4-H office in the Grange Hall, pretended to study and drove home with Mom. I was no good in school any more. I couldn't think straight. I never answered in class. But I could see things I hadn't seen before. I could see into the hearts of That Element; The Trailer Trash and the Gelders. And I was just like them.

If a teacher tried to force me to answer I would just stare at him. The teacher would flinch and fume and pretend to laugh, but he couldn't make me talk. Then the teacher would send me to the office. Big Deal.

I told my old pal the principal, hey I was just being real quiet in class, that's supposed to be good, right? Wasn't I being good? Wasn't I good? Wasn't I? The principal would sigh and look all concerned and gaze out the window again and tap his little pencil and tell me if there was anything he could do to help.... I shrugged and cocked my head over and squinted up my eyes at him too and asked him exactly what was he going to do?

I was going out to the barn to ride, and when I put the tack on Sam he started to shrink, and kept shrinking till he was the size of a cat. Sam was too small and weak to carry me, and I would scream come back come back come back and then I would wake up and it was another horrible morning in my horrible life.

I had this dream almost every night. It was the worst nightmare ever, and I woke up with the cold sweats when I dreamed it, although what was happening in it didn't seem half as horrible as the stuff I was dreaming up during the day. I got in bed with Evvie one night after having it and told it to her, because I was afraid of going to sleep and having it again, and maybe she could make it stop.

Evvie shut her eyes and thought about it so long I thought she had dozed off. Then she said,

"Sam is Dad. Dad is Sam."

"What's that supposed to mean?"

"I dunno."

I started taking the bus home right after school and sitting on Sam again because I was dead scared he was going to shrink up and disappear on me. I sat on him making braids in his mane and un-doing them again, like Evvie and I had done after the horse show. I stopped thinking about murder and arson and just day-dreamed, there in the barn.

Late one cold clear afternoon there was golden-rod colored light pouring through the stall window, and a little hoof-paring of a moon setting over west. That color sky reminded me of something long ago, when I was little, and happy.

As I was trying to remember what that something was, I caught sight of a small person walking up the road and turning into our dooryard. It was Jinnae, knocking on our front door. After a few knocks she headed out to the barn and found me sitting on Sam. Jinnae had dark circles around her eyes but it wasn't makeup. She looked so pale and tired and even thinner than usual and she was carrying some kind of parcel under her coat.

"How do," she said.

"How do," I said.

Silence.

"Thought I'd come up hollow and say g'bye, and show you the kid. Going to live on Paulette's ranch out west." Jinnae slipped into the stall and unbuttoned the top of her coat, turning round to show me a flat little gnome face, red like an apple, its eyes squinched shut, almost hidden under a snow white knit cap.

"Evvie around?" said Jinnae, buttoning up again.

"She stays with Mom at the Library ever since…He's cute, what's his name?"

"She's a girl. Name's Evelyn. Don't fuss now, BooBoo." Jinnae joggled herself up and down.

"You and TJ not getting married?"

"He wants to, but I said no. I'm sick of men pestering me."

"That why'd you let your damn Dad pester Evvie? Why didn't you tell your Ma?"

"I dunno. I guess I thought that's just how Dads did. He done Paulette and then Monique and then me the same. Nobody ever said anything about it being bad."

"So how come your Ma didn't stop him? How come you and your Ma don't get Frenchy and John to knock his teeth in and throw HIM out of the house and then YOU could stay there!"

"Ma won't hear no word against him, she needs his assistance check to get by."

"I–I think somebody ought to take a gun and shoot him!"

"That's what T.J. says."

Silence.

"Jeez, Ruthie, he's my Dad, he's the only Dad I got."

"You telling me you still love him?"

"I guess."

"You people are all stone CRAZY, Jinnae Willett."

"Speakin of crazy, you wanna to tell me why you're sitting on your old horse out in the barn?"

"Because, because..."

"I gotta go, Ruthie. Byron's takin' me to the bus. Just tell Evvie g'bye for me, OK, and I'm real sorry about what happened."

Jinnae adjusted the bundle under her coat. I slid off Sam and walked her over to the barn door.

"See ya."

"See ya."

I watched her go; she took the shortest way back, trudging kitty-corner across the frozen cornfield, not climbing onto the road till our land ended and the woods began.

I looked at the golden-rod sky fading to green to blue, and finally I remembered what it reminded me of. It was the time Dad took me night skating on this little woods pond downstate.

It was just him and me, skating under the moon and stars with our feet throbbing with the cold. He showed me how to ice-dance, holding hands with our arms crossed. I sang "The Skaters' Waltz," *Smooth O'er the Ice, Gli-i-ding Along,"* while we whirled around and around. When we got home we had cocoa with marshmallows and Dad lit a fire in the fireplace and he rubbed my frozen feet till they were warm again. His hands had so much heat in them.

I almost yelled out, because I missed my Dad so much, because I wanted to be Daddy's Little Girl again...

Usually when Jinnae told me things I didn't figure out what she meant for a week. But that evening I understood her right off. I couldn't stop hating my Dad, and I couldn't stop wanting my Dad. So I guess I figured out the minster's definition of hell, too.

The Last Battle

Dear Jean-Claude,

Happy St Pat's. It will be my 15th birthday in two weeks, so wish me happy birthday! There is still snow on the mountains here and it doesn't feel like Spring is ever going to come. It's cold and grey and I am all alone and have nobody to talk to except you.

I was in the kitchen for once, because Dad was downstreet and Mom was out somewhere with Evvie. I had my pal's letter spread out on the kitchen table and I was writing back to him in my school tablet.

Dad is crazier than ever, he went and shot my friend's horse. He kills any wild animal he sees, including this beautiful shining white buck that used to live in our orchard. He accuses me of poisoning his food and makes me sleep in the barn. He is always sharpening up his hunting knife and talking wild about wanting to cut off my arm. Please, I beg you, don't let your Mom tell Bea or Ed anything more about what my Dad is doing to us because you'll only make things worse. We are dead scared to tell anyone or go to the police because he'd kill us all for sure.

A shadow fell over the panes in the door; then the door opened and there was Dad. Shit, his car was in the garage today and he'd been in his shop all along. We stared at each other a long time without moving.

Dad shrugged his shoulders and ducked his head.

"Hi," he said.

Silence.

"What are you writing?" He came over picked up the envelope to Jean-Claude's letter.

"Who do you know in Canada?" he said.

"You think nobody in Canada would want to know me?" I snapped; Dad turned red and squinty eyed; he grabbed Jean's letter, which was spread out on the table. I sprang at him screeching like a wild-cat.

"You can't *read* that, that's *private,* it's Mine, MINE MINE!"

He whipped the letter behind his back saying "Don't you use that tone of voice with me Young Lady."

"GIVE IT HERE!" I howled. "Give me my *goddamn letter*, you have NO RIGHT TO READ MY LETTERS!"

"I'll read what I please in my own house. I decide who has rights here, not you. As long as you are under my roof and eating my food, you will….."

"This isn't YOUR roof! This isn't your HOUSE! YOU don't put any food on this table! You think you're SOMEBODY? You're NOBODY!! You live off YOUR WIFE'S SALARY, you no-good lazy BUM!" I shrieked at him. "YOU got fired from your job and NOBODY would take you back, not even your OWN MOTHER would take you back, because you're a big Fat FAILURE and *Everybody Hates You even Ed,* and EVEN MOM DOESN'T WANT YOU HERE!"

Silence.

We stood facing each other, breathing hard, shaking. Dad's face went from red to dead-white. My heart was thumping so loud I knew he could hear it. He dropped the letter back on the table, but I never took my eyes off his eyes.

"OK." Dad said. "That's it. I'm through with you. I'm sending you away for good; and I'm calling Kennedy's right now to come with a van and take that goddamn nag."

"Go ahead. *Call* them! What do I care?"

Silence.

We stared at each other. Nobody flinched. Then Dad turned his back on me and went to the phone. He paused, and back at me looked over his shoulder. His lips were twitching and pulled back off his teeth. He picked up the receiver and began to dial.

"AAAAAHHHH!" I bolted out the back door, heading for the woodshop. Just like I imagined I was opening the door, throwing the latch on the inside and grabbing the hand-ax that hung on the wall. I was taking that ax to Dad's beautiful hand-worked laminated-hickory re-curve hunting bows as they hung on their rack, hack, hack hack.

I was screaming like a pig and bunching up some old newspapers and pouring turpentine on them; I was grabbing a box of matches off the workbench. My hands were shaking, but I had a match lit when I heard Dad howling and pounding on the door with something heavy.

The door shrieked and opened backwards; Dad had yanked the hinges off. He was standing in the doorway with a crowbar in his hand. The match flame was burning my fingers. I yelled and dropped it and it landed on the papers. And went out.

Dad came at me. I knew he was going to kill me and I didn't care because he would go to jail and rot there forever. But I still dodged him, throwing tools and chunks of curing hickory wood at him. We both kept on screeching and cussing.

"*Stop it right now the both of you*! What in God's name are you DOING!" Mom was driving her pickup through the yard and practically into the shed, and jumping out of the cab like fury.

"*Both of you get inside the house this minute*!" She said, She was not yelling, but she was mad, she was furious as she herded us both into the kitchen.

"You are going to have this over right now, and I *mean* it," Mom said, rounding on Dad. Dad, once more all red in the face, had commenced bawling that I had *deliberately* tried to burn his shop down. Mom looked daggers at him and he shut up.

Then she turned to me. Her eyes were wide with a calm and terrible rage.

"Listen to me, and listen good," she said in a voice that was soft and hard. "Your dad is trying very hard to start over," she said, "and what makes it so hard is that he thinks you despise him."

"I DO despise him! He won't *look* at me, he won't *talk* to me except to say I'm bad and I can't do anything right. So now I am bad, so what, why shouldn't I be? He said he was going to sell Sam to Kennedy's and I said go ahead, I don't care anymore!!"

Mom whirled around on Dad again. "Did you hear what she just said? Does it sound familiar to you at all? Now you are the Father here and your child has asked how it might be that she could ever win your approval and your love. How *might* that be, Dave? Are you going to tell her how, or are you going to take away the last thing that she cherishes in this world, the animal she pours her love into because her father turns it down? Are you going to treat *her* the way *they* treated *you*? Do you think that's going to work? *Do you?"*

Dad's mouth flopped open but no words came out. Then he crumpled up and sank to the floor sobbing, and the sobs came out half yelping and half choking. Like somebody dying. Like a dog being run over. A terror like nothing I have ever known before or since shot through every vein in my body.

I started to shake and gasp and sob, from the awfulness of my fear and pity seeing my Dad crying for me.

Mom swung me around and held onto my shoulders and talked fast and low. "I know this is hard for you to understand, but this year your father has had to grow up all over again. His parents hurt him terribly and he feels just like you, and he knows it now and he doesn't want to pass this curse on to you.

"And Ruthie, I know it's unfair that he has to grow up while you are growing up. I know it's almost killing you. You two are so much alike, that's why you get all locked up fighting each other. It's like fighting yourself, do you see?

"Right now you are *dead even*. Now is the time to stop the fight and end the curse. *Just stop it, right now."*

Mom let me go and I doubled over and collapsed on the floor. My father reached out for me and I crawled into his arms. We were both sobbing and rocking each other and trying to talk. All we could say was "It's all right, It's all right," over and over. It's all right. Mom sat down and cried on the kitchen table. Not her old helpless way. She was just happy that the war was over.

Who's Boss

Say the Word and you'll be Free. –Lennon/McCartney

Two days after the Last Battle Mom and I were alone because Dad and Evvie went to a sports show to sell the things in Dad's shop I had not ruined. Before he left I made Dad a promise to work in the shop to repay all the damage I had done. That seemed only fair, and I was sort of looking forward to it.

Mud season was almost here again and soon nobody would be able to walk anywhere except the road, so Mom and I decided to take a woods hike, down Lovers' Lane and over Mitchell's to chat with the Connor ladies.

We looked at the new barn built over the old foundation hole after the Connors had cleared away the ashes and bulldozed them across the street near the pit silo. The charred pile was ugly, but in a year or two the worms would eat it and grass would grow over it and everybody would forget the fire ever happened.

We sat and took tea with Ma and Grandma Connor around the stove, and Grandma took my hand in hers and said

"Land of Heart's Desire,
Where beauty has no ebb, decay no flood,
But joy is wisdom, time an endless song."

You have your Heart's Desire, young one," Grandma said. "I see it, plain as day."

On our way home we stopped and sat on the log bridge over Mitchell's Brook, listening to the water running as the ice melted.

It would be Spring before we knew it. I would turn fourteen soon and Mom and Dad and Evvie were planning a party. With cake and candles.

"Well, Ruthie," Mom sighed, "I have to apologize to you for so many things. I never guessed how bad it had gotten between you and Dad. I had…well, 'worries at work,' and I wasn't paying you enough attention."

"That's OK. I'm sorry too. I was trying to make Dad go away. I was sort of keeping it secret from you I guess."

"I would never have driven home that afternoon if Bea hadn't called me to say she heard some wild story from her in-laws in Canada that something terrible was going on with Dad. I didn't really believe her but she insisted…"

Mom sighed. "I owe you an explanation as well, Ruthie.

"You know, when you were little your Dad was so scared he could never support us and buy you the things you wanted. And his parents were always belittling him and leaning on him to move up in the Company. They thought that nothing in the world was good enough for their son, including the things their son wanted to do and the life he wanted to live.

"Your Dad yearned for the outdoors. He hated working in an office, but he was afraid to go against his Dad, and he was afraid of MomMom's—well, MomMom's comments. When he lost his job his parents punished him. They made him return all the loans and gifts they gave us to help us get started. When Dad decided to keep the farm and sell the house to pay them off, they disowned him."

"So since his parents always made it clear that they wouldn't love him if he failed, he believed nobody loved him at all. I thought that if I just kept telling him I loved him no matter what, that he'd get over that belief. I guess he hated himself so much he couldn't believe me, and he acted the only way he knew how; he took it out on all of us. My mistake was to let him do that.

"Then Bea," Mom went on. "Bea! what a friend she has been through all this! She told me to finish my sentences and stick up for myself a little. That's when the trouble started. But I guess the trouble needed to start." Mom threw a twig into a channel of free running water in the brook and watched it float away downstream.

"Your dad still has a way to go before he forgives Bea."

"Was that why he was so rank to her at the party?" I threw a twig in the brook.

"What do you think?" said Mom. "Anyway, I took him back. Your Dad and I tried several times to make peace with his parents but nothing worked. PopPop is an out and out bully, and MomMom…She took pains to let me know that I wasn't…I shouldn't say things like this to you, so I'll stop there. They're still your grandparents after all."

"They said you weren't as good as the ski girl, right?" I said.

"Never mind about the ski girl. What I want you to know is Dad wanted to love us always, but he was afraid to, he had been so mortified, do you know what that is?"

"Kind of like his spirit was broken?"

"Exactly. It's a wound of the soul."

"Bea said Ed got a wound of the heart once."

"A soul wound is even more terrible. It means you don't know what you need to live.

"Dad didn't know what he needed. When he was upset he'd snap back to doing the same things his parents did to him, over and over again. He tried to bully and belittle you into minding him, didn't he? And you dug in your heels and refused didn't you?"

"Yes."

"But what he needed so desperately all along was not your obedience but something he was much too scared to ask for. Love is something you can't bully a person into giving you. Love was the forbidden word in your father's family. Do you understand that?"

"Like 'pony' was the forbidden word in our family once."

"It's the same. Can you understand how horrible Dad's life was when he couldn't say 'love?'"

"Eyuh."

Mom looked at me sort of surprised. I was surprised myself.

"How come you are suddenly wise enough and grown up enough to see your way to forgiving your Dad?"

"Well, because it was me yarning him around, too. After a while I wanted to let bygones be bygones, but I couldn't stop trying to get him back for what how he treated me, until you drove in and made me stop for good and all. But come to think of it I had lots of helping hands along the way, trying to make me stop, just like you said. Bea, and Byron and Analiese and Evvie and, even Daphne and Delilah, in a dream I had. Shoot! I almost forgot Sam."

"Sam?"

"Eyuh, Sam. He can talk you know." I threw a twig into the water.

"OK Ruthie, I believe you. What did Sam say?" Mom threw in a twig.

"Well." I threw in another twig. "I never used to believe Dad when he said there was no such thing as love. But then I did believe it, when he left and I knew he didn't love us. That day I went out and... I yarned Sam around. I hurt him. On purpose. I felt so awful but I couldn't stop doing it."

"What happened then?"

"Sam ran off and I yelled at him to come back and get kicked some more. I threw rocks at him, as if that would make him mind me. I knew I was ruining everything and he would never love me any more, and I hated myself, but I did it anyway."

"Then what?"

"He forgave me."

"Sam knew what you really wanted, didn't he?"

"Ayuh."

Mom hugged me and we sat there close and cozy and didn't say much. We watched the ice melt and tossed some more twigs into the water. Those twigs were like bits and pieces of our old accursed life, floating away from us, down Mitchell's to Green Creek, and the Otterkill and the Hudson River and into the Atlantic Ocean.

So after all that hurting and hating, Dad was my Boss. I did what he told me to do.

Dad and I got along OK. He didn't yarn me around any more. He didn't say he wished he never had kids. He didn't call me a pig or ugly. He didn't accuse Mom of spoiling her kids. He didn't complain about anybody's cooking. Because Dad and I were doing the cooking.

Dad didn't ever talk much to anybody really. He and I worked side by side in silence or tramped the woods and fields, enjoying each other's company the way horses do. I came to see that under all his bluster and stomping, that my father was a very shy man. Dad kept working in silence through the years and making beautiful things; he stopped making guns and bows and commenced to carve animals out of wood– birds, deer, foxes– they reminded me of the wonderful horse he carved for me when I was nine.

Farmers, hunters, duffers, all sorts of locals who couldn't stand him before now came calling, just to sit and swap stories and watch Dad work. They asked him to go fishing with them. Sometimes he went, but he wouldn't hunt any more. As his carvings got more beautiful he got more quiet and peaceful.

Mom kept her town jobs and served some terms as Alderman. Evvie and I sang for money at weddings and funerals and worked as farm hands. It took me a long time to realize that Evvie had been so heart wounded by Dad leaving and then by Bob Willett messing with her that she probably never would be able to talk about it; not to me, and certainly not to the cops or a judge and jury. But she mended herself in her own way. Evvie wrote fairy stories for kids' magazines, and took in all stray and injured animals; dogs, cats, chickens, even wild things, keeping a sort of orphanage for all creatures great and small. She also boarded horses, taming and re-training the rank crazy ruined ones, and folks paid her. Funny that she, not me, became the horse trainer. Maybe because I just loved Sam.

Here at the End of All Things, Sam

*Cast me not off in the time of old age; forsake me not
when my strength fadeth. –Psalm 71:9*

I remember the last time I ever rode my good horse Sam. I was just finishing my master's degree in Liturgical Music and already conducting a choir in New Hampshire. Mom and Dad had retired to Florida. Evvie had stayed on the farm, dividing her time between writing stories and rescuing animals. She got as skinny as I used to be, and I kind of chunked out.

Only Sam had stayed the same. He never slowed down. He was always so strong, so steady, always eager to go go go. Sam stayed the same the way the mountain stayed the same, or the moon and stars stayed the same. I guess I believed that he was immortal. But one late autumn I got a call from Evvie.

"Come up soon," she said. "We have a decision to make." I knew what she meant but I couldn't, wouldn't accept it.

I always wept for joy when I turned off onto Mitchell Hollow road, driving past Glen's, past Jinnae's old house—flatlanders owned it now—past Byron's, where the twins had set up matching trailer homes alongside their Dad's. Then into the woods and out between the fields. There was the barn and over it the great sheltering ridge of Argue Mountain.

My sister came out on the stoop in a cloud of yelping dogs; we hugged and cried a bit before going inside where there was a fire going in the stove.

I couldn't talk about the decision right off, so Evvie and I started by looking at our scrapbook, which contained mostly photos of girls on horses over the years. We turned to the last page.

"Look at that one, that's last spring Sam looks really fit! He'll live to a hundred!" I said.

A slim young girl sat on a bald-faced horse whose pumpkin-orange winter coat was shedding out in raggedy clumps. The horse is standing at parade halt, holding himself proudly. The girl's name was Evelyn Willett.

"Ruthie," sighed Evvie, "Sam's almost forty years old. His teeth are falling out. The other horses pick on him. Now is the time, if we do it this year."

Before the ground froze too solid to dig the hole.

"It's a gift to an old horse, Ruthie. He won't have to suffer and waste away or colic because he can't chew his food."

"I know, I know. I just never thought we would come to this day. Can't we wait just one more year?"

"Hm. He has a few pairs of teeth that meet. I guess I could blanket him and feed him in the stall. The others drive him away from the hay rack now. He doesn't like being bottom horse."

"I just want to be with him just one more summer, and then. We'll put him. Down."

"OK, we'll do that then. I'll separate him and blanket him and he'll do OK."

"Thanks. I can help pay for fencing the paddock for him. Now, that's settled," I said, laughing and wiping my nose on my sleeve. "Tell me the gossip."

Here's what had happened to our friends and neighbors. Ed Pilcher was crippled up with arthritis and couldn't walk. Bea took care of him and had helped run the financial end of things for Wayne and Laura, until Laura died in a car accident.

Wayne was doubly heartbroken, even more so because his and Laura's only son, Larry, had never had any interest in farming and wanted to be a commercial artist. Wayne, who had encouraged me to go into music, was furious with Larry, but let him go the Rhode Island School of Design. Left with no heir to take over his farm, Wayne partnered up with a cousin of Laura's, who also happened to be a distant cousin of old Frenchy's named Jimmy Devereux. Jimmy wanted to reclaim the farm in Trace. Wayne and Jimmy tore down the old haunted house and built a new house on the site for Jimmy's family. Then the two men cleared the abandoned farm, planted fields and meadows, grew their herd and prospered. So the curse of the Pelletiers and the Pilchers and was finally put to rest, and Bea and Ed were contented that this be so, til the end of their days.

Ronan O'Ryan had died peacefully in his sleep at age 100.

Annaliese was the new Doctor Mueller; she married another doctor, but she kept her old name on her shingle. Bob Willett, Esq., Prop. was in the State Pen for molesting a minor; Lu Monique and her kids had moved back to Canada. Jinnae still lived on Paulette's ranch, working as a rodeo trick rider, paying us visits when her shows toured in the East.

She, Byron's wife, having survived lung cancer, was still going strong. We called on her now and then at the trailer, where she held court in the parlor, hooked up to a big oxygen tank by a plastic tube snaking into her nose. She gave us detailed accounts of her sufferings, pausing only to remove the tube and take a drag on the Camel cigarette that smoldered between her fingers. She's casual mixing of fire and oxygen made me fear for my life, and also made me rethink my theories about who had actually burned Byron's house down.

Daphne and Delilah worked their way through several husbands apiece, produced a flock of kids, but they still loved drinking and getting into the kind of bar fights that make it into the papers. When Byron and Evvie and I went in together on an old Farmall H tractor and a rake and baler, the twins insisted on helping us get our hay in every year. They were polite to me in the field, but they yelled and cussed at their Dad and their kids and each other. It was hard to see it, but the Westfords loved each other, in their way.

One hay day Daphne headed into the barn with a lit Camel dangling from her mouth. I lunged between the door and her, saying "uh, don't....." Daphne squared around, fists up, then realized I was not looking for a fight. She dropped the cigarette in the barnyard muck and stepped on it, flashing me one of her eye-rolling grins. Then she swung up in the mow and stacked bales. I sat on a rock out in the paddock till I stopped shaking.

Evvie and I finished off the evening by telling Sam stories.

"D'you remember when we were cantering to the top of that hill in Byron's pasture and a flock of turkeys flew up right in our faces? And then Jeff Letique took a shot at them from the other side of the hill, right over our heads? Scared? Remember how you screamed at him to hold fire? But Sam froze like a bird dog!"

"Well, he never was one to spook at a little thing like that."

"D'you remember the time you took Sam to the fair and Byron bet you that you couldn't get Sam to load in his truck? Sam stopped dead at the door, whuffing with his eyes bugging out. I do believe he thought he was being sold off. You said, 'Come on, Sammy, there's money riding on this,' and he just followed you in. And stayed in."

That night we never went to bed, we just talked and dozed all night in our chairs surrounded by dogs and cats basking by the fire; dreaming like Bilbo the Hobbit "of meadow-flowers and butterflies in summers that have been."

The next day dawned bright and clear with a dusting of sugar-on-Wheaties snow; I thought I'd take Sam for a ride, for Auld Lang Syne. He looked thin but chipper. I cut him out from Evvie's boarders and adoptees and brushed him off, remembering how Evvie and I used to do it, one kid on each vast orange side, polishing relentlessly until his hair-coat shone like glass. It would never shine that way again, but at least his winter fur was coming in fairly thick.

I tacked up and soon we were prancing down the barn lane just like old times; Sam and me, alone with each other and the bare silent hills. We crossed the road and walked up the Greenway. The old lane skirted Byron's meadows, washed in pale-gold morning sun. Shadows of the leafless trees made stripes across our path. Sam walked quietly, almost on tiptoe, as I scanned the ledges for deer and birds. It was right before hunting season; the wild things watched us silently and unseen. When we went into Byron's pasture and approached the trail up Amon Hen, the old humming song started up in Sam's chest, and I heard his old hip bones creak under me as he gathered himself. My horse veered toward the trail and I let him do it because I wanted to see the whole neighborhood from on top of the hill as much as he did.

"All right," I said, "but no madcap dashes. Cantering only." With a snort and a curvet he was off, bounding up the trail, and the grass flowed beneath our feet, as in the storied days of yore.

As we leveled out on top we were going fairly fast and I was up in the irons crouched over Sam's neck. Then I saw a large woodchuck hole in our path.

For years I had trusted Sam to spot chuck-holes, and he always performed perfectly, never deceived by the grass-veiled "back-door" sort of hole or the last-year's partially caved-in hole, or even old tractor ruts. He was terribly particular about where he put his feet.

But I knew in a sickening moment that if he had noticed this hole at all his reflexes weren't up to stopping, turning or jumping over it. We froze for an eternal second above that yawning hole; then his foreleg came down in it, his face hit the ground; I heard a crash and a groan as I was launched forward through the air. I thought, Oh Lord he's broken his leg, Oh Lord he's broken my saddle tree, Oh Lord, he's going to flip over onto me. With a second crash and groan I lit on the turf, dislocating my shoulder.

When I got up I saw that Sam was up too, his leg was not broken and the saddle was intact. But the old horse stood trembling with his head low. I went to him and picked the reins up off the ground. He turned and looked full at me with a great weariness in his pale eyes, and I heard him say, quite distinctly,

"I'm done carrying you, Ruthie. You can walk on your own."

"It's all right Sammy," I said, leading him a few cautious steps. He seemed OK to walk. I eased the reins over his head and tucked them up under a stirrup leather. Then I turned him loose, holding my elbow with my hand to ease my throbbing shoulder. Sam walked free by my side, just like the old days.

We picked our way down the hill and walked out of the pasture onto the street. We were two miles from home. Halfway up hollow we met my sister and Byron in his truck.

"We've been down and I'm hurt," I told them. I got into the truck and Byron drove me to the hospital, and Evvie and Sam walked the last mile home.

Hast thou given the horse strength? Hast thou clothed his neck with thunder?... He paweth in the valley, and rejoiceth in his strength...he mocketh at fear...he swalloweth the ground with fierceness and rage...he saith among the trumpets, Ha, ha. –Job, 39 vss19-25

The End

Author's Note

This is a made-up story, but yes, there was a Farm and yes, there was a Sam. He did many of the things that happen in this book and would have done the rest if the opportunity had arisen. The real Sam was put down by the vet and buried in his home pasture the year he and the author fell into a real chuckhole.

The Bible quotes are from the King James Bible.

The poetry quoted in the Chapter "Who's Boss" is from "The Land of Heart's Desire" by W.B. Yeats.

About the Author

Susan Larson has been an opera and concert singer, a professor, a journalist, painter, gardener and grandma. She loves horses, dogs, birds and the rest of the natural world; and she loves her biologist husband Jim. She lives in a small town in Massachusetts, close by her kids and grandkids.

CPSIA information can be obtained at www.ICGtesting.com
Printed in the USA
BVOW041758231212

308981BV00002B/45/P